DEALING WITH THE DEVIL

Other books by the author:

A Wing And A Prayer (The First Book Of Gabriel)

Belladonna (The Second Book Of Gabriel)

A Long Way To Die (The Fourth Book Of Gabriel)

Past And Future Sins (The Fifth Book Of Gabriel)

DEALING WITH THE DEVIL

THE THIRD BOOK OF GABRIEL

ERNEST OGLESBY

iUniverse, Inc.
Bloomington

Dealing with the Devil
The Third Book of Gabriel

iUniverse books may be ordered through booksellers or by contacting:

iUniverse
1663 Liberty Drive
Bloomington, IN 47403
www.iuniverse.com
1-800-Authors (1-800-288-4677)

ISBN: 978-1-4759-3603-2 (sc)
ISBN: 978-1-4759-3604-9 (hc)
ISBN: 978-1-4759-3605-6 (ebk)

Library of Congress Control Number: 2011901153

Printed in the United States of America

iUniverse rev. date: 02/19/2013

This book is dedicated to the memory of my parents.

Prologue

Achille Ratti felt his years these days. He had lived a lot longer than he had ever thought possible, partly to do with his Faith in God, and partly to do with the remarkable properties of the Blood of Christ which he had imbibed many years previously.

Blood of Christ was what they euphemistically called it, but it was actually the blood of another remarkable individual, known as Gabriel, one of the original 'Angels' of a bygone age. Legends had grown up around him and his kind, legends which the Church found intermingled with their own, over the centuries.

Since Gabriel had helped in Ratti's own scheme to oust the former leader of the Sword of Solomon, Alonso Borgia, Ratti had now claimed the chair in the infamous Council Of Vampires, a pseudonym more apt than many people had previously realised, as Borgia's vampirism had been well concealed from the world at large and within.

Now Ratti had a chance to put the Sword Of Solomon back on track, in line with it's original aims of furthering and supporting the work of the Church, where more mundane and usual methods failed. Borgia had corrupted this in recent years, for his own personal agendas.

In gratitude for his help, Ratti had agreed a truce with Gabriel, vowing no more harassment of him or his friends, provided Gabriel voluntarily submitted a pint of his unique blood each year. This was not enough to stockpile, but would enable the existing recipients to continue their necessary boosters, so that the Council could survive, and leave a little left over for their scientists to continue their research.

The unique blood had kept Gabriel alive through the centuries, regenerating his cells, and repairing minor injuries, and when imbibed by a normal human, it prolonged life, and kept prolonging it, for as long as the blood could continue to be imbibed. Its affects were noticeably lessened in ordinary humans, but it had tremendous benefit for the whole of mankind if it could be duplicated or synthesised in some manner. Despite many years of trying, the Church scientists had not yet been able to do this.

Ratti studied Gabriel's file. First reported contact had been made by Borgia himself, in the 15th Century. Reports were sketchy, till modern times, though instances of contact with others of Gabriel's strange forgotten race were more commonplace, and they too were documented in their own files.

Old tales reported these winged beings in Roman times, at the birth of their modern Catholic religion. Only seemingly immortal, they could be killed, had even been dissected in their laboratories. Tales of the properties of their blood came out of Roman Britain, from the Druids who had first discovered its gifts.

Some of these 'Angels' had come into the possession of the Church, over the years, and had reluctantly become guinea-pigs for their scientists, in their fervour to analyse and synthesise. Regretted, but even he saw the necessity for it. Their last surviving guinea-pig, Michael, had been sacrificed in an ill-fated attempt to snare Gabriel in England, and that had also resulted in the death of their own Father Ryan as well.

The daughter of Gabriel and Laura, Belle, had now left the Church, and even her weaker blood was now denied them, all thanks to Borgia, after she had also been used as a pawn in Borgia's greater game. Sister Angelica, one of Borgia's operatives, had likewise disappeared after the debacle at Borgia's nightclub, and her whereabouts were currently unknown. It was understood that Belle had been maimed by her during the affair. Presently they did not know if surgery could restore the limb.

Ratti had also read through Belle's file, and he realised the Church owed the woman a lot, as it did the mother. Hardly surprising they had turned against the Church when the truth was made known to them.

Marco Falcone's report was also on his desk, and contained his own insights into the last operation. Ratti appended it to Gabriel's main file.

Ratti then put down his pen, and reached for a blotter, now finished with his latest notes on Gabriel's file, which one of his staff would later type up on his word-processor. Ratti was a man of simpler times, and a lot of today's modern technology was distasteful to him.

What to do with the man called Gabriel, Ratti wondered? Should this truce hold? Doubtless Gabriel would take precautions in just how he would have the blood delivered, but Ratti already had people working on that, who would backtrack the consignment, in an attempt to locate it's source, and thus Gabriel's base of operations. It would not be easy, but the attempt would be made. Today's allies could easily be tomorrow's enemies. Fate had a way of working against you like that.

He looked into one of the few mirrors in his apartments, and studied his dark mottled skin which even the miraculous Blood couldn't improve, and realised he envied Gabriel his seemingly permanent youth. Far older, he looked in his prime, whereas Ratti's own age was merely disguised, not erased. Wisdom did not rely on age, and only partially on experience. Ratti's mind had not dimmed over the years, and remained as keen as ever. Whether it would be a match for that of Gabriel in the years to come, remained to be seen.

Chapter One

Gabriel looked out of his study window, onto the spacious lawn beneath, where Laura and Belle lounged on sun-beds, talking, and enjoying the hot Argentine sun. It had been mere weeks, yet the stump of Belle's hand was now fully healed over. The girl, if girl she could be called at her actual age, still didn't know what to make of it. Automatically, she still went to use it as though the hand was still there, where it had been for more than sixty years, and cursing when she realized it was not. A trick the nerve-endings played on the body.

Gabriel could still 'feel' his own wings, though in fact they had been severed from his body almost two thousand years ago. His shoulder-blades still twitched occasionally, the muscle-groupings still there and still eager to exercise, yet they would never know such exercise again.

He had given Belle's problem much thought over the last few weeks. A physiotherapist had been booked to help his daughter acclimatize herself to her lost limb, and an artificial prosthesis had been commissioned. Belle was ambidextrous, like her father, and so could still write, but reading was something she now had to do one-handed, as were most of the other things in life she had taken for granted, such as washing and dressing herself etc. Even fastening a pair of jeans one handed was awkward and a chore.

Going over to one of the paintings on the wall of his study, Gabriel pulled it on its hinges away from the wall, revealing the hidden safe behind it. Fingers twirled the combination lock this way and that, until the final click was heard, and then Gabriel pushed the tumbler inwards, releasing the final lock, before operating the handle, and drawing the heavy door open.

Inside this safe, Gabriel did not keep money or documents, but it did indeed contain treasure of a sort. He drew out the shiny segmented metal belt, scepter and amulet, which had gathered dust in there since the safe was first installed.

Gabriel had first obtained these articles over 1500 years ago, and had kept them in various secure establishments over the years, but had recently had them scientifically examined in one of the many research labs he secretly funded. The findings had been vague enough by themselves, but put together with what Gabriel knew of their origins, and a very different picture emerged.

The dull coppery-looking metal plates of the belt were some sort of solar panels, though the metal itself remained unidentified. X-rays revealed inner-circuitry. A simple switch on the side of the buckle caused the belt to vibrate. Gabriel had measured the frequency of the vibrations. Presumably whoever was wearing the belt at the time would also be made to vibrate at that same frequency, though he had yet to try the effect upon himself.

The amulet also had a switch, a small depression on its underside, hardly big enough for a fingertip, which when pressed caused a sudden burst of radiation lasting barely a millisecond. Gabriel could only guess at its function. The rest of the necklace seemed purely ornamental.

The small scepter-like wand was a complex little device, with numerous settings. Broken now, yet perhaps it could be repaired by 'someone' with the right knowledge. Certainly, human science couldn't repair it.

All these items had been stolen by Gabriel from their former owner, who had valued them quite highly, and it was Gabriel's firm hope that he valued them still. They were Gabriel's only hope of obtaining his aid in restoring Belle's hand. Gabriel had brought the severed hand back to Argentina with him, and it resided in a basement facility, maintained at a constant sub-zero temperature. It could be stored indefinitely if need be, but it was Gabriel's hope that it could be re-attached within weeks.

"I haven't seen those for a while," Manuel commented, as he brought a tray of coffee into Gabriel's study. Gabriel smiled wistfully.

"Stolen property, Manuel. I hear there is a reward for their return. I just hope the owner doesn't hold their theft against the thief," he mused, a wry grin momentarily appearing on his face.

Manuel put down the tray on the desk, and poured his master a cup of coffee. The little twinge in his back meant he was feeling his age, though still generally sprightly for a 54 year old. Gabriel added the cream himself. "You never did tell me all the details, Sir," Manuel prompted.

He regarded Gabriel, as he gave the suggestion thought. Gabriel never looked or felt his true age, and Manuel had just a tinge of jealousy. Over two thousand years old, his Master looked no older than a human in his late thirties. Olive skin, and black hair, gave him a Mediterranean appearance, which fitted in well here, in Argentina. Average height added to that appearance meant he could fit in just about anywhere, without standing out in the crowd, which was how he preferred it.

"Details escape me, Manuel. It was a long time ago. Perhaps I need to refresh my memory." He took a sip from the coffee, and ruminated for a few moments, savoring the strong caffeine.

"Regression?" Manuel asked. Hypnosis was one of Manuel's many skills, and had been employed to regress Gabriel on a few occasions, when his master wished to recall details of former events in his long-lived life. Gabriel nodded. "Do you want both Madame Laura and Belle to sit in on the session?" Gabriel frowned at the suggestion.

"I'm not very good at 'sharing', am I, Manuel?" he criticized himself. "That character-flaw was partly responsible for the two of them getting in too deep with Borgia. Perhaps this time it might be best if they learnt a thing or two about my past," he reached a decision.

"I still remember some of the things you told me. You're not seriously thinking of going back over there? I still don't understand how you did it the first time, or how you got back in one piece. If Malevar is still alive, he's not one of your biggest fans. He tried to kill you, remember?"

"I remember. But if he's the only one who can help Belle, I have to go to him. Whatever his price, I'll pay it."

*   *   *

Out on the lawn, the two women in Gabriel's life were sunbathing by the pool. Laura had her blonde hair down, after a swim, and it was still matted as it dried out in the hot sun. Belle's jet black hair was a gift from her father, naturally sleek and shiny. The water had matted the curled perm, though it was slowly drying out as she lay there.

Gabriel's daughter looked in her late twenties, and Laura only slightly older, though each was *much* older. Laura didn't like being reminded of her true age. There was still a hint of vanity there, though she was happy enough with her appearance, which showed no sign of the passing years. Belle was in fact born in the Second World War, and Laura had seen that war at first hand.

Belle was trying to read a magazine, and getting frustrated every time she wanted to turn over a page, which necessitated putting it down on her lap, physically turning the page over, and then picking it up again. It was the simple things she had taken for granted which were causing her fits of temper, cursing at her own stupidity, and cursing the thing called Angelica that had done this to her.

Beside her, Laura could only watch her daughter in silence, and she tried to do it discreetly. Belle didn't want sympathy from anyone. She just wanted to get on with her life. Gabriel had promised if there was a way to restore her hand, then he would do whatever was required to make it happen.

The vampire they had fought had nearly killed both of them. Only luck and the sudden intervention of Gabriel and Falcone had saved them. Laura put a hand to her freshly scarred throat. By now ordinary scars would have healed. These were fading, but slower by far than she had become used to, with her new regenerated blood accelerating her metabolism.

Gabriel had killed Borgia, but what about Angelica? What had happened to her? Belle was reminded of Angelica every time she tried to use the hand that was no longer there. She carried Jessica's ghost along with her, and now a physical reminder of the woman's hatred as well. Some day. Some day, she promised herself.

She remembered waking up in the clinic, horrified at the bandaged stump where her hand used to be. Until she actually saw it for herself, she had hoped against hope it was all a bad dream. Angelica had taken Jessica from her, and now a hand.

The reunion with her father, when it came, had been emotional to say the least. She saw the hurt look in Gabriel's eyes, and she tried to reassure him that none of this was his fault, but ended up sobbing in his arms as he held her against him, letting her emotions express themselves in tears as they ran freely down her face.

She used the stump to push back her sunglasses on the bridge of her nose. At least she could do some things with it. The artificial prosthesis, she was definitely not keen on, though it might help her balance and depth-perception.

"Will you stay here with us? Have you decided yet?" Laura asked her daughter. Belle looked across at her.

"You think this truce with Solomon will hold?" she asked.

"Maybe. Ratti has the respect of the rest of the Council. I trust him much more than any of the others. He's promised to leave us alone as long as Gabriel sends him a pint of blood each year, and he has already done this. It seemed a good enough compromise. Otherwise they leave us alone, and we leave them alone."

"If that is the case, there is no need to remain in hiding," Belle mused. "It's nice here, but whether I would make it my permanent home is too early to say. Maybe I'll go back to my modeling," she suggested, laughing briefly. "Do you know there is one model who has metal springs instead of feet? I wonder what they'll make of me with this?" she held up her stump.

"Don't . . ." Laura urged. "It's not something to joke about."

"I'm trying to look on the bright side, 'Mother'. There, I called you it. Is that a positive sign?" she forced a strained smile. The anger was still there, simmering under the surface.

"Belle, your father and I love you so much. We want you here with us, but only if you want us as your parents. We have so much lost time to make up for. We've grown up apart, and are still strangers. We need time together. Don't give up on us too soon," she urged.

"This isn't your fault," she said, holding up the stump of her wrist, "and it's not his fault either. Don't go off on a guilt-trip on my account. If it's anyone's, it's my own stupid fault! I allowed myself to become complacent, allowed myself to get angry. Emotions are your worst enemy in a fight like that. I just couldn't stop that red-mist coming down. I beat myself," she admitted.

Laura put out a hand to rest on her daughter's shoulder. "If Borgia hadn't drugged you, you'd have beaten her. I know you would," she tried to reassure her.

"But he did drug me, damn it!" She shook her head in frustration. "Caught me with one of my own tricks, and I fell for it. All I wanted to do was kill that bitch, and I couldn't see he was setting me up for her." Belle was getting angry again. "One day, Laura," she promised. "One day I'll find her, and I'll take my time with her, just like she did with Jessica!" she vowed.

"We found you. Maybe we can find Angelica, too," Laura suggested. "But don't devote your life to revenge. It's in the past, now. Why not leave it there?"

"I was raised an Italian. Vendetta is in the blood, if not literally in my own case. I thought she was dead." Belle laughed ruefully. "Did a good job of keeping out of my way in all of my years with the Sword of Solomon organization. She's good," she admitted. "Finding her won't be easy. You found me because I remained in plain sight to draw Gabriel out. She'll have gone to ground now Borgia's dead," Belle cautioned.

"Perhaps Ratti can be persuaded to help? She was Borgia's protégé," Laura suggested.

"So was I, if you remember. I doubt that Ratti would want to help me," she glowered. *No, revenge was a dish best served cold. She would wait and bide her time, she decided inwardly. The two women hated each other with a vengeance, and they both had a lot of time on their hands, sorry, 'hand'. She smiled wryly at her inner joke.*

"Well, there are other ways to find people. I never did tell you how we found you, did I?" Laura mused. Belle turned to regard her mother. "Let's go for a drive. The mountain air might do you some good," she smiled, quizzically, and got up from the lounger.

She reached for her robe, and Belle did the same. Laura put her robe on, deliberately turning her back so she wouldn't have to see Belle's struggles to perform so mundane a task. She didn't offer help because she knew Belle would refuse, and be insulted at the offer itself. She had to get used to her disability, in her own time, and in her own sweet way.

The two women walked back across the lawn towards the house. The terrace window was still open, and they used it to go inside out of the hot Argentine sun. The slight breeze from the ceiling fan felt refreshing after the heat. It was always cooler indoors with the marble floors, which took a lot of time to warm up during the day, but gave the heat out again at night to maintain a nicely average temperature. Here in Buenos Aires, they never really had to worry about inclement weather in the moderate climate all year round.

They went up the ornate staircase to the upper floor where they each had bedrooms. Although Laura shared the master bedroom with Gabriel, she also had a separate bedroom, albeit with adjoining door, as she needed extra wardrobe space for her clothes. Gabriel was trying to organize a builder to come and fix things up, but builders were notorious the world over.

Laura changed into a light tee-shirt and shorts, and then waited patiently, listening to the mild curses through the next wall. She managed to refrain from asking her daughter 'do you want a hand?' which under the circumstances, would probably not be appreciated.

Five minutes later, Belle appeared in a white silk shirt and tan slacks. "Ready when you are," she announced, finally, and the two women went back downstairs, meeting Manuel, who informed them of Gabriel's wish to see them in the lounge.

*   *   *

The two women followed Manuel along the corridor, to where Gabriel was waiting for them. "Darling, can this wait? We were about to go for a spin up in the mountains," Laura announced.

Gabriel looked to Manuel, and then back at the two women, shrugging his shoulders. *The change of scenery would do Belle good, he thought, for she had cloistered herself in the villa since arriving in Buenos Aires.*

"It's waited nearly fifteen hundred years, so I don't see why not. We'll discuss it after dinner tonight, assuming you're going to be back by then," he smiled.

"I'm taking Belle to see Juliana," Laura announced.

"Oh," Gabriel was slightly nonplussed for a moment, but then smiled once more. "Well, give her my love when you see her, and watch out for that stick of hers," he warned. "The old bat uses it far too frequently," he joked.

Laura giggled, though Belle felt left out of the conversation. "Don't worry, she'll like you," Laura reassured her daughter. "It was Juliana who helped us find you. We'll be back for dinner, don't worry," and with that she linked arms with her daughter, and the two women went off, leaving Gabriel and Manuel to make the most of the afternoon by themselves.

Chapter Two

Laura drove the 4x4 with the top down, enjoying the feel of the wind through her hair. The road through the foothills was narrowing as it approached the tree-studded slopes in the distance, but Laura maintained her speed. She liked to drive fast.

"You say she's a witch?" Belle asked her mother.

"Sure seemed like it to me at the time," said Laura. "Don't worry. Juliana took a liking to me, and I'm sure she'll do the same with you. Gabriel met her about forty years ago," she explained. "He and Lucifer rescued her from some nastiness with the previous military junta. Her husband was executed, I believe. Since then she prefers to live a life of seclusion up there in the mountains. Just an old shack by a stream, with no electricity or modern conveniences. That's how she likes it, I guess."

"What you don't have, you don't miss, huh?" asked Belle, still moody, and Laura turned to glare at her daughter. "I'm sorry, I didn't mean it like that," Belle apologized. "I'm dealing with it, okay?"

Laura shrugged. "It's not something I can help you with, or I would. So I guess you'll have to," she stated. Then she turned her attention more onto the road as it began twisting and bucking, starting to wind it's way into the tree-line. Dust spewed out from behind her rear tyres as she engaged four wheel drive. The road would shortly be turning into a dirt track before much longer.

Belle was still moody as she studied the stump of her right arm propped up on the window's edge. The sleeve of her shirt partially obscured it, but the slipstream pulled it back, the new flesh still white. Would she ever get used to it? She had rejected the idea of a prosthesis, but would she remain as adamant as time went by? Doing things one-handed was a chore. Even her ambidextrousness didn't help. You needed to hold as well as manipulate.

Technology had advanced with artificial limbs, but not to the extent where you could superglue a new limb onto a human body. You still had to use straps and bindings to hold the limb in place, and weight was always a problem. She had done a lot of reading in the last few weeks. She supposed she should think herself lucky it was only a hand she had lost. Yes, only a hand. Angelica had taken first a lover, and then a hand from her. She just hadn't thought she could hate anyone more than the Cannucci's.

They drove along in silence for a while, as the hot sun had disappeared once they had entered the thick tree-line, climbing higher into the foothills. Truth to tell, the scenery was splendid and helped bring Belle into a better frame of mind, and she even managed to swear at the speed with which Laura continued to drive along narrow roads. Laura just grinned defiantly, as she drove the 4x4 to its fullest capacity.

Belle gasped as they tore along the edge of a gorge, the road so narrow she had to lean out of the window to see that the wheels on her side were still on it. A hundred feet or so below, a mountain stream splashed over shiny wet rocks and stone. Then they were running through a narrow pass, sheer stone sides which towered above them.

They were back into more trees less than ten minutes later, and the road flattened out once again, before climbing gradually once more. Laura finally pointed out the wisp of smoke above the tree-line in the distance. "That's where we're heading," she announced. She turned off the road, following faint tire-tracks which were partially overgrown with grass. The suspension kept the discomfort to a minimum, and within a short while, the cabin came in sight.

Laura smiled as she saw that Juliana had been busy. Her cabin showed a new coat of creosote to weatherproof it on the outside. Juliana was walking back from the nearby stream, carrying a bucket of water, as she heard the 4x4 approach, and she looked up, recognizing the vehicle, and waved. Laura waved back, smiling as she pulled up and parked.

Belle stayed back, feeling out of place, as Laura went to greet the old woman, who put down the bucket, and accepted Laura's affectionate hug. "Ahhhh, it's good to see you again, child." Her weathered face broke into a grin as she greeted Laura. The two women obviously well pleased to see each other again. When their embrace ended, Juliana turned to look at Belle, who still hung back nervously, and Laura grinned broadly. "And you certainly need no introduction, girl," she smiled affectionately, sensing the Belle's skittishness. "I'd know you anywhere," she admitted.

"Hi, I've heard a lot about you." Belle offered her hand, her left hand, with more than a touch of awkwardness, and Juliana smiled wryly as she took in the reason for the girl's nervousness. Juliana held the hand warmly in her own small hands, and gasped lightly, as she looked deep into Belle's eyes.

Juliana's eyes seemed to bore into Belle's soul, and Belle found it difficult to meet her stare. The grey eyes still held their sparkle, despite her advanced years. Not Belle's idea of a witch at all. Grey hair, tied back in a small bun at the back. Juliana stood just under five foot eight inches, and she stood tall, not stooped with age as a lot of old women. She still looked fit and sprightly. The reclusive lifestyle obviously suited her.

"A gifted family indeed . . ." Juliana mused, catching Laura's eye. "Come inside, and I'll make some coffee on the stove." As the pot boiled on the old range, Laura filled in the details on the reunion with her daughter, telling Juliana of the horrible experience in Borgia's arena. The memory of it all was still so vivid in her mind.

*   *   *

Laura went suddenly immobile at the surprise of seeing a second set of fangs, and then came the pain and pleasure of the bite itself. Belle was just plainly horrified, and sat back on the sawdust, as the 'thing' in front of her tore open her mother's throat, red blood quickly staining the white robe she wore. She gawped helplessly as Angelica then let her mother drop semi-conscious to the sawdust of the arena floor.

The face that turned towards her, open maw crimson with her mother's blood, was like nothing she had ever seen on this earth before. Fangs, so white and long and sharp. Then the old Angelica was back all of a sudden, as she closed her mouth, hiding her true appearance from the watching masses, whom were unsure what they had just witnessed. "Now it's your turn, little girl!" she hissed, picking up the short sword once more while Belle remained motionless and shocked on the ground before her. "Borgia wants you alive," she spat out. "But guess what?" she grinned evilly. "I don't!" and the sword rose and then fell savagely, and all Belle could do was to put a hand up to ward it off.

*   *   *

Juliana shook her head. "Vampiro!" she exclaimed. "Ahh, let me see the wound." Leaning closer, Juliana examined the faint marks on Laura's neck, rough fingertips delicately tracing the fading but still pronounced bite-marks.

"I've been worried about it," Laura admitted. "We know so little about this sort of thing. I thought vampires just fiction until that bitch bit me."

"Fiction and fairytales aren't always men's imagination, child. Some far-fetched tales are based on fact. Best be careful. What you don't know could get you killed," she warned, as she scrutinized the wound. "The bite is healing, and wasn't deep enough to drain you. Don't worry, you will not turn into such a creature of the night. What you need to worry about more is that this thing has tasted your blood. That makes you susceptible to its influence, and if it so desires, it can find you, wherever you are. I would take care," she cautioned.

"Then we both have a reason for killing Angelica," Belle butted in.

"I'd kill her regardless of what she's done to me. She's hurt you, Belle, and you're my daughter. I don't want to let anyone hurt you," she promised. Belle could sense the sincerity there in her words, and managed a weak smile.

"Come here, child," Juliana beckoned Belle forward. She shuffled forward on her rickety chair, and Juliana took her left hand once more. "Your beauty from your mother, and your 'charm' from your father, eh?" Even Laura chuckled at that one, though Belle glared at her for doing so. "Be still, now," Juliana scolded, peering intently into Belle's eyes. Belle held her stare defiantly, not wanting to flinch before the old woman, witch or not. "You take after him more than you know, child," she nodded her head, as if satisfied with what she saw. "And you,"

Juliana rounded on Laura, now, "the last time we met, your magic helped mine. Have you thought on that since then?"

"*My* magic?" Laura asked, incredulously, taken aback by the woman's sudden statement. Belle looked at her mother in a new light, suddenly amused by her uncertainty.

"Of course," Juliana confirmed. "It runs in your family, too, you admitted."

"Well, maybe way back a few generations. All I ever had were visions. Some called it foresight, but I was on medication a lot at the time, and it was probably nothing more than rambling. That's not what I call magic," Laura protested.

"Magic is magic. Whatever form it takes," Juliana insisted. "Your blood and Gabriel's blood, bound by my own, which was already in the pot when we added yours. Three special bloodlines combined to reveal your daughter to us. You have power, child. You both do, to differing degrees. In this world, there are ordinary people, and extraordinary people," she added. "Your family is hardly ordinary," she stated simply. "We must talk of this again. At a later date," Juliana smiled. "I will help you explore your birthright more fully," she promised.

"Can you help me find Angelica?" Belle asked Juliana, hopefully. The old woman smiled ruefully, shaking her head slowly.

"There is no blood-link between you. She only took from Laura, she did not pass on her own blood, and you should be thankful of that," she cautioned. "There are limits to what even my magic can do," she apologized. "I would need something personal to use in my conjuring. Unless you have that, I cannot presently aid you in your search."

*   *   *

On the drive back down from Juliana's cabin, Belle mused on what the old woman had told them. "So we're all witches together?" she laughed. Laura found Juliana's comments hard to believe, too.

"What is witchcraft these days?" she pondered. "There are rumors of it in my ancestry, but in those times they used to denounce anyone as a witch, for the slightest thing. I wasn't kidding about the premonitions I sometimes get, though," she explained. "More like waking dreams, if you know what I mean. I don't get them that often, but when I do, they're usually right," she said sincerely.

"In that case, I look forward to learning more. You are planning on coming back to talk with her about it aren't you?" Belle asked. "She's weird, but I kind of like her," she admitted. "I almost burst out laughing when she called you 'child' as well as me," she admitted. "Despite your looks, you must be older than her."

"Watch that mouth, young lady," Laura admonished. "I don't like being reminded of how old I really am. Do you?" she asked. "I suppose it's something we'll get used to if we live long enough," she joked, lightening the mood. Belle chuckled with her, and Laura was pleased the visit with Juliana had helped put her in a better frame of mind. "Look at the sky," Laura pointed out. "I'd better put my foot down, or Manuel will skin us alive for missing dinner."

"I'd like to get there in one piece, if you don't mind." Belle cautioned. "You drive fast enough as it is," she stated. "I don't make a good passenger," she admitted.

"Do *you* want to take the wheel?" Laura asked, with a defiant grin on her face, this time making a pointed remark about her missing hand.

"Now you watch *your* mouth, 'Mother'," Belle scowled, then couldn't resist a chuckle, poking her tongue out. "Okay, you win. I'll smile more," she conceded. "I know I've been lousy company since we got here. Que sera, sera."

"What will be, will be. Your father says he'll find a way. I've learned to trust him over the years. He wouldn't have mentioned it unless he was confident. It's not his way to build up your hopes needlessly."

"We'll see," Belle said, and settled back to 'enjoy' the ride. Could it be done, she asked herself? She knew enough about her own body's metabolism to know now that her unique increased regenerative properties worked against her in this instance. Before her hand could be reattached, that regeneration process would have to be halted or suspended to allow her body to accept the hand as part of her own body. Medical science couldn't do it. The Church had conducted enough experiments on captured angels in the last century, but their findings on this were inconclusive. They didn't know how it worked, or how to control it. The blood was the key, but it defied analysis.

Chapter Three

Over dinner, Gabriel asked the two women how their trip up into the mountains went. "Looks like you got back in one piece after all. What happened, did she break that stick of hers?" he mused.

"She only uses it on you, she says," Laura taunted. "Says you're the only one ever gives her any trouble. Not?" she shared a mischievous glance with Belle, who chuckled behind a napkin.

"I never find it that funny," he admitted. "You wouldn't either if your bones were hollow like mine," he added. "She does it on purpose, to wind me up," he complained, only half in jest.

*   *   *

After dinner, Laura and Belle soon joined Gabriel in the main lounge, where Manuel was serving a fine cognac. Laura poured herself a glass, and did the same for Belle without being asked. Belle said nothing, but accepted the glass graciously.

On the coffee-table in front of Gabriel were the metal belt, scepter and amulet he had taken out of the safe earlier that day. Neither of the two women had seen these articles before. They gathered they were of some significance, though both waited for Gabriel to explain their relevance.

"Laura, I mentioned to you before that there might be a way that Belle's hand could be re-attached," he started to explain, when Belle interrupted him.

"Look. Let's not kid ourselves," Belle interrupted. "My hand got cut off. The way my body's regenerative abilities work, it can't ever be reattached. That's what you said," she accused, then instantly regretted the venom she had just directed at him, biting her lip.

"What I said was that no one on earth was capable of re-attaching it. What I also told your mother was that I knew someone who could. Someone *not* of this earth," he explained, and waited for his words to sink in. Belle looked dumbly at him and then at Laura.

"What are you on about? I thought we'd heard all the weird stuff for one day." she asked, puzzled.

"I've been to places other than this world we live in," he began. "These things are proof. I've had them scientifically examined, and the metallurgy is unknown, as is the circuitry within the metal."

"You've already told us you aren't human. Are you now telling us that you're an alien?" Belle interrupted him again.

"Not quite. But perhaps it's better if you hear the whole story," he explained. "I haven't been to another planet, but I have been to another place, a different dimension I think. Maybe this world, but at a different time. It's hard for me to understand, let alone explain, though I've read up on the latest theories. Someone there has the technology to help you regain the use of your hand, Belle." he promised. "His name is Malevar! He's a sort of scientist, though like none you've ever seen before." The two women looked at each other, not quite knowing what to make of this revelation. "You both know how I lost my wings," Gabriel continued. "At the time I thought I was seeing things, as that High Druid managed to open some sort of rift in the air, and it was like looking through water." He found the memory coming back to him easily and painfully.

*   *   *

As Gabriel lay there, trying to ignore the pain of the emasculation and the burning tar, the High Druid turned away from the stone altar, and raised one of the dismembered wings over to the faerie ring. "Lord Malevar, accept my offering, and aid us against our Roman foes!" the Druid spoke aloud to his followers. Then, he began chanting in an unknown tongue, forming sounds Gabriel had not known a human throat could utter, he made invocation to unknown deities, allowing the droplets of blood to *spatter the small stones that formed the circumference of the ring itself, and a hushed awe fell upon the whooping Celts as the air itself slowly began to distort.*

Gabriel thought he was swooning, imagining things, as his vision blurred. It was as though he was peering through water, he could see, but not clearly. The space above the faerie ring looked more liquid than air, and a voice both grim and yet distant now spoke, cowering the painted Celts, and even the High Druid himself bowed as the voice rang out. "Your offering pleases me. But it is not enough."

"The wings now. You will have the angels themselves by the next full moon. Surely you would not begrudge us some of their blood for ourselves? You know its properties to my kind." The High Druid made his excuses, only too aware of who it was with whom he was speaking.

"My kind has aided yours for centuries. If you wish that aid to continue, then hold true to your word, druid. The next full moon, and no later. Now, give unto me the wings." the voice commanded. The High Druid thrust the first severed wing forward, the air obscuring it as though he were immersing it in a stream. Then it just seemed to disappear altogether, as the rest of the Celts gasped in awe. The other severed wings followed, disappearing before Gabriel's hazed eyes. He was as awestruck as any of the Celts. This was true magic indeed. The ethereal voice rang out once more. "Be true to your word, druid. At the next full moon, the angels must cross over."

"As you will, my Lord Malevar. I will keep my word." The druid was quick to reassure the unknown entity.

"Be sure you do. The Dark Elves are not known for their compassion," he warned. The druid bowed his head in supplication, and the swirling air began to return to normal. The gateway to wherever else had closed. The night was no longer charged with eldritch energy.

Gabriel swallowed hard, and turned to where Lucifer lay bound with him on the altar, but his friend was unconscious again, and had not witnessed any of this. Hope of some sorts then . . . They were not to be killed out of hand, but given over to what? He had heard the legends of the 'little people' who were supposed to haunt this land since before the coming of mankind, though had never witnessed anything like that which he had seen this night.

*   *   *

"Many years later, Lucifer and I had scoured most of the known world for the rest of our Aerie, which had fled north to escape the incursions of Rome. Not a trace did we find. All the time the memory of that night came back to haunt me, and I found myself thinking that might be what had happened to them all. This Malevar, whoever he was, wanted Angels, and as there now seemed to be none left in the known world, I thought they perhaps might be in his world." He paused to take a sip of cognac, as the two women looked on, interested now in his tale. "I determined to seek them there, and Lucifer and I returned to Britain in search of the clearing where our wings were taken from us."

"Is that where you got these things?" Belle queried the strange devices on the coffee table. "They don't look typical of the design of artifacts from Roman Britain, or Celtic for that matter."

"They're not. Souvenirs I brought back with me from Malevar's world. This was fifteen hundred years ago, so bear with me when I say I don't clearly recollect everything. At the time, with what I knew of the world, I thought everything was magical and supernatural. I didn't know about dimensional theory or any of the modern day stuff about teleportation, and phased universes etc. I was bright for my time, but within known limits. I was about to experience the Unknown for the first time," Gabriel explained.

"This is where I come in," explained Manuel. "There have been times when Master Gabriel and I have indulged in hypnotic regression, where I can make him recall in detail events hundreds of years in his past. He wants the two of you to be present when he undergoes this next session." Laura and Belle looked at one another. Both were fascinated to hear more.

"Okay, how do we do this?" Laura asked.

"You don't. It just takes me and Manuel," Gabriel explained. "But I think this time the two of you had better listen in, and get to know all I know about Malevar and his world, because I have to go there again!"

"What?" Laura exclaimed.

"He can't come to me, so I have to go to him. I believe the belt is his method of transportation into our world. While I have it, he has to stay in his own world. Malevar is the only one who can re-attach Belle's hand," he said simply.

"What makes you think this Malevar is still alive. Is he immortal like you?" asked Laura. Gabriel nodded.

"We have a lot in common," Gabriel confirmed.

"Hold on a minute," complained Belle. "My hand's gone. I'm getting used to it. I'll live with it, okay?"

"But suppose you didn't have to?" Gabriel argued. Belle didn't know what to say, yet Laura was quick to voice her feelings.

"I know better than to try and talk you out of this. You're too stubborn by far," she accused.

"You should talk," Gabriel countered.

"Alright. If you're sure this is the only way, *and* if you're sure this will work," she went on. Gabriel shrugged his shoulders.

"Hey, I got back okay last time, didn't I?" he argued. "Besides, this session will help me recall everything, and view it in light of what I know today. I'll get a totally different slant on it this time around. I should be able to understand more of what I saw at the time. What seemed like magic should be better understood as science. If it isn't, then we might have a problem," he admitted. "Who knows, maybe time has mellowed Malevar."

"Suppose it hasn't?" Laura acted Devil's Advocate.

"Then we'll see how badly he wants his trinkets back." Gabriel tried to make light of the situation.

"I'll draw the curtains, and then we can begin," Manuel said, and he went over to the silk curtains and drew them against the pale moonlight coming in from the French windows. Manuel then took a small candle and box of matches from out of the desk drawer. Gabriel lay back on the soft leather sofa, making himself comfortable.

Belle and Laura made themselves comfy on the adjacent chairs, each eager to learn these secrets from Gabriel's past. Manuel lit the candle, and then blew out the match. Laura went over and switched off the lights. The small flame didn't give out much light. It was just there to focus on. He held it closer to Gabriel's line of sight.

"Look into the flame," Manuel said softly. The two women focused on Gabriel himself as they saw him relax, his eyes staring intently at the small flame, the flickering light reflecting in his pupils. "Let yourself relax," Manuel advised, and Gabriel allowed his body to shut down, slowly losing all sensation. Only the flame existed now. Small, flickering, holding his attention. "Sleep," commanded Manuel. Gabriel's eyes closed almost as soon as he had said the words, for he was used to this hypnotic regression, having done it on numerous occasions in the past with his manservant. "Remember," Manuel spoke softly. "Remember Malevar." Gabriel's mind voyaged back through the dim dark centuries. Malevar. The name was important. Seek him out, an inner voice said. "Tell us about your first meeting with Malevar, from your own point of view, and include what you learnt later from Lucifer."

Gabriel felt himself drifting into a deep sleep, mind and body drifting, searching through his memories. Back through the years and centuries, to darker times.

Chapter Four

The Viking longboat cut through the thick fog. Only the constant dip of oars into the water was heard. It was like sailing between worlds. The sea swell was light, yet the steersman held his course according to the magnetic seer-stone he held suspended by a length of twine. This ship had made the crossing to Britain many times before, carrying raids up and down the northern coastline.

They were prepared for battle now, though hoping to find none initially, for Gabriel had offered a large purse of gold to get them safely onto the British mainland. What they did once he and Lucifer were on dry land was their business.

Gabriel peered ahead through the fog, yet beyond the dragon-headed prow he could see nothing but grayness. From time to time, an archer would fire a burning arrow ahead into the murk, which would disappear from sight. After many minutes, and many arrows, one flame remained in the distance, and oars were shipped as landfall approached.

The long barren strip of beach was deserted as the longboat was run aground. Planks were lowered to disembark Gabriel, Lucifer and their blindfolded horses. This was done quickly and in silence, as the Norsemen got their bearings by sending scouts quickly up and down the beach in both directions.

Satisfied, the two scouts returned and conversed with their captain Rolf Greybeard. He was quick to give both Gabriel and Lucifer a hearty handshake, and wished them well. Then he was quicker to put out to sea once more, and the two of them watched as the fog swallowed up the longboat. It turned to the north once more, and ran parallel to the coast, as it gradually faded from sight. Thick, clammy, damp fog, smothered the sounds of the oars dipping into the water.

The air was damp and there was a chill, and both Gabriel and Lucifer drew their cloaks tighter about themselves as they rode their horses up the beach, seeking solid land. They had no seer-stone themselves, so needed to get out of the fog to get their bearings, and needing to travel south and east from this landing point.

"I'd just gotten used to warmer climes, friend Gabriel. Now you bring us back to this country. I had forgotten just how damp and miserable it could become in the winter months."

"Mayhap not for long, Lucifer. If our quest is fruitful, and we find our lost brethren, maybe we will decide to stay with them. There must be a reason we cannot find them in all our travels. Perhaps they have found a place more to their choosing than this world in which they are hunted and persecuted."

"Even so, did we have to land so far north? We have many days travel ahead of us until we find the welsh mountains again." Lucifer complained.

"The Roman Legions still occupy the lands to the south, Lucifer. Word has it that they are finally leaving this country to fend for itself. Too much trouble back home to keep foreign armies occupied overseas. But they haven't all gone yet. Best keep out of their way," he advised.

"What makes you think we'll find a druid after all this time? I thought the Romans had put them all to the sword," Lucifer asked.

"Not all. They are like a plague upon the earth. Some still survive up in the mountains. Hermits and such. They will know the secret of the faerie-circles."

They rode south along the beach, until they found a place to cross into the mainland pastures, and then skirted a thick forest to the west. As they rode further inland, the fog gradually cleared, and a feint winter sun became visible in the grey skies. The wind picked up from the north, though, and so they still needed their thick cloaks about them.

Medieval Britain in the so-called Dark Ages was splitting into principalities as the Romans retreated southwards. Every so-called noble was trying to grab as much land as he could. Alliances were formed amongst themselves, to allow them to prey on the weaker farmers and fiefdoms.

*　　*　　*

Eight days riding saw the welsh mountains finally visible in the distance. Another two, and Gabriel and Lucifer skirted the dark woods where they were made land-born forever. "It was a long time ago, yet some nights in my sleep I can still feel the knife," Lucifer admitted.

"I know what you mean, Lucifer," replied Gabriel. "If there were a different crossing-point, I would use it. But our knowledge here is limited to our own experience. Only the druids know the secrets of those rings, and they cannot be trusted." He wheeled his horse around, and headed north towards the distant smoke which came from one small settlement.

They kept their swords close to hand as they approached the hamlet, aware that strangers were looked upon with suspicion in these dark times.

The language hadn't changed much in the time they had been overseas, and they found it quite easy to converse with just enough of a local accent to get by. A small inn was found where lodgings and food could be obtained. Ale was provided, which the two of them drank next to a roaring fire, after ensuring their horses were adequately stabled.

As the young boy brought food, his curious mind led him to converse with the two strangers. "What do you here, sirs? Strangers are rare in these parts," he admitted, and both Gabriel and Lucifer shared a warning look. It was Gabriel who answered the boy.

"We come from the north, where the Picts are raiding across the wall more often, now the Romans no longer man it. The local lords will only patrol their own little stretch, yet the Picts are finding it easier to cross in many places."

"I have heard similar tales, Lord," said the boy, laying down a fine plate of roast mutton and potatoes. "The Romans brought law to a savage island, if nothing else. Dark times are ahead, now they pull back further to the south coast."

"I heard they had a large battle near here, some years ago," Lucifer butted in. "Anglesey I think the name was . . ." The boy's eyes lit up as he remembered.

"Aye good sir. The last of the legions cornered what was left of the Druids up there. What they didn't slaughter, they dispersed to the far winds," he recounted.

"Where did they all go?" Gabriel asked offhandedly. "The Romans couldn't have put them all to the sword?"

"Not all, sir. What few that were left were scattered far and wide. Most live lives of seclusion now, like old Daeffyd. Too frightened to come down from the mountains for fear the Romans are still chasing him."

"Daeffyd? Is he a druid?" asked Lucifer.

"Was, Lord. No more," the boy admitted. "He be half-mad with loneliness these days. We leave food for him, but hardly any of us ever catches a glimpse of him, so frightened is he of the rest of us. The food is always taken though, so we know he still lives."

"More ale, boy. Then tell us more of your madman," Gabriel smiled.

*   *   *

A day's riding to the south was the haunt of this mad recluse. Daeffyd Wildwood was his name, when he used to answer to it. One or two of the villagers remembered him from his youth. Some of them still left food for him, to supplement his diet of berries and shrubs. Gabriel and Lucifer both went with the villagers the next time they left the food for him, and then they settled back to wait for the food to be collected, camping out in the woods.

It was another three days before the gaunt, wild-eyed man appeared. What was once a white robe now hung in rags from around his skeletal frame. His hair and beard were wild and unkempt. He still moved nimbly for one of his obvious advanced years, and he still had a mind about him, whatever drugs and roots he took to maintain himself in the wilds.

Gabriel and Lucifer had discussed how to handle this druid. Subterfuge wasn't likely to work. What they wanted of him was too specific, and he would soon guess their motives if they tried to trick him. Best just take him captive, and force the information out of him.

He turned and ran as soon as they made themselves visible, long wiry legs soon putting distance between them as he sought the refuge of the mountain slopes once more. Lucifer rode him down, throwing himself from his horse to bring the druid to the ground, where a fierce struggle quickly ensued. The old man was stronger than he looked, and Lucifer swore as he narrowly evaded the edge of a wicked sickle-shaped dagger the old man pulled from within his brief clothing.

"Die, damn you!" the old man cried out, as he lunged at Lucifer, and only the thick material of his jerkin prevented the mad old man from drawing blood.

"Careful, Lucifer. There's life in the old dog yet!" Gabriel warned as he dismounted to aid him in subduing the old man.

"Aiiieeee!" Daeffyd squealed, as the dagger was twisted from his grasp, and the two strangers wrestled him to the floor, where they used rope to bind his hands. "Don't kill me, sirs. I meant no harm. I have no money. Why do you attack a poor madman like I?" he squealed.

Gabriel eyed the blade with interest. A sacrificial knife, such as had been used on the two of them that fateful night. Wildwood cursed as he found his wrists tied securely. Lucifer added a gag to put a stop to the old man's curses.

Wildwood was tied by rope to Lucifer's saddle, and forced to march behind his horse as they rode slowly into the dark woods. The hermit fell as he struggled to keep up, and Lucifer dragged him along the ground until he found his feet once more. Neither of them had much love for druids. Wildwood soon learned not to fall, as his captors would show him no mercy.

Wild eyes stared as he eventually recognized the route the two men were taking, and it was confirmed when finally, after two hour's traveling, the clearing came into view.

The two horses stopped on the edge, as Gabriel and Lucifer saw once more the scene of their emasculation. The large stone altar had been rebuilt since Michael had overturned it in his fury. There, to one side, was the plain stone circle, which was the reason for their return to this land. Smooth pale stones, some partially overgrown with moss, but they retained a strange lustre.

There were similar stone circles up and down the length and breadth of this country, and legends abounded as to their origins. Strange sights and stranger beings were often seen around such circles, usually during the dark of night and at certain times of the moon. Legends said they were gateways to arcane realms, and Gabriel's own vision had seemed to prove that correct. Did they all lead to the same world, or did each lead to a multitude of worlds?

This was the only such 'gate' that Gabriel was sure of. Through it he must go, in search of his brethren, and the druid was the key. "Bring him forward," Gabriel spoke to Lucifer, as he dismounted and tethered his horse to the branch of a tree. Lucifer dismounted also, and unfastened the rope from his saddle, which he handed to Gabriel.

As Lucifer tethered his own horse, Gabriel pulled the druid forward into the clearing. The man stared wild-eyed and defiant into Gabriel's face, as Gabriel tore the gag away from his mouth. Wildwood spat on the ground near Gabriel's feet. "I know you, Druid. Not you personally, but your kind," Gabriel stated.

"And what kind is that, that would cause you to bind me and bring me to this place?" he asked defiantly.

"You worship the wood!" Lucifer answered. "You made sacrifice to your gods on that very altar," he pointed, accusingly. Wildwood grinned.

"Your kind almost sacrificed the two of us on that same altar!" Gabriel revealed. "When they did so, a gateway formed in the air above that circle," he pointed. "I wish to pass through that gateway. You will open it for me. Do this and you will go free upon my return," he promised. "This I promise. I offer death if you refuse," he added grimly. "Then I will find another of your kind and offer him the same choice. I care not how many of you I have to kill, "he revealed, coldly.

Wildwood remained silent as he appeared to consider Gabriel's request. "The Dark Elves come less frequently to this world in recent years. Why would you seek them in their own world?" he asked, revealing now his knowledge of another world beyond their own. All the time he was studying Gabriel's face. Then, he turned his attention to Lucifer, and noted the similarities in physiognomy. The two could be brothers. One dark, the other blonde.

"I have my reasons. They are not for you to know," Gabriel answered. Wildwood smirked.

"Before my time, I have heard legends of this place. No human sacrifice has been made here for hundreds of years. But I know of you," he accused. "So the legend is true, and the winged ones still live?" he laughed, "and now you seek my help?" He laughed again.

"I don't seek your help, druid. I demand it! Aid me and you live. Fail me and you die. I will have no hesitation in slitting your throat. I have no love for your kind," he admitted.

"And I have none for yours!" Wildwood snarled in return. "The Roman persecution that destroyed my religion was brought upon us by you and yours. Rome all but wiped us out at Anglesey. Only a few of us still know the old secrets," he warned. "Kill me and you will likely not find another who can help you."

"I'll take my chances," warned Gabriel. "How badly do you want to live, Druid?" he asked. Wildwood remained silent for a moment, as if considering. Then he raised his head once more.

"Very well. I will aid your crossing. I must first gather some berries and plants to make a potion." Gabriel nodded, and as Lucifer went to accompany the druid into the wood, Gabriel began to set up camp on the edge of the clearing. They still had a couple of hours until dusk, and he wanted to waste no time. If truth be told, he was not looking forward to this 'crossing', but it was something that had to be done.

Wildwood scoured the surrounding woods, gathering up plants and berries from various bushes and trees, mushrooms and lichen, pieces of tree-bark, all of which he secreted within the scraps of his clothing. Lucifer held onto the rope tether, ensuring the druid could make no escape attempt. He never turned his back on him the whole time he was in the woods.

Aware of the attention he was getting, Wildwood allowed himself a secret smile as he continued with his foraging. He knew who they were. The legends were true after all. Angels without wings, now seeking the Dark Elves. He would aid their crossing indeed. The pact between Malevar and the druids had been broken by the lack of sacrifices. Perhaps tonight would make amends, and the resurgence of his religion might result with renewed aid from the Dark Elves.

Like most druids, he knew the legends of the Realm of Faerie. Knew that these angels would not last long once they had crossed over, for he knew from stories passed on, over the years, some of what Malevar did with the angels that had made the crossing previously.

*   *   *

Night came finally, bringing even deeper darkness to an already dark wood, and Gabriel had lit a small fire around which the three of them sat. The feint cries of nocturnal beasts and birds were strangely absent from this part of the wood. Lucifer provided utensils from out of his saddlebags, and Wildwood mixed his herbs and plants in a small pot, which was now boiling slowly over the fire, whilst the druid muttered strange chants over it.

The two angels watched Wildwood suspiciously as he slowly concocted his strange brew. "You expect us to drink that?" Gabriel asked. Wildwood grinned.

"We all will drink," he replied. "You will not die of it, that much I promise you," he smiled. "It is nourishing and it will aid your crossing between the worlds," he assured.

"I will cross. Lucifer will remain here with you to ensure I get back safely. Whatever door you open, I wish to remain open until I return," Gabriel warned. "No tricks, Druid!"

"Don't worry," Lucifer reassured his friend. "Any tricks and he'll regret it." Wildwood allowed himself to smile as the two angels conversed. Surreptitiously, he took a few small berries from his clothing, and put them to his mouth, chewing slowly, as if merely peckish, as he tended the boiling pot.

Chapter Five

The moon was fully overhead by the time Wildwood deemed the broth ready to drink, using the ladle to blow on the hot liquid. To show the mixture was harmless, he was the first to drink, licking his lips after he swallowed. "Not the best-tasting soup I have ever made, I'm afraid," he apologized, as he handed the ladle to Gabriel.

Gabriel dipped into the pot himself, blowing on it as he raised it to his mouth, and sipped. Tart and thin, it took some swallowing, but he forced it down, and then handed the ladle to Lucifer.

"Why do we all drink?" Lucifer asked "if only Gabriel is to cross over to the other realm?" Wildwood smiled.

"Are you not hungry? Well, for no other reason than to show good faith, and allay your friend's fears that I would poison him. I have drank already as you have seen," he pointed out. Lucifer grunted, and raised the ladle to his mouth as Wildwood watched, willing him to swallow, though trying not to make an issue of it.

Lucifer did indeed swallow, his stomach rumbling. He took a few mouthfuls, then, finding the broth not much to his taste, he went to break out some strips of dried meat from his provisions. Wildwood contented himself with clearing up the utensils.

"Now what, Druid?" asked Gabriel. Wildwood turned to regard him, a keen fire in his eyes.

"Patience. You will cross soon enough," he advised. Leaving the warmth of the fire, Wildwood went over to the Faerie circle, his rope tied to a tree and just allowing him enough freedom to reach that far.

He began making strange signs in the air with his hands, and muttered in the high speech that Gabriel remembered from his last visit to this clearing. Only the High Druids knew that language. Finding Wildwood had been fortuitous indeed.

Gabriel felt the warming effect of the broth inside him, and was aware of a strange heightening in his senses, as he watched the druid at work. This time though, there was no rippling effect in the air above the stones, though this did not seem to faze Wildwood, who continued in his incantations.

Lucifer watched warily, suspicious of the druid. The chanting went on for more than twenty minutes. A high mist had covered the moon, obscuring the stars, and enveloping the clearing in a strange silvery luminance, when Wildwood at last beckoned Gabriel forward.

"The gateway has opened," he announced, although neither Gabriel nor Lucifer could see any difference in the faerie circle. "Step forward into the ring of stones," he waved Gabriel forward with his hand. "If you dare," he smirked.

Gabriel glared at him, hiding his own fear. Taking a grip on the pommel of his sword, he stepped forward, striding boldly into the faerie circle, and then turned and stood looking back to Lucifer and the druid. The strange luminescence was affecting his vision. It was like looking back through mist, and the sight of his friend was growing dimmer, dimmer . . . .

*   *   *

Lucifer watched in awe, as Gabriel began to fade from sight, his body becoming transparent, until suddenly he was gone. The faerie circle was empty. "He has made the crossing," Wildwood announced. "We had best make camp. We have no way of knowing when your friend will return," he advised.

"Yes. You are right on that account," Lucifer admitted, feeling a great lethargy coming into his bones. He added more kindling onto the fire, and then broke out some sleeping furs from his and Gabriel's saddlebags.

Wildwood smiled furtively as he noticed the yawn coming from Lucifer's mouth. The broth's only purpose was that of a strong sleeping draught, and had no part in the ability of Gabriel to make the crossing.

Angels, he had learnt from his teaching, could make that crossing at will, just like the Dark Elves themselves, whereas humans could not. The faerie circles welcomed them as their own.

Lucifer was now feeling the effects of that sleeping draught. The berries Wildwood had been discreetly chewing were an antidote to the potion, and would enable him to remain awake whilst Lucifer slumbered. Freedom and revenge for their ill-treatment were on his mind.

Tonight, not one, but both angels would cross over into the realm of the Dark Elves. Nevermore to be seen in this human world.

*   *   *

In another time and another place, Gabriel stood seemingly in the same ring of stones, though now looking about him at a totally different landscape. Above him even the very stars looked different.

His senses were all on fire, nerve-endings tingling, his skin itched like never before, and he sank to his knees, shaking helplessly as he tried to come to terms with what was happening with his body.

It took long minutes to adjust to what he was feeling. Even the air tasted differently. His eyes, ever keen, seemed sharper and could make out more details in the darkness around him. He was still in a wood, though now there was no sign of a clearing or an altar. Around him the wood reverberated with the nocturnal sounds of hunter and hunted as the animal kingdom re-enacted it's own laws of survival.

His limbs felt heavier than normal, and it was an effort to stand upright once more. He felt tired, strangely tired. He started to walk, stepped out of the circle of stones, and walked into the trees. His breath was becoming shallower, his sight growing dim. Once more he sank to his knees, and this time he could not get up again.

Gabriel fell backwards, and lay prone. He tried to move his arm towards the hilt of his sword, but could not. His vision was losing focus, and the last thing he saw before he blacked out were the stars through the trees, and the pale moon that shone down on him.

*   *   *

Wildwood grinned as he surreptitiously watched Lucifer stir uncomfortably as the lethargy crept upon him. The druid was seemingly asleep, and Lucifer needed to stay awake to guard him, but his eyes kept closing, and it was an effort to open them again.

Lucifer had looped the rope around the branch of a tree, so that Wildwood could not approach him, without the tugging rope waking him up again. At last, his eyelids closed and did not reopen. The druid's eyes now opened wide, noting Lucifer's breathing as the draught took effect. His chest rose and fell in a light rhythm, as he fell asleep.

Nothing moved in the clearing for a full ten minutes, until the druid was sure Lucifer was well under, and then he threw off his furs and stood up. The rope tugged at Lucifer's wrist, but there was no reaction from him as Wildwood unfastened the rope from around the branch, and moved closer to Lucifer's sleeping form.

Kneeling, he searched through Lucifer's clothing for the sickle-shaped dagger, and used it to cut the bindings around his wrists. Then, rubbing to restore the circulation, he stood up and aimed a hearty kick into Lucifer's mid-section, enjoying the feel of the foot sinking into his soft stomach. Apart from a deep groan, there was no other reaction from Lucifer. The potion was potent indeed, and he continued to sleep through it, as Wildwood laughed.

"Now it is your turn, my pretty one," he grinned. "You know far too much about our ways, and I know more about you than you think. The legends tell of your blood, and I would have some of it before you cross over." With effort, Wildwood began dragging Lucifer over towards the restored altar.

It took less effort than he thought to lift the angel onto the crude stone slab, and all the time Lucifer remained unconscious. He looked in both sets of saddlebags for suitable containers, and found a flagon of wine, which he emptied onto the ground. It would serve to contain something far more precious.

Stripping back the sleeve of Lucifer's tunic, Wildwood took the sickle-shaped knife, and cut deep into the exposed arm, holding it out over the edge of the slab as he positioned the empty flagon. The blood flowed red and thick, and Wildwood smiled as the flagon began to fill. If the legends were true, then one mouthful of this creature's blood would double his own lifespan. He had a whole flagon of the stuff to himself. It must be preserved at all costs.

The wound in Lucifer's arm was closing as the flagon was finally corked, and Wildwood was well content with this night's work. Now to prepare him for the crossing into Malevar's world, and with luck the Dark Elves would breathe life into his dying religion, now it was seen that the druids had renewed their pledge of servitude to their Dark Lord.

*　　*　　*

A hot sun finally woke Gabriel from his drugged slumber, and he awoke to an aching back, and a strange throbbing in his temple much like a hangover after too much ale. He rolled over, looking about him to get his bearings. The circle of stones was there, a short distance away, but no clearing, as such. The trees were different, too, green and full of leaves, when Gabriel suddenly realized it was a different season here, in the full of summer unlike the first chills of winter he had left behind. *What was this world?* he asked himself as he got to his feet.

Around him, the sound of the forest, and the birdsong was quite normal. *Where had this 'gateway' taken him? To a different part of the world, or out of it altogether?* He remembered how differently the stars had appeared after his crossing, though that might have been more his disorientation than anything. He needed to explore this strange new environment more fully before making his mind up.

Finding a suitable tree, Gabriel began to climb, and was soon up in the highest branches, his light bodyweight enabling him to clear the leafy covering of most of the surrounding forest before the branches started to sag beneath him. He looked around, seeing nothing but forest for miles, thinning vaguely to what he assumed was the north, where a wisp of smoke could be seen. Signs of life that would need investigating.

Chapter Six

Gabriel headed in the direction he perceived as north, from the angle of the sun, navigating his way through thick woodlands.

He had first started to hear the strange whispers in his head shortly after he had set out on his journey, and they were still there on the edge of his consciousness, coming and going like a swarm of insects. He managed with difficulty to put them to the back of his mind and ignore them for the most part, though occasionally shook his head as though trying to get rid of an insect that had flown into his ear.

The woodland was a mixture of color, as the leafy covering overhead increased and decreased in density. All the lush colors overwhelmed his senses at times. Even in the height of summer, and the glorious changing autumn of his own world, he had not experienced such a rich tapestry as this. He knelt, and picked up some of the soil, running it through his fingers, crushing it and sniffing. The soil itself smelt more alive somehow.

His mood changed with the colors, so that he felt light and cheerful as he experienced the warm shafts of sunlight breaking through, yet felt eerily somber as the wood darkened, sometimes into a blackness so deep, it seemed to take on a life of it's own, and he found himself unconsciously avoiding those places. Even the voices in his head seemed to change as he neared them, and it was harder to ignore them, almost making sense of them as they pulled at his awareness. But some inner instinct told him to stay to the lighter paths, and he went on his way, unaware of the many eyes that followed him as he wandered through the woods.

The butterflies he noticed gradually. One, then another, would flit into his line of sight, before disappearing just as suddenly as they arrived. One, then two, sometimes more than that, fluttering out of the trees as if to take a curious peek at him, before vanishing again. Strange butterflies, larger and more colorful than any he had seen before on his travels, even in the Far East.

The wood itself was lush. Thick, heavy trees, which moved and rustled lightly above him in the breeze. Lichen clung to a few, and there were plenty of plants and flowers just as colorful all around him. A pleasant land indeed, thought Gabriel. He heard the sounds of wildlife at a distance, though he had not yet come upon any of the woodland animals. Just as skittish as in his own world.

Before long he came upon a stream, and knelt at its bank to drink, scooping up some water in his hand to bring to his mouth. It tasted good, cold and clear. Very refreshing. Gabriel studied his features in his reflection as the ripples eased, gradually making out his features in the water. But then, as he watched, those features seemed to change, becoming a different face altogether, one which looked out at him seemingly from beneath the surface. A strange thought came to the forefront of his mind, one not his own, asking "What is your name?" Startled, he jumped up and back.

Cautiously, he leaned forward again to take another look, and this time the face looking back appeared to be his own, and so he took the strange incident as imagination. As he went on his way, behind him the rippling water sounded almost like faint laughter. If he had looked closer, he might have seen the surface of the water break as though a fish had come to the surface in search of a fly, yet this particular fish was shaped strangely like a human hand, before it vanished back beneath the cool flowing waters once more.

Gabriel continued to head north, or so he hoped, stopping occasionally as he heard the noise of wildlife in the wood, like the sound of a skittish deer. For all his woodland skills, he still made too much noise to be able to creep up on such.

The vegetation was thinning now, the gaps between the trees increasing and more and more sunlight was filtering down through the lush green foliage.

*　　*　　*

The sudden scream of terror rooted him momentarily to the spot. It was so unexpected. Male he thought, and then the sound of a wild beast snorting and bellowing as it attacked. Drawing his sword, Gabriel dashed ahead towards the sounds, closing the distance in long purposeful strides.

A large wild boar was attacking a hollow fallen tree-trunk, large tusks ripping the dead wood apart slowly but surely. The screams from within told of a frightened man or boy, hiding within, his bloodstained face visible as he peered, frightened and dazed through a hole recently torn through the bark.

As Gabriel ran out into the small clearing, the huge boar turned at the sudden intrusion, and wasted no time in attacking a fresh target. Gabriel leapt high to avoid the long tusks, as he struck down with his sword. The blade cut deep into the beast's shoulder, and it squealed, turning unbelievably fast to continue the attack, and this time one tusk caught in Gabriel's tunic, and the beast shook him violently, slamming him against the bole of a tree, before drawing back to begin another charge.

Head down, and those frightening tusks lowered, it came at him again. Dazed, Gabriel could only stab his sword forward hurriedly, bringing a squeal of renewed pain as the point cut across the brow of the beast, blinding it in one eye.

Then, from within the fallen hollow trunk, a tiny man crawled out into the sunlight, wiping the blood from a wound on his forehead with the back of his sleeve. Gabriel thought he was seeing things as the diminutive fellow then drew a wicked looking dagger of his own, and attacked the boar from behind, sticking the blade deep into it's hindquarters.

Following his reflexes, Gabriel got to his feet, and attacked the boar again, as it turned to try and deal with the rear assault, and Gabriel's sword plunged deep into it's side, and he twisted to find it's heart, which finally gave out, and with one final bellow, the huge beast slumped to the ground, dead. Gabriel leaned on his sword, getting his breath back, as the tiny man picked himself up from the ground, and cleaned his dagger.

"I am indebted to you, sir," the dwarf spoke, in a dialect that Gabriel hadn't heard in years, but which was still recognizable. No, dwarf was the wrong word. He was just 'tiny'. Proportionately, from a distance, he looked as normal as Gabriel, yet he stood barely three feet high. A pointed beard assumed he was a grown adult, yet Gabriel had never seen his like. Clad in brown leather britches, and a darker brown jerkin, made of what looked like hemp. Small black boots, of a similar style to Gabriel's own, proved that there were still some similarities between this world, and his own. Gabriel was dumbstruck for a moment. "My name is Brin, and from the look on your face, I take it you are a stranger here?" the little fellow asked.

"Yes, I am. My name is Gabriel," he introduced himself, then pulled his sword free from the carcass, releasing a dark flow of blood to stain the soil. He cleaned it with some grass, and then put it back in its scabbard.

"If you will help me carve up and carry the best of this beast back to my home, I will feed you and make you welcome, good sir. It is best not to be out in the wood after dark, and twilight even now approaches," he warned.

"You need to get that head-wound bandaged up," Gabriel pointed out, and the little man wiped at it again, the blood caking slowly.

Gabriel took out a sharp poniard, and helped Brin to carve off the thick meaty haunches from the carcass, and then followed Brin through the woods to his humble home. It wasn't quite tall enough for him to stand fully, but he made do without complaint. Brin was in his debt, and eager to be helpful. Any information he could get from him would be of great help in his quest.

*   *   *

"We do not see many humans in this world," Brin began, as he roasted one of the haunches on a spit over a fire. "Certainly none such as yourself, walking free and with weapons."

"How do you see them, then, friend Brin?" Gabriel asked.

"In chains generally, for such as you are kept as slaves, doing manual tasks in the cities and farms," he admitted. "Not my idea, or my doing, by the way," he hastened to add. "Such is the way of it in the city, by Malevar's decree, and few dare stand openly against the Grey Priest," he warned. "Humans do not share the same longevity as we, and we must seek permission to replace them with others from your realm."

"I have heard of this Malevar," Gabriel admitted. "I believe he has answers to many questions."

"Oh, knowledgeable he certainly is, with his magicks, and devices. But he answers to no man or elf. He commands and we obey," Brin explained the way of things. "His coming is lost in time, so long ago that few alive can recount the tale, even handed down by our ancestors. Immortal is he, and he now rules our world, or at least what we know of it, for we do not travel afar as you humans are known to do. I have been to your world, in my youth," he admitted suddenly. "The wee folk, the little people, of your legends, we are known as. Curiosity served, few of us visited the savagery of your human world again, except where ordered by Malevar. We took the odd man, or woman, sometimes on a whim, but mostly as directed by Malevar. Manual labor built his castle, and his places of magick. Many human slaves died in its construction, and many more died within its walls after it was built. But only Malevar knows the truth of that, all I tell is the tales that were told to me." He broke off from his tale to take the roasted meat down from the spit, and began cutting it up for himself and Gabriel to share. "Legend has it that this world was a far more pleasant place, before Malevar came here. Since then it has become darker, the woods no longer safe after dark, for strange things prowl and hunt in the shadows. This world is dying," he admitted, sadly.

"It seems not that way to me," admitted Gabriel. "Even the very air has a fresher taste here, to my thinking."

"Twas better, believe me," said Brin, biting into the hot cooked meat, juices running down his chin into his beard. "Since Malevar came to this world, abominations now roam the landscape. Goblins and Hobgoblins. Other things as well. Best seen from afar, and they shun the daylight, so ashamed they are of their own appearance. But at night, they roam freely, and I have heard some horrible sounds and screams echoing through these woods after dark."

"You say 'since Malevar came to this world' . . . Is he human then, like me?" asked Gabriel.

"Nay, for I have seen him once. Taller than myself, he is shorter than thee. His skin is grey, his head bald. I have not seen his like before. No one knows from whence he comes. But he quickly rose to power, usurping our own king. His magicks are powerful, and no one will stand against him," Brin revealed. "But tell me of thyself. How came you to this world?"

Gabriel shrugged his shoulders. "I come in search of my kinfolk. I crossed over into this realm through one of the faerie-circles of stones. I was aided by a druid."

Brin snorted. "I know of them. Evil men who claim to respect the wood. All they respect is its power. They do not honor it. They seek to use its power to their own ends."

"Indeed, I have no liking for them myself. He needed a little persuading to help me make the crossing. A friend holds him captive till I can return," Gabriel explained. "He and his brethren have persecuted my own people for centuries. For I am not exactly human myself." Gabriel loosened his tunic, and shrugged it off his shoulders to show Brin the scars on his back. "Once I had wings, till the druids took them from me. Others of my kind were forced through these strange portals into this world. Your Malevar was interested in my kind, I believe."

Brin examined the scars with interest. "If that is your reason for journeying here, then I feel you will find only sadness. I have heard of your winged brethren being taken to Malevar. They were all taken to his castle or his places of magick. None ever returned," Brin admitted. Gabriel was suddenly saddened by this grim news.

"I must seek the truth in this myself, friend Brin. For there *are* no more of my kind save one in the human world any longer. Malevar is my only hope," Gabriel admitted.

"Then I caution you, approach him with care. If he does harbor an interest in you and your kind, it would be well if he thought you just another human drudge. To reveal your true ancestry would not be wise," Brin advised. "I will escort you to the city, for no human is usually seen traveling alone." Brin outlined his plan to Gabriel, of how he thought best to aid him. Gabriel listened attentively, for he was a stranger here. This world was a lot stranger than the one he was used to.

*   *   *

Back in the world we know, Daeffyd Wildwood stripped the unconscious Lucifer of his clothing and weapons, intending them for his own use. Almost a full day had passed, which Lucifer had spent in drugged slumber. Wildwood needed the full moon to complete his chanting. The angel was stripped naked. Lucifer would have no need of clothes once he crossed over into the Realm of Faerie. He chuckled as he pulled the drugged body over to the stone circle, and rolled it over, till it crossed the boundary stones.

Stepping back, Wildwood watched and waited. It wasn't long before Lucifer's body began to grow fainter, less solid, as it attuned to the strange pulling vibrations of another world, and slowly faded from sight altogether. Speaking in the familiar High Speech of the Druids, Wildwood dedicated the human offering to Lord Malevar, imploring the ruler of that foreign realm to renew his pledge with the Druids. He received no answer. The woods remained silent as he waited in vain, and then reluctantly, he turned to un-tether the two fine horses. It wasn't a totally wasted night, after all.

* * *

As Gabriel settled down for the night in Brin's home, Lucifer slept naked and still drugged, deep in the wood, having finally materialized in the same spot that Gabriel had entered this world. The wood was slowly coming alive with nocturnal sounds, some of which were like nothing heard in his own world. Silence, grim and foreboding, followed those sounds, till the scream of some captured, tormented animal rent the night air.

Lucifer came awake slowly, the night-chill sinking into his naked body. He shivered, wrapping his arms around himself as he came to his senses, slowly becoming aware of his surroundings, and cursing his own stupidity for allowing the druid to trick him. He noted the still healing wound on his arm where Wildwood had obviously bled him, and for a second debated whether a loud curse would carry to wherever the druid had now fled.

Lucifer saw the stones then, spaced evenly apart in a circle around him, and realized what the druid had done. He had sent him through after Gabriel, and now how would they get back to their own world?

The noises carried far across the darkness of the night, and Lucifer's hackles rose instantly, for he was skilled in wood-lore, and was familiar with all the creatures that inhabited these woodlands. He was not familiar with the noises he was hearing, fortunately at a distance, though definitely getting closer.

He quickly assessed his position, naked and defenseless, and quicker still, decided that flight was his best option until he knew more of his surroundings. He quickly took to the trees, leaping high with his strong legs, and climbing rapidly up into the thick foliage. He found a suitable branch to rest for the night, obscured from sight from the ground below, yet still allowing him to view the ground in patches. He settled down to wait for the approaching creature or creatures to come into view.

Lucifer did not have long to wait. He heard the sounds of moving foliage coming from his right, and the harsh deep breathing of two creatures betrayed their presence before they stepped into view.

Short they were, and would come almost up to chest-height, but they were hunched over, big barrel-chests, and huge loping muscled arms dragged knuckles along the ground. One of them carried a large hand-axe, whilst the other carried a crude club, obviously broken off some tree. Their faces were a grotesque parody of Lucifer's own, with features twisted out of shape. One of them had a huge nose which almost obscured the gaping drooling mouth. The other's eyes were large and close-set, as he sniffed about, catching the scent of something that Lucifer was afraid was himself. They had clothing of a fashion, yet roughly thrown together and torn in places. Their feet were large, and bare. Lucifer saw claws where toenails should have been. These things, whatever they were, were not human.

"What is it you smell, brother?" asked the first of the ogres. He lifted his own head, trying to taste the air.

"Sumfing . . . . not sure . . ." he grunted in reply, and Lucifer shrunk down in his leafy hideout, hoping they wouldn't look up into the tree itself. He hardly dared breathe, as he waited for the two monsters to make their move. Looking up, he knew he would be able to climb higher than the two of them with his lighter body-weight, but if they saw him or heard him, all they had to do was wait him out. He couldn't stay up there forever.

After what seemed like a lifetime, the two creatures moved away from the tree, and Lucifer heard the noises they made as they went through the undergrowth, putting distance between them and himself. Breathing a great sigh of relief, Lucifer decided to stay up in the safety of the tree, at least until dawn, and settled down to sleep as best he could under the circumstances. He would be uncomfortable by morning, but still alive.

* * *

Lucifer awoke just after dawn, as the sound of the woods coming alive around him woke him from his uneasy slumber. The birdsong in the adjacent trees seemed as normal as in his own world, as did the sounds from the ground below. The wood looked less fearful in the light of day.

Before climbing down, Lucifer decided to climb up, seeking the sky above the treetops to get his bearings. As did Gabriel before him, Lucifer spotted the smoke coming from Brin's cottage in the distance, though at this time he did not know it's source, but chose as did Gabriel to explore it, it being the only sign of human life for miles around.

Lucifer climbed down to the ground, crouching warily as he alighted, senses alert for anything untoward, such as the reappearance of those two strange hybrids that had passed by last night. Then he straightened up, trying to get the aches out of his body from his uneasy sleep. His back ached, no matter which way he twisted and stretched. Best try to walk it off, but first he paused to urinate against the tree-trunk, to relieve the pressure in his bladder.

Walking lightly in the direction the smoke had seemed to be coming from, Lucifer too noticed the way the wood seemed to change character as the foliage above thickened and blotted out the sun. The darker, cooler places seemed less inviting, especially after last night, and so he picked his path with care, enjoying the warm sun on his back.

The whispering started shortly after the sun rose, and he shook his head, thinking he had some wax in his ears, but it wouldn't go away, just stayed there on the edge of his consciousness. The first butterfly fluttered to a sudden stop as Lucifer walked into the clearing, hovered a moment in mid-air, and then hurriedly flew off into the trees. Lucifer thought nothing of it, even when the whispering in his head seemed to increase, and more and more of the butterflies began appearing again, as if curious with this new stranger in their midst.

One of them flew close, skimming out his line of sight as he momentarily gasped, certain that he had glimpsed something odd about the butterfly's body, but it moved too quickly to be sure. Some of the whispers seemed like laughter, though shrill and tinny to his ear.

Trudging on, he sighed with satisfaction as he heard the rippling waters of a stream, and finally saw it meandering across his path. Kneeling on the water's edge, he dipped his hand into the water to scoop some up to his mouth. The cold clear water tasted better than the finest of wines, and he savored the feel of it trickling down his throat. Then, his thirst assuaged, he began to walk into the waters, seeking to wash himself, gasping as the coldness of it squeezed his privates, and he lowered himself into the waters.

As he began to wash himself, the water seemed to move gently around him, stroking him, caressing him. It felt so soothing that he lay back in the water, and let the eddying current wash over him, the waters almost feeling like a woman's fingers, running over his body, but that was absurd.

Sitting up, Lucifer wiped the water from his face, studying his reflection for a moment in the rippling surface, and then gasped as he watched that reflection change into a woman's face. "Gods!" he exclaimed, quickly standing up, and splashing noisily for the bank of the stream, climbing up and out of the water.

"Don't be afraid . . . ." a whispering, rippling voice seemed to echo in his mind, and Lucifer paused, kneeling on the bank, ready to flee if the need arose. He looked back into the stream, to see the waters there swirling about, and as he watched, they took the shape of a woman, slowly rising naked from the water itself, to stand finally before him, her flesh slowly assuming normal skin-tones, till she appeared as solid as Lucifer himself, who remained kneeling there, and gawping at her beauty. He could do nothing but gawp at the vision who now stood there before him, ankle deep in the stream. Otherwise nude, her long hair hung down to partially cover her breasts. It was green, and halfway between seaweed and moss in it's texture. The hair at her loins matched that on her head. Her eyes were a deep azure blue, and her lips pale and yet sensuously full. She had no shame in her own nakedness, and looked upon Lucifer's own unclothed state as natural as her own.

"My name is Rhiahne. The spirit of this stream. Its essence is my own. You are a human. I thought the other human a mystery, but now there is a mystery twofold," she smiled, though made no overt moves to harm him, and so Lucifer stood up before her.

"Lady, I have heard of you water-elementals, but did not think to ever meet with one. You are beauty itself, and I apologize for bathing in your waters," he said, sincerely. Rhiahne smiled, and raised her hand to him. Lucifer moved forward to take it tentatively, surprised to find it felt like living flesh.

"Do not be surprised, sir. I may take human shape as I wish, though for the most part, I prefer to suffuse my essence in my living waters. I sometimes choose to interact with the other species who inhabit this wood, but you, sir, are a stranger here, as was the other human who passed this way."

"That would be my friend. I am looking for him." Lucifer admitted, trying to keep his eyes on her face, and only too aware of the effect her innocent nudity was having on him. His own nakedness made the problem quite apparent, and he was having difficulty controlling his own body. If she noticed, she gave no sign. Her face did not disguise any mischief or malice.

"I tried to speak with your friend, but he was alarmed and ran off through the woods before I could explain," Rhiahne told him. "I meant him no harm, nor do I wish harm to you. You are beautiful for a human," she said, complimenting him, and looking down the length of Lucifer's body for the first time. She touched his shoulder, her fingers cool and soothing, as she ran her hand down his arm, and then over his chest. "Stay with me but a while, and I will aid your search for your friend. My life-waters run through this wood and beyond. Many things are known to me. Many creatures come to partake of me, and they share their knowledge with me."

"I would indeed like to stay, lady," Lucifer admitted, "but my search for my friend will permit no delay." Rhiahne came closer, her nakedness having now a profound effect upon him, as her cool fingers gently caressed him.

"Just for a little while," Rhiahne pleaded, and then her lips pressed to his own, and Lucifer found himself surrendering his will to hers, responding to her fresh kisses, as the two of them sank to the ground.

*   *   *

Dawn came to Brin's cabin to find the elf and the human both already awake, and readying provisions for the journey ahead. "You will have to leave the sword behind, for no human, not even a slave, is allowed to carry weapons openly. The dagger you may hide about your person," Brin advised. Gabriel was loath to leave the sword behind, but unless he passed for one of the human slaves, he doubted whether he would get very far into the city.

"Very well," he agreed, using strips of leather to fasten his dagger to his forearm where it would be concealed under his sleeve, but remain easily accessible should he need it.

Brin took a leather collar, from which hung a small metal box. The metal box had been damaged. "This you will wear around your neck. It was how Malevar subjugated the humans. Something in the box sapped their will. Don't worry. It's broken, and doesn't work any more. That's how my own slave ran away," he admitted.

"You had a human as your slave?" Gabriel asked.

"Yes. Don't look so shocked. Having a slave was a status symbol, and we had to control them somehow. The human women we kept in the whorehouses, but the human men, being bigger and stronger, we needed to control more fully, else they ran amok amongst us." He handed the collar to Gabriel.

"Are you sure this thing is broken?" he asked, examining the object, though not understanding it at all. Malevar's magic.

"I have no talent for repairing the thing, I assure you. I seek not to trick you, friend Gabriel." Tentatively, Gabriel put the collar around his neck, allowing the clasp to close and fasten it in place. He felt no different. "There. Now you look like any other human walking around the place. Just look dumb and do everything I tell you to do in public."

"How far is it to the city?" asked Gabriel.

"About half a day's travel to the north. We should get there by noon." Brin finished packing a couple of small satchels with provisions, including joints of cooked meat from the slain boar. "Malevar makes an appearance on the steps of his palace once a day to hear petitions from the townsfolk and civic dignitaries. You'll get to see him alright, but what you do after that will be up to you. He has his guards, and he has his magicks. People live in fear of him, and although most would like to see him gone from this land, their fear is his most potent weapon."

"What is that castle of his like?" Gabriel asked.

Brin thought for a moment. "I don't often go into the city, so my memory isn't that good. But it seemed a difficult place to get into. Built within the city itself, it backs onto a river. As I said, a broad set of stairs leads out from one entrance into the city square. There is another larger entrance to the city to the west, where provisions and wagons enter, though it is heavily guarded. I have heard he uses the tower of the castle overlooking the river as his laboratory, performing arcane magicks there. The surrounding walls are high, and no window is close to the ground, even for a human to reach. No trees near the walls to climb, and the nearest building is too far away to overlook the walls. I do not see how you will get into the place," he admitted.

Gabriel was already thinking. He had seen enough castles in his travels around Europe and Asia. A river meant sewage and effluent outlets, which usually went unguarded. Messy but effective. If the walls were rough enough, he could even scale them by hand. "I'll find a way," he assured his elf-friend.

*   *   *

Gabriel and Brin set out for the city. There was a pathway of sorts through the woods, meandering this way and that, and they followed it as Brin pointed out the various features of the wood, laughing as a swarm of the large butterflies came rushing their way, only to stop and pass by to one side. "They are curious, that's all," Brin explained, then saw the puzzled look on Gabriel's face. "You haven't met them yet?" he laughed. "Come my friend, the Faerie await . . . ." and he beckoned Gabriel forward with one hand and beckoned to the fluttering 'butterflies' with the other, and as they came forward, Gabriel got his first real look at the Faerie-folk of legend.

Slim of body, and humanoid in shape, male and females alike fluttered about, though still cautious of coming too close. The whispering in Gabriel's head grew louder, and now as understanding dawned, he found himself able to begin to make sense of the faint chatter. No butterflies these, but faeries true. Tiny folk, dressed in garments so fine, only spider-silk could be spun so smooth and thin enough to clothe them. Dyed in a variety of colors to match the varied pigmentation of their natural wings.

He laughed at his own stupidity, and the sound was infectious, as the tiny tinny sounds moved all about him. "The Faerie Folk befriend elves and the odd human only rarely these days, friend Gabriel. They too have known suffering since Malevar came to these lands and are now no longer safe even in their own woods, for evil things of Malevar's creation now run free. You have seen the dark places in the woods, best skirted in the daylight, for that is where these creatures now make their home, and at night they roam far and wide," he explained.

Gabriel stared about him, fascinated and smiling stupidly at the dancing faeries who fluttered about him. One of the bolder ones, a female, with a striking coloration of purple and blue wings, flew suddenly up close to him, then paused, fluttering just in front of his face, and then, laughing, flew off as he tried to raise a hand gently to her. She was beautiful, and mischievous, and looked to be the equivalent of a young girl, not yet in the full bloom of adulthood. "The stuff of legend in my world," Gabriel explained. "Marvelous." He was awestruck. "I have been hearing these voices in my head since I got here. I didn't know what it meant."

Brin suddenly looked puzzled at Gabriel's admission. "You hear their voices in your head? Now that is strange, for only the faerie-folk themselves can 'speak' silently to each other like that." And as Brin watched in astonishment, Gabriel held up his hand, and the young female faerie flew back, settling gently in the palm of his hand, as if fearing nothing. Gabriel laughed softly, and the faerie laughed with him, then flew up to kiss him lightly on the nose, before flying off back to the rest of the fluttering swarm, as the whispering in his head grew louder, as many more voices were suddenly more agitated. Gabriel laughed anew at the unexpected event, and then as Brin and he watched, the faeries began to drift off back into the woods, as silently as they had come.

"Consider yourself honored, Sir, for that was Pfil herself who took a fancy to you. Pfil, daughter of Ragnar, King of the Faerie-Folk," Brin explained.

Brin and Gabriel then resumed their march towards the city, and finally came into view of it shortly after midday. The woods led down into a plain, and sited on which was the large city, and the overpowering castle in the distance, backing onto the winding river as Brin had said. To the west, in the distance, lay a formidable mountain range, while across the river, to the north and east, the plain continued into the distance. "Let's circle around, cross the stream, and approach the city from the east, so I can get a good look at the castle," suggested Gabriel, and they changed direction.

*   *   *

Back in the woods, the hot midday sun awoke Lucifer, who found himself still wrapped in Rhiahne's arms on the bank of the stream. Guiltily, he realized half the day had passed, and began to raise himself up. Rhiahne stirred beside him. "I have kept you long, I know," she admitted guiltily. "Yet, do not think ill of me, for it has been many years since I last took a human lover. I know you must go to seek out your friend, for that is your human way. He went to the north, to the cabin of the elf Brin. He will be safe with that elf, and you both shall be safe within these woods, despite it's perils, should you only stay close by my waters. I will protect you both from harm. My magicks are powerful. I would not keep you, but I would ask you to visit with me again, if it is possible." Her face was beauty itself, and Lucifer didn't know how to refuse her.

"Lady, were it for myself, I would never leave your side again. I have never known a woman more beautiful than you. Yet you are right in that I must seek my friend. He is in peril, though he knows it not. If it is possible, I will indeed seek to find you again, in this world, or the next," he promised her, and bent down to kiss her sweet lips once more, before helping her to her feet.

Rhiahne smiled hauntingly, as she walked slowly back into the cool flowing waters, and as Lucifer watched, all color disappeared from her skin, as it became translucent, and then as clear as the water itself, slowly losing shape, and sinking back down to merge with the rippling waters of the stream. He heard a faint sigh, and then Rhiahne's essence had merged fully back into the stream once more.

Chapter Seven

ucifer took Rhiahne's advice as he traveled through the woods, keeping automatically to the sunlit sections of the woods, and avoiding the darker places.

The whispering returned now and then, as did clouds of butterflies flitting through the trees at a distance. Sometimes flying closer, before flying away again as he turned to look at them. He tried to put the strange feelings he was experiencing to the back of his mind as he concentrated on making up for lost time as he headed north.

He found Brin's cabin deserted, after approaching it cautiously. The door was unlocked, and so he went inside, noticing Gabriel's sword almost at once, which was worrying in itself. It was unlike Gabriel to leave a weapon behind, yet Rhiahne had assured him that his friend would come to no harm from the elf.

Looking around the cabin, Lucifer noticed clothing, though far too small to fit him. Yet there were some animal skins, and he noticed a small set of tools to work the leather. First things first. He couldn't run around this world naked, so he set about trying to fashion some clothing from the animal-skins.

"Manling." Lucifer heard the voice at the back of his mind, and whirled suddenly to see one of the large butterflies hovering there in the doorway. Large white wings, feathered with dark green veins, adorned his back. "You understand us, don't you?" an amused voice asked him, though the faery's lips did not move.

"What?" Lucifer looked closer, the body shape of the faerie now apparent. "My God! Is there no end to the wonders of this world?" he asked aloud.

"Manling, but not human. For humans would not understand our talk," the faerie explained. "Brin is our friend, and this is his cabin. Would you steal from him?" Again, the words seemed to burn directly into his head, yet it was not real sound. Lucifer stared about him, wary. Was there any threat to be had from this tiny winged being?

"I just need some clothing. I mean no harm. I'm just trying to find my friend," he explained.

"The dark one? We have already met your friend. Pfil was quite taken with him. He and Brin journey to the city to the north. They go to seek Malevar. Your friend is a fool. Malevar will kill him," the faerie warned. "He has killed many of my kind, and all of yours."

"What do you know of my kind?" asked Lucifer, afraid of the answer he knew was coming. The faerie fluttered up and down as though nervous.

"Long ago, others of your kind, though with wings, crossed over into this world. They came one by one, and yet we sensed them. Some we talked to, but could not save. All were given to Malevar. Most died at his hands," the faerie explained. "They were the lucky ones. A small number were 'changed', and they now roam the dark places of this world, and some have even crossed over into your own."

"I think I saw two of those things last night," Lucifer admitted.

"Then lucky they didn't see you. For they feed on elf and human as they do the beasts of the forest. This is a realm of magick, yet Malevar's magicks are by far the most fearsome. None can stand against him. He is slowly poisoning this world."

"This is a fool's errand then. We came to this world in search of our lost brethren, and now you tell me that none survived." Lucifer was dismayed.

"All consigned to death in Malevar's castle, where he performed his foul experiments upon them, as he does every species, from elf to faerie to humans, and their tainted offspring. Few survive, and those that do are shunned by the faerie-folk."

*　　*　　*

Laura, Belle and Manuel all listened attentively to Gabriel's account of his first exploration of Malevar's castle. The darkened room, dimly lit by the single candle, brought a closeness which they could all experience. The air lay heavy and expectant as they hung on every word that Gabriel recounted.

*   *   *

As Gabriel and Brin neared the outskirts of the city, Brin bade him fall in behind his 'master's footsteps, and Gabriel did so before he caught sight of the first inhabitants. Laughing 'children' even smaller than Brin were playing in the fields, and they ignored the two of them, happy and carefree in the innocent games they were playing.

As they entered the city itself, Gabriel noticed the varying architecture of the dwellings. Simple structures of mud and wattle, much like in his own world, made up the perimeter buildings, whilst much finer structures of mud brick and some stone structures could be found further towards the city centre. The city was a scaled down version of similar habitation in his own world. Basic sewage, and buildings grouped together in a more or less ordered fashion.

The sight of his first human reassured Gabriel that Brin's strategy had been wise to accept, for the lifeless character walked obediently at hand with his elf master, ready to do his bidding or protect him from harm. He did not look malnourished or ill-treated at all, and was reasonably well-dressed, but his eyes were vacant, soulless in fact. He had no obvious will of his own. Around his neck was a similar device to that around Gabriel's own, obviously working all too well.

Gabriel adopted a similar blank gaze and he did his best to follow Brin as the elf nodded and greeted a few folk he knew, who commented on his new slave. Brin shrugged off their enquiries with good nature, where he needed to. He had obviously told the truth about his lack of a slave for many years. Gabriel hoped that they didn't ask too many awkward questions.

As they entered the city square, Gabriel found it quite crowded with applicants all vying to be heard, and it was difficult to see from this distance just what was happening on the steps of the castle. He used the opportunity to study the structure well, and indicated to Brin that he wished to study it further.

Brin lead the way around the crowd to the west of the city square, and then they headed north towards the river. Gabriel noted the architecture of the castle, which at one point jutted out into the river itself, where a narrow structure housed a large water wheel. Gabriel at first thought it provided water to the castle, but the architecture itself was strange, with large metal protuberances and shiny metal cables. The walls were indeed rough enough to climb, though about thirty feet high, yet he would be in plain sight all the time he was doing so. A more surreptitious approach was called for.

They crossed the small stone bridge over the small tributary of the river, back to the west side of the city, and moved upstream of the castle to where the waters of the river flowed deep, before running shallow near the castle itself. Many small boulders in the water, perhaps left over from the castle's construction, broke up the even flow. Scouting along the river bank, he noticed the green algae on the rocks, drawing his attention to the outfall, barred by a rusted metal grille.

As Brin kept watch, Gabriel waded out into the river, and then submerged himself, letting the current carry him downstream, and slowly swimming in towards the shadows of the rear wall of the castle. The distant figures of the guards on the battlements weren't paying close attention to the river, more concerned with the gathering in the city square, but Gabriel was taking few chances.

He half crawled out of the water onto the wet, foul-smelling rocks. The grille-work was secured in place by an old lock. He felt certain he could pick it with ease, but was unsure whether to do so now, without letting Brin know what was happening. To gain entry while everyone was occupied had it's advantage, yet it might be better to wait for nightfall, so that the occupants would be mostly asleep, and give him greater freedom of movement.

Satisfied he had made the right decision, Gabriel lowered himself back into the water, pushing off with the current and letting it carry him downstream, to the eastern side of the castle, where Brin was now waiting for him.

Stripping off his wet clothes as he got out of the water, Gabriel began hanging them on bushes to catch the hot afternoon sun while he dried himself off, and warmed up, and he explained his plan to the elf.

*   *   *

That evening, Gabriel slipped into the cold water once more, repeating his approach to the locked grille-work. He used the blade of the poniard to manipulate the working of the lock, fearing for one moment that the rusted metal would refuse to budge and possibly snap his only weapon, but eventually the metal moved, and the lock snapped open. He worked the grille off slowly, not wanting any noise to carry up to the battlements above. Finally, Gabriel slipped inside the sewer outlet, and paused, letting his eyes grow accustomed to the gloom, and his nose accustomed to the smell.

Finally, Gabriel began to move, finding his way more by instinct, knowing roughly how the sewage system would be designed. The narrower passages would lead to small private or public privies. He wanted an access into the kitchens, where a large amount of slops would be disposed of, and thus the larger diameter passages were of more interest to him. All of them were navigable, having been constructed by human slave labor, but he needed a large enough opening to make his exit.

Following his nose, literally, Gabriel managed to identify the aroma of rotting food, and soon found numerous rats running this way and that, proof that his route was true. They scattered out of his way as he left them to feed, and he made a cautious exit out of the slop-hole and into the lower kitchens. Empty now, he used the opportunity and the sluice to splash clean water over his hands and face, mopping at the worst of the filth on his still-damp clothes.

Still feeling decidedly uncomfortable in his damp clothing, he began working his way through the darkened chambers and passageways. The deathly silence unnerved him. Normal castles such as this would still have servants and retainers carrying out their duties at all hours of the night or day for that matter. Such was not the case here, for the creatures with which Malevar obviously trusted his personal safety were obviously under instruction to secure the perimeter and leave the inner chambers to Malevar alone.

It made things easier, if one could breach that security as Gabriel had done. He padded softly and silently in the general direction he assumed Malevar's inner sanctum lay, navigating stairways with caution, but climbing ever higher. Most of the walls were simple bare stone, though here and there were hung a few rich tapestries, depicting mainly woodland scenes.

Eventually, the torches that hung in iron baskets on the walls grew fewer, and began to be replaced with strange shining stones, which gave off light much like the fireflies and certain phosphorescent algae. Dull and suffused, but light nevertheless. Gabriel examined one such stone in awe, feeling it smooth and cold to the touch. Some strange unknown mineral, he assumed.

There were more of these glow-stones, the higher he climbed into the tower. He realized he had finally reached his goal when the first of the strange metal boxes came into view. Dull, and yet shiny at the same time. Small brightly colored jewels adorned this box, in a pattern with which he was not familiar. Strange metallic wires connected this large box to others of the same ilk, as Gabriel looked around. The chamber was filled with these strange boxes, some large, some smaller. Colored wires connected some of them to each other, and others seemed to tether these boxes to some sort of manacles on the walls, though they looked far too heavy for a thief to make off with, even should one gain admittance to this chamber as Gabriel had done. Other strange mechanical apparatus filled various niches, and decorated a number of tables, but Gabriel had not seen their like before, and was thus at a loss as to their purpose.

Gabriel entered the room warily, putting his hands on the first of these boxes, feeling the vibration coming from within, and the slight warmth from the metal. He didn't know what to make of it, and began touching some of the jewels, one of which suddenly shone so brightly at his touch that he recoiled in shock momentarily. It seemed to react to his touch. Best not to touch it again he thought, and so continued his search, passing out of this chamber, and into another which housed strange glass cubicles, slightly reclined, against one of the walls.

He froze as his gaze swept along the many such cubicles, until he came to one which was occupied, by one of the strange semi-human creatures which Malevar used as his guards. It was motionless, and the interior of the cubicle in which it was housed was filled with a strange grey mist, which coiled itself about the creature's body, as Gabriel drew himself closer to examine it more fully.

It stood more or less chest-height on Gabriel, though the limbs and musculature were much thickened. Fingers and toes were twisted and deformed into virtual claws, with long ragged nails. The face and jaw structure were bestial indeed, and Gabriel couldn't help think of the wild boar he had slain in the woods, as though this creature were somehow related to such a wild beast of the wood. It was either dead or asleep, for it moved not, and showed no reaction to Gabriel's examination. He touched the glass, to find it strangely chilled, and the imprint of his hand remained on the glass for a few seconds after he removed itMoving on, Gabriel continued his exploration to the next chamber, which seemed to be a library of sorts. One heavy tome lay open on a small table, and Gabriel perused it eagerly, though it was written in a language he could not decipher, lavishly illustrated in a mixture of strange symbols. The sketches that accompanied the strange text seemed to be biological in nature, detailing joints and musculature. Gabriel had traveled far across the known world, yet his discoveries here continued to astound him.

Exploring further, Gabriel marveled at some of the strange unknown devices he found in the remaining chambers. He was familiar with machines, though mainly those of a siege nature, yet he had also had experience working with a locksmith, and knew the intricacies of manipulating metal. Further travels in the Far East had broadened his horizons further. Still, he knew not what to make of what he saw here.

Strange elongated and interconnected metals rods were hinged and seemingly suspended above a long table. There were leather restraints attached to the table, which indicated that they were used to bind something or someone. On the ends of the metal rods were strange metallic implements, some of them looked razor-sharp. The whole thing had an unpleasant look to it, an obvious place of torture to Gabriel's mind. He shuddered as he envisaged himself strapped to that table, and quickly moved on to the next chamber, where he suddenly gasped, and stared helplessly up at the stone wall where the skeletal remains of an Angel where nailed there in an obscene display.

So it was true, then. Angels *had* been delivered to Malevar. Was this their fate then? Gabriel went to step forward to touch what remained of one of his people, but found himself unable to do so. In fact, he could not move a single muscle in his body. What magick was this? He rolled his eyes, staring frantically from side to side, breathing still, but with difficulty, yet he could not otherwise move. What was happening to him?

"Do you have any idea what I do to curious and uninvited souls who dare to trespass within my castle?" Gabriel heard the voice behind him, strangely sibilant, in the same dialect used by the elf Brin, but the words seemed not quite as flowing. He could not turn to see who it was, though he tried his hardest. Movement out of the corner of one eye directed him to his first glimpse of Malevar himself.

He stepped around Gabriel slowly, observing him at his leisure, sizing him up as would a butcher about to prepare a piece of meat. Gabriel stared in awe at the strange creature as it came into sight. Malevar the Grey was aptly named, for his grey lizard-like skin was like nothing Gabriel had seen before. Shorter than the creature in the glass casket, Malevar was only head and shoulders taller than Brin the elf, yet his physiognomy showed vast differences. His arms and neck were disproportionately long, and one of those hands held a strange glowing scepter before Gabriel, as though using it's radiance to examine him more closely.

Gabriel examined Malevar in turn, his face emotionless and almost featureless. Malevar's head was out of proportion to his slim, small body. The skull seemed to swell, and the grey skin was stretched over it. A small thin mouth below two small holes in the centre of his face, for Malevar seemingly had no nose to speak of. His eyes were large, and totally black, like obsidian. There was a reptilian aspect to them, in the way he blinked, as lids opened and closed from the sides, instead of above and below. Five longer fingers on each hand were extremely slender, and seemed to end in small pads. He was dressed in a fine muslin robe, which was cinched about his narrow waist by a metal belt of what looked like broad copper-links. The buckle of the belt was adorned with four of the strange shiny jewels he had noticed in the first laboratory chamber. Malevar's small mouth appeared to smile, as he realized Gabriel was examining him in turn.

Malevar reached for the collar around Gabriel's neck, and he pulled it off roughly, though Gabriel could feel it not. He might as well have been made of stone. "Broken. But by you, or someone else? A mystery indeed," Malevar chuckled. "You look too intelligent for the usual human drudges we keep about the city." He puzzled over Gabriel's appearance momentarily, and then studied the significance of Gabriel's last movements towards the skeletal remains nailed up on the wall. "Could it be?" he mused. Going back behind Gabriel, he took a small sharp knife from within his robes, and used it to slit up the back of Gabriel's rough jerkin, peeling back the pieces to reveal the symmetrical scars on Gabriel's shoulder-blades, and he cried out in triumph. "Yesssss. Fate is smiling on me at last," he exulted, returning within Gabriel's limited vision once more, though Gabriel had no idea of what had just happened. "Take a good look, my friend." Malevar pointed up at the grim exhibit on the wall. "Such was the fate of your brethren in years gone by," he admitted. "I conducted my experiments upon them all, furthering my knowledge of your uniqueness. Sadly they all died before I reached my conclusions, but now I have you, wings or no wings, and you will do nicely!" Malevar promised, leaning closer, waving the glowing scepter in Gabriel's face. "Your fate will be different, I promise you," he cackled. "I will not harm such a magnificent body. I have already learned as much of it as there is to know. It will serve my purposes well."

Gabriel tried and tried, but he could not move. He remained motionless as Malevar sized him up like a slab of beef. What magick spell had been cast upon him? If only he could move, this scrawny creature could not stand against him. Yet he was helpless.

Malevar waved the scepter one more time, its glow changing in color slightly, and Malevar spoke once more. "You can now speak, so tell me how you came here. I would know how you came to this world which is not your own. None of your kind have made the crossing for many years now."

Gabriel found he had limited movement in his neck and he moved his head from side to side, opening and closing his mouth, which was strangely dry. He cleared his throat. "I came seeking my brethren, murderer!" he accused. Malevar stood there nonplussed at his allegation. "I was almost given over to your tender mercies many centuries ago, but my people rescued me from the Druids. Now my people are gone, and I have searched the world over for them without finding even a one. This realm was my last hope. Are they all dead then?" he asked, forlornly.

"All who made the crossing, aye," Malevar confirmed. "But their deaths served a purpose, in that they enabled me to finished my genetic research and verify the results of the breeding program which was interrupted many centuries ago. You have no idea of my frustrations when the last of your kind perished on my operating tables, before my technique was perfected. But now I have you." Malevar came closer, and Gabriel was at a loss to read the emotions in such a strange face. "You are a fine specimen," he promised. "With your body, I will once more walk amongst men in your own world."

"I would kill you, monster!" said Gabriel, with effort, still trying to move despite the obvious spell he had been placed under. Malevar made a sound which Gabriel took for laughter, so high-pitched as to be almost inaudible.

"Wherefore do you think you will succeed, where all others have failed?" and with that, Malevar raised his scepter before Gabriel's eyes once more, and it's tip glowed brighter, forcing Gabriel to close his eyes, and as he did so, he lost consciousness.

*　　*　　*

Lucifer hurried through the wood, feeling a sense of dread he had never felt before. Guilt over the easy deception by the druid Wildwood, and fear for the unknown fate of his friend Gabriel, who had surely been lead into a trap by the druid's deception.

All through the long night, he hurried north along the faintly moonlit, well-worn path. He could brook no delay, and where he heard noises in the black shadows, he drew his sword and challenged boldly "Come then, if you would challenge me! Come and taste my fine sword!" he warned. None came forward, whether they existed only in his imagination or otherwise. Lucifer was in no mood to waste any more time. Only the blackness of the night slowed him at all. He made steady progress, and by dawn he could see the spires of the castle in the distance as the trees thinned out.

A small man, an elf by the description the faerie had given him, was leaving the city by the same pathway. Lucifer strode boldly on, determined to ignore the diminutive fellow, when the elf stopped in his tracks upon seeing him, and pointedly noticed the sword at Lucifer's hip, if not the crude nature of the leathers that Lucifer had fashioned for himself.

"No slave are you, and I recognize that sword!" Brin accused, pointing. Lucifer paused, mouth half-open in surprise at the elf's words.

"You recognize *this* sword?" he asked in return.

"Aye, for it was left in my safekeeping," Brin admitted.

"You know of my friend Gabriel?" Lucifer asked. Brin regarded him warily.

"I know of him, aye. But what of you? What is your name?" the elf asked.

"I am called Lucifer, and if you know of my friend's whereabouts, then tell me, for I fear he is in peril."

"Indeed he is," nodded Brin. "Anyone foolhardy enough to brave Malevar's castle puts himself in peril, but he would listen not to my warnings. Daylight has come without his return. I could not do anything to aid him by myself, and I have few friends in the city, and so I had no option but to return to my cottage in the forest and wait and hope for his safe return in time, though I fear otherwise."

"Mayhap the two of us together may prevail in aiding my friend." Lucifer replied. Brin nodded.

"Come then," agreed the elf. "I will show you where he entered the castle, and we will seek to follow him, if that is your wish."

*　　*　　*

As if through a mist, Gabriel was aware of movement around him, though he still found movement impossible. He was strapped naked and supine onto the table he had seen earlier. Above him, strange mechanical arms and other devices moved as if of their own volition, though he gathered Malevar or some of his goblin assistants were causing them to move by some means he had yet to fathom.

One of these goblins now came forward, with a small bowl of water and a soapstone, and he used this to wet Gabriel's head. Gabriel noticed the strange headbands these goblins wore. Their behavior was strangely subdued. Could this be another form of control device used by Malevar like the collars the humans were forced to wear? Taking a small but sharp dagger, the goblin began to scrape the hair off Gabriel's head, taking his time, till eventually Gabriel's skull was bald. Malevar himself then came forward with a strange device which he clamped to Gabriel's skull momentarily, before removing it once more, and deliberating as he studied the device.

He went over to one of the strange metal boxes, and began pressing some of the small jewels on the surface, in a rhythmic fashion. Gabriel could just see what happened next out of the corner of his eye. An apparition began to form above the box. What looked to be a human skull hung there, slowly rotating, as lines began to crisscross it's surface, some black and some red. He did not know what to make of the strange vision, though Malevar thought little of it, obviously. Gabriel knew it boded ill for him, and tried desperately to move, but it was as though he no longer had any control over his own body, the straps were irrelevant.

Malevar came and stood looking down at him. "You will forgive the crudity of what is to come, but resources are somewhat limited these days." Incredibly long grey fingers ran over Gabriel's skull, examining the bone structure. "Most of the operation will be computer-controlled, but my 'assistants' will still need to perform some of the physical tasks when we transfer the brains. Don't worry, you will not die as a result of this operation, for you will find yourself controlling my body, at least until such time as I am sure the operation is a complete success, and I will no longer need my old body. Then you may do with it as you wish . . . ." he chuckled. "Rule here in my stead, if you will, for I will then cross over into your world. In your body, and immune to the pollution of my own lungs by your atmosphere, I will be free to seek out my legacy." Malevar's words were lost on Gabriel. He understood little of what the priest said.

One of the goblin assistants then wheeled another table in alongside the one which currently held Gabriel.

*   *   *

Lucifer and Brin padded wetly along the lower chambers of Malevar's castle, after using the same sewer entrance as Gabriel to enter the castle unseen. The short swim had taken only minutes, with Lucifer aiding Brin against the current, and they had entered through the grille left unlocked by Gabriel.

They hid from a few of the goblin retainers that scurried about the castle. Bigger than Brin, they were still dwarfed by Lucifer, and he carried a good length of steel to defend himself should the case arise. Stealth was still required, for they were greatly outnumbered. "Your friend sought Malevar's castle, where the fiend carries out his alchemies on my people, and yours before. We must go up and to the east," Brin advised. Lucifer nodded, and the two of them moved swiftly and silently. Brin lead the way, and Lucifer gasped as the elf revealed some of his strange powers unconsciously. Whenever Brin stepped into the shadows, he disappeared from view. Seeing Lucifer's astonishment, Brin reappeared with a smile on his face. "Fear not, friend Lucifer. Tis but a little thing I do. My people cross over into your world by an adjustment to our inner-vibrations. I myself did not understand how this works until Malevar's coming, and he explained to my people how he had been able to duplicate what we thought were natural powers. He explained that everything vibrates, and that my people could adjust their own internal vibrations at will, enabling us to step between worlds under certain conditions, and where weakness in the fabric of space exist, and this control can also allow us to fade from sight in certain conditions, such as deep shadows. We do not actually disappear, more 'blur' our image, but this is well hidden in poor visibility," he explained. "Malevar constructed a belt of power, which gave him similar powers, and that was how he followed one of our people into the realm of Faerie."

"So how do humans come into this world of yours?" Lucifer asked.

"Physical contact with one of us as we cross. Our inner vibrations are passed on into whatever we touch," Brin explained.

"But Gabriel and myself did not accompany any such as you when we crossed over. How is this?" he questioned. Brin shrugged his shoulders.

"I do not know. Perhaps, despite the difference in our size, we are related somehow? Your mother may have slept in a faerie-circle one fine summer's night," he chuckled, reminiscing fondly.

"Tis magick, to be sure." Lucifer didn't fully appreciate Brin's explanation, just as Brin himself had not understood it when he himself had first heard it. "Yet Malevar duplicated it. He must be a powerful magician indeed." Brin nodded, and then took the lead again, vanishing eerily from sight when he strode into the dark shadows being cast by the ornate drapes hung against the bright sunlight streaming in from the windows. He reappeared again after a few feet, and Lucifer followed eagerly. Together, they made their way towards the laboratory complex without encountering any of Malevar's retainers, then, hearing noises ahead, they slowed to a more cautious approach.

They heard five individual voices coming from the chamber ahead of them. One high-pitched, which they assumed to be the Grey Priest himself, and the other four, the subhuman assistants of his. Lucifer drew his sword, slowly. Brin took a quick peek beyond the doorway, assessing the situation.

Malevar was stood by one of the metal boxes, pushing the brightly colored jewels in seemingly random sequence, though nodding to himself as he did so. The now bald Gabriel was secured to one table. A second table, presently unoccupied, was beside the first, awaiting an occupant.

One of the long hinged metal arms was slowly moving to a position behind Gabriel's head. "I will supervise the first part of this operation myself, before surrendering myself to the mercies of my well-trained assistants. A risk enough in itself, but you have no idea how long the millennia have chafed upon me. I would leave this place, and return to my own people. This has been denied me since my body began to reject the poisons and toxins in your atmosphere," he explained. "I have been dying for centuries, as the poisons I breathed in over many years in your own world took their toll." The attachment on the end of the metal arm rotated, and a wickedly shaped device now neared Gabriel's skull.

Lucifer assessed the situation in a second, and although not understanding anything Malevar had said, it was obvious he intended harm to Gabriel. It was time to act. In silence, he nodded to Brin, who pulled out a dagger from within his own tunic, and then the two of them rushed into the laboratory, as startled goblins looked up from their tasks.

"Gaaahhhhkkkkk.!." one of the goblins fell screaming, skewered by the long length of Lucifer's sword. Brin ferociously leapt up onto the chest of another of the goblins, driving the cold blade of the dagger into the creature's throat, even as Lucifer turned to attack another of them.

No weapons were on view within the laboratory complex, which meant it was purely a physical fight, not counting the weapons they wielded themselves. Malevar had obviously thought himself secure in these towers, for even his hobgoblin guards were not allowed within.

A third goblin fell, and as Lucifer turned to help Brin with the fourth, a startled Malevar reached for his scepter, brandishing it before him, and pressing one of the jeweled studs on it's hilt. As he did so,

Gabriel suddenly found he had movement. The scepter was somehow responsible for his paralysis, yet now Malevar used it for a different purpose, and a beam of brilliant ruby light shot out from it towards Lucifer, who had the presence of mind to turn the struggling goblin between himself and the brilliant light.

The goblin's eyes went wide and then rapidly dimmed as the smell of burning flesh rapidly became apparent. The body went limp in his arms, sagging towards the floor as Lucifer fought to hold it up as a shield against Malevar's strange magick.

With a supreme effort, Gabriel lurched his body this way and that, and managed to cause the table to which he had been secured to overturn, falling against Malevar, and knocking the scepter from his hand. "Don't let him get his hands on it again. It's some sort of weapon," Gabriel warned, and Lucifer dropped the dead goblin, leaping forward as Malevar tried to retrieve his scepter. Brin slid forward, kicking the scepter away from Malevar, who snarled as he whirled around, and punched another of the brightly colored jewels on one of the metal boxes. Instantly, a loud wailing noise could be heard, as some sort of alarm rang out across the castle. Like the buzzing of a thousand hornets.

Malevar ran back towards one of the distant antechambers, as Lucifer began to free Gabriel. Brin recovered the scepter. "Careful with that thing. Who knows what else it can do, or how it works?" Gabriel cautioned. Lucifer secreted it within his jerkin. "You can tell me how you got here later, friend. For now, my gratitude knows no bounds. I was a fool to come here, and even more of a fool to come here alone," he admitted.

"One learns from mistakes, friend Gabriel," Lucifer nodded. "Let us hope we both learn from this one. Come." He helped him to his feet. Gabriel drew his dagger from the makeshift sheath within his tunic.

"I still seek a reckoning with Malevar, sorcery or no," he snarled. "The deaths of our brethren cannot go unavenged," he insisted, and as Lucifer protested, Gabriel ran after Malevar in the direction he had fled. Lucifer and Brin could only follow, knowing that the still-wailing alarm would bring the fearsome hobgoblin guards. This was not good. Unless there was some other way out, they would be trapped here in the laboratory complex.

Gabriel charged forward recklessly, keen to catch up with the fleeing priest. His blood was up and only more blood would calm him now. Lucifer and Brin moved to follow, watching the rear for the pursuit they knew would shortly follow.

Malevar fled through three more anterooms, filled with apparatus and more metal boxes such as Gabriel had never seen before. Giving them only a cursory glance, Gabriel was intent on catching the Grey Priest. Finally, Malevar led him to the easternmost tower, in a room filled with large glass vats of colored water, some of which contained the bodies of both whole and partially dismembered bodies of humans, elves, goblins and hobgoblins alike. A storeroom of sorts for the human tissue Malevar used in his alchemies.

Gabriel cried out as he caught sight of Malevar struggling to open a concealed doorway in the stone wall, through which he obviously sought to escape. Furious, Malevar whirled around, as Gabriel attacked, dagger held high to plunge into his grey chest. Malevar's hand reached down to the ornate buckle of the copper-segmented belt around his waist, an emaciated fingertip touching one of the bright jewels that adorned the buckle, and his mouth drew back in a strange grin as Gabriel lunged, knife-hand plunging down, but to no avail.

It was as though the air itself had thickened in front of Malevar. His plunging dagger had at first slowed as though someone had grabbed at his forearm, and then it had stopped altogether. Gabriel screamed in fury, working has hand back and forth. Then he raised it again, and tried a second time to bury the blade in Malevar's chest. Again, the blade was stopped mere inches from the Grey Priest's flesh.

Malevar's hand dipped inside his own robe and re-emerged clutching a small wooden rod, which was scarcely of a size to fit his small hand.

Rounded ends of the rod just projected either side of his palm, and he struck out at Gabriel with this seemingly ineffectual object.

Pain blazed up Gabriel's arm as Malevar had no trouble at all in hitting home. The lightest touch at Gabriel's elbow made him scream with pain, and his fingers flew open, dropping the dagger. Malevar snarled as he dashed forward to take the fight to Gabriel, but not before Gabriel clutched the knife in his other hand before it could fall to the floor. He struck again at Malevar, but with only the same effect as before. It was like trying to strike through molasses.

As Malevar lashed out once more, Gabriel, wary this time, side-stepped, and flung himself bodily at the Grey Priest, and they both went crashing into one of the large glass containers with force enough to send it rocking, and finally toppling over to smash onto the floor and discharge it's contents, fluids and body-parts all.

As the fluids spilled around Malevar's feet, bolts of bright lightning flashed in a wild pattern around Malevar, as though the fury of the heavens had come to earth. Malevar screamed, body threshing wildly, till finally he convulsed, and sank to the ground, mouth frothing as though he had suffered a fit. Gabriel himself had not been harmed by the strange lightning storm. Standing over Malevar's body, Gabriel raised the knife once more.

He whirled suddenly at the sound of fighting from the antechamber behind him. Lucifer and Brin were engaging the first of the hobgoblin guards, who were attacking with pikes and axes. This wasn't a battle they could win in such small numbers. He was loathe to refrain from taking vengeance upon Malevar, but he quickly joined the fray, adding his own dagger to the fight, overpowering Brin's foe as Lucifer ran the other hobgoblin through.

"We must leave, and quickly," he warned. "Follow me," he advised, and led them quickly to the secret doorway that Malevar was trying to open. He and Lucifer managed to get the partially ajar doorway fully open, and they rushed Brin through. Pausing to take Malevar's belt as another trophy, Gabriel also tore from around his neck a small decorative amulet on an impulse. Noises from the antechamber alerted them to more hobgoblins rushing to Malevar's aid, and Gabriel shut the door quickly, hoping none of them knew of Malevar's bolt-hole.

Brin delved within his belt-pouch, and struck a flint-box to give them light within what turned out to be a stairwell, and they quickly followed the steps downwards, hoping this secret passageway lead to safety. They could hear the consternation on the other side of the wall as the hobgoblins surrounded their fallen leader and slaughtered compatriots. Doubtless they wondered where their foes had vanished to.

Down and down went the stairs, which they descended as fast as they could, till at last they came to what at first appeared to be a dead-end, but then the light from Brin's flint-box revealed a lever set into the stonework, and when Gabriel pulled it down, a doorway slowly swung open in the outer wall of the castle, close to the river's edge. Gabriel had not spotted this doorway in his earlier surveillance of the exterior, so it must be well-concealed. "Quickly now, we must be away before pursuit is launched."

*   *   *

Back in the laboratory, Malevar was slowly regaining consciousness, furious with himself for being overcome so easily, fuming at the loss of his belt, he also noticed the missing amulet, and guessing where Gabriel and his friends had gone, he revealed the secret doorway to his guards, and they were quick to follow on Gabriel's trail.

*   *   *

The woods to the south were the nearest means of covering their trail, and so Gabriel, Lucifer and the elf Brin plunged into the undergrowth as fast as they could, eager to put distance between them and any pursuit. Speed was of the essence, initially. Stealth would come later.

They ran as though pursued by the Devil himself, though these fearsome hobgoblins came a close second. They were excellent trackers, Brin knew. Alone he might have a chance, but these two humans were unknown quantities. Mighty enough indeed, they needed woodlore to get out of this predicament, and he began whistling in a shrill discordant manner.

Lucifer was about to caution him to be quiet, when the first of the faeries began to appear. One lone male, followed then by another, and another, then a female., till a small swarm soon fluttered around Brin, who hastily conversed with them in a strange sibilant language that Gabriel couldn't understand, though Lucifer seemed to be catching the grasp of what they were saying. The swarm then flew off rapidly, as Brin ushered the two men forward. "They will help as best they can, but we must still hurry." He took off through the dense woods, and Gabriel and Lucifer did their best to keep up with his small legs.

*   *   *

As the hobgoblins entered the woods, they were instantly beset by a swarm of flying insects, faeries, bees, wasps. The insects had their own bodily weapons, whereas the faeries used tiny blowpipes to attack the huge beast-men, their darts covered with toxins not known in the human world. Their cries of pain and anger could be heard at a distance behind Gabriel and his fleeing friends. The cries of pursuit faded, but did not diminish altogether, for some of the hobgoblins had forced their way deeper into the dense foliage, past the stinging darts of the insects and faerie-folk.

Lucifer cried out as he caught his foot on a tree-root as he ran, and went down heavily. Gabriel paused to help his friend up, frowning as Lucifer began limping. "It's sprained. Go on without me, I'll lead them away."

"We're in this together, friend. Lean on me." He took Lucifer's weight, and Brin came back to see what the delay had been. He shook his head, and then turned to continue on his way. Behind him the two men did their best to keep up, but the faint sounds of pursuit were getting gradually louder now.

"One sword, and two daggers. Not much. You'd better take the sword," said Lucifer, handing it to Gabriel, and taking back the dagger.

"Keep going," Gabriel urged, as a cry went up behind them. They had been spotted by one of their pursuers. "Hurry." He pulled Lucifer along, struggling down the bank of a small stream and splashing through the waters. Too late, now, to conceal their tracks, and he cursed inwardly. How many were there behind them? Only three or four and they stood a chance. Any more, and they would be overrun, captured and returned to Malevar's not so tender mercies.

They were still in the water when the first club whistled past Gabriel's ear, smacking into an overhanging willow tree, and gouging a huge chunk out of the bark. He and Lucifer scrabbled up the bank, determined at least to use the higher ground to best advantage. They turned as Lucifer leaned against the tree-trunk for support. Brin returned, upon realizing what was happening, and the three of them determined to make a stand against the eight huge hobgoblins that rushed eagerly down the opposite bank of the stream.

Bellowing loudly, and brandishing their clubs, pikes and axes, the hobgoblins were keen to close the distance between themselves at their prey. The waters of the stream were disturbed angrily by their threshing feet, muddying those waters and sending ripples and small waves back across the stream. In the space of a few seconds, those selfsame ripples suddenly grew to the size of small waves, and those small waves then grew larger still, as a veritable maelstrom seemed to churn the waters of the stream, revolving around the hobgoblins in it's centre.

The poor doomed creatures halted in midstream, squealing at the strange phenomenon which was building around them. Some of them turned to flee, but to no avail, as the waters surged, rapidly sloshing back and forth, pulling them off their feet, and under the waters themselves as they screamed in fear. One by one, the wretches vanished. Flailing limbs broke the surface, threshing helplessly, till finally they all vanished beneath the churning waters.

Gabriel, Lucifer and Brin watched on in awe, as their pursuers perished within less than a minute. The wood was finally still and silent once more. "Rhiahne." Lucifer gasped, realizing what had just happened, and slowly, as they all watched, the waters slowed, stilled, and began to flow upwards, taking on a human shape, feminine undoubtedly. Its human torso projected above the now calm waters of the stream, as they heard the tinkle of its laughter.

"Sweet human. Malevar is powerful, but he has limitations. Others in this world have power also. The wood will always stand against him." Lucifer hobbled forward to the bank, and reached out a hand to touch the humanoid face, which rippled lightly at his touch.

"Lady, my friend and I thank you from the bottom of our hearts."

"Yet you would leave me . . . ." the voice was tinged with sadness and resignation.

"I must, for this world, for all it's beauty, is not my own. Mayhap I may come again to this place, if it is possible. For it and you hold a beauty I have never found anywhere in my own world," he admitted.

"Then I must content myself with that. Should we meet again, let us recapture the magic we shared together."

"Lady, my heart grieves at this parting. More than you know."

"Go then. Do not grieve, for I am as timeless as thee. I await," and with that, the water elemental raised a hand to Lucifer's face, stroking it once, before liquefying once more, and merging with the gently flowing stream.

Lucifer stood there a moment, and then turned and slowly hobbled back to his friends. "I'm impressed," Brin admitted. "Rhiahne rarely reveals herself, let alone takes such an active role against Malevar's minions. His reach is long, and he hates the wood with a passion. He seeds it with his night-creatures on purpose, hoping to destroy it from within," he explained. "Come, let us return to my dwelling," he suggested, "and I will find you some furs or leather to furnish you with clothing," he said to Gabriel, who was still naked.

*   *   *

"And that, is the story of my first meeting with Malevar," said Gabriel, finally coming out of the slight hypnotic trance that Manuel had place him under. "Needless to say, myself and Lucifer managed to cross back over into our own world once more, even without the aid of the druid. It seems that somehow Brin was right when he said we were somehow related. I can cross over at will, at least within one of those faerie circles. They seem to be gateways of some sort, and they feature prominently on junctures of leylines throughout Britain." He sat up on the sofa, smoothing the wrinkle out of his trousers, as Laura went to turn up the lights.

"Wow. Far out!" was all Belle could bring herself to say. The lights brightened, and Laura returned to sit next to her daughter. Manuel went to pour brandies for all concerned. He poured one for himself also.

"It's a rather tall story," Laura complained.

"I've had a long time to convince myself it all really happened. We also have the physical evidence." He pointed to the copper-segmented belt, the amulet and the small scepter on the table. "I've had them tested, and most of the metals with which they are made, remain unknown to modern science. They are not of this world," he stated pointedly.

"Alien, then? Your description of Malevar certainly sounds like one of the popular descriptions of an extra-terrestrial," Laura went on.

"Still not sure, even after all this time." Gabriel took a soothing sip from his brandy. "I don't know whether the realm of Faerie is another planet, another dimension, or just another world co-existing with our own, yet slightly out of phase. There are a lot of theories, but I still haven't made my mind up. Suffice it to say, that things are different over there. Creatures from that world used to cross over into our own, and had become the stuff of legends and 'fairy-tales'. Both creatures natural to that world and also the result of Malevar's experimentations. He was a scientist of sorts, interested in genetic manipulation. Having dissected and studied my own kind over the centuries, I believe him to be an expert on my unique body-chemistry. Thus if anyone can reattach Belle's hand, I believe it to be him." Belle looked at her mother, and then turned back to her father.

"Dad, you don't have to do this. It's just a hand. Something I'm getting used to living without. Malevar might even be dead by now. You said yourself, he admitted he was dying, whether he had a lifespan as long as your own or not. If he is alive, he doesn't owe you any favors. He wanted to put his brain in your body for Christ's sake."

"That might be a bargaining ploy," Gabriel mused. Laura rounded on him in an instant.

"Don't you even go there!" she warned.

"I'm not going to offer myself up on a platter," he explained. "I'll take precautions. I'm going to offer the return of the belt, amulet and the scepter first. The scepter has a multitude of functions, one of which is some form of neural scrambler. It can also emit a powerful laser. I can't duplicate some of the broken internals, but Malevar may be able to. One of the jewels seems to be cracked, and I think they are the power-source. I have no way of making a replacement. Other functions I have yet to fathom. The belt puts out some sort of resonance-field which harmonizes the body's inner-vibrations to be able to cross over into Malevar's realm. At the same time, those frequencies seem to cause some sort of force-field effect. Malevar got shocked when he got liquid over him, but the belt seems to be undamaged. The amulet defies examination. Apart from a small burst of radiation, I don't know what it does. Malevar will, so we'll see how badly he wants them all."

"It's how badly he wants you, that I'm worried about," admitted Laura.

Chapter Eight

Manuel made the reservations to fly to England. It was finally agreed that Gabriel attempt to make contact again with the Grey Priest Malevar. Laura and Belle would await his return, with Juliana there as a backup should anything go awry with Gabriel's plans. Gabriel might be able to make the crossing unaided, but how were the rest of them to help him if he needed assistance? Gabriel had assured them that Juliana's powers were a match for any Druidic earth-magic. She would be able to send one of them through the faerie circle without the aid of any belt, should it prove necessary.

Laura and Belle went to see Juliana again, to request her aid in the forthcoming trip, and recounted to her, all Gabriel had revealed about this strange new world. Juliana kept nodding as they spoke, for she had heard the tale before. While they were there, the conversation swung around to Laura and Belle's own inherent powers. "Child, I sense within you a strong affinity to power. One or more of your ancestors practiced earth-magic," she told Laura. "You, Belle, are your father's daughter. What is inherent within him, should also be inherent within you. It goes with the blood. You may find you can cross over into this realm unaided," she assured her.

"I'm not sure I want to." Belle admitted. "I'll live with this," she said, holding up the stump of her wrist.

"Your father doesn't want you to have to live with it, Belle." Laura spoke. "Perhaps it's guilt that drives him. I don't know. But he loves you, and would do all in his power to help you."

"I know that, Mother," Belle replied. "We haven't been a 'family' for very long, but I already feel a closeness to both of you that I never felt with the Cannucci's."

"Your father is a good man, child. One of the best I have ever known. If I had not been married when first I met him . . . ."Juliana had that faraway look in her eyes for a second. "Ahhhh, but an old woman dreams. Nice dreams though," she chuckled, and both mother and daughter joined in the laughter. "Gabriel is unique in this world. Human and yet not human, for the power is strong in him, though he refuses to acknowledge it. Perhaps his mother did indeed fall asleep within a faerie-ring one summer's night, and his father was not of this reality. He has a strong affinity to the earth. He can indeed match his inner harmonies to the required frequency he needs to cross between the realms. He can understand if not communicate with some of the creatures native to those worlds. Perhaps he also has other powers, I don't know, for he is stubborn in examining his inner self."

"You said 'realms', as in plural," Belle interrupted her.

"Of course, child," Juliana nodded. "There are many such realms, of joy and nightmare. Tis only a thin line that exists between fantasy and reality, between sanity and madness. In places, where those boundaries are weak, some people can cross such lines at will. For others it is an effort, but the lines can indeed be crossed."

*　　*　　*

Back at the villa, on the computer screen, Manuel and Gabriel perused Ordnance Survey maps of England and Wales, superimposing upon them, overlays of known ley-lines, taking note of the junctures, as Gabriel scanned his memory to identify the location of the faerie-circle whereby he had crossed over into Malevar's world. It had been hundreds of years ago, and much had changed in Britain since that time, land had been developed, the courses of rivers altered.

He had been back to Wales some years ago, when he had accepted a secondment to 22 SAS as a Special Instructor to help the Mountain Group hone their climbing skills, though his stay at Stirling Lines had been brief, and not enough time to get too acquainted with much of modern day Wales. His time there had been spent up in the Black

Mountains, supervising training, before being shipped out to Oman and the Green Mountain and Jebel Mardar ranges.

"About there." Gabriel pointed at the screen, and Manuel did a screen-dump to the printer. "That looks to be the place," he confirmed, enlarging and studying the area in detail. The ley-lines crossed in what was still an expanse of woodland, as yet undeveloped, which was surprising given the country's population explosion in recent years. More and more people were being allowed into the small island, despite its lack of space and adequate housing. Developers were continually cutting away the woodlands and moors and open spaces to build houses for its ever-growing multi-cultural population. "It's only a few hours drive out of London. We'll find somewhere local to stay. I don't envisage this thing will take but a few days, one way or the other."

"Sir, are you sure you've thought this thing through?" Manuel cautioned. Gabriel smiled.

"Not all the way, Manuel. Depends what I find when I confront Malevar again. Best be flexible in my approach."

"You'll 'wing' it, sir?" Manuel looked at him reproachfully.

"Exactly," Gabriel chuckled. "I do my best thinking on my feet," he admitted. "If Malevar isn't swayed enough by the return of the belt and the scepter, I might even throw in the amulet, then there still might be a way I can persuade him to help. He seemed hampered by the lack of what we think of as modern technology in that world. I can transport some of that technology over to him, if he needs it. Modern scientific apparatus might mean I can give him the ability to create a new host-body without endangering my own. Scientists here can now clone animals. Sooner or later someone will clone a human being, not just an embryo. With my DNA, Malevar could clone a body for him to inhabit."

"That doesn't seem a wise move on your part, sir." Manuel shook his head.

"On the contrary, Manuel. I am on Interpol's Wanted list in more than one country for some of my past misdemeanors. Having another me around might be advantageous. They might well pick up Malevar by mistake, as long as we don't tell him he's a wanted man in this world," he chuckled. "That would leave me free to wander around as I please," he added.

Manuel smiled wryly as he understood Gabriel's strategy. "Not exactly 'playing the game', sir," he admonished.

Gabriel's smile turned grim. "Malevar butchered every one of my people he got his hands on to further his genetic research, Manuel. I am not a very forgiving man as you know. I haven't forgotten and I certainly haven't forgiven. I'll have my revenge, one way or another," he promised. "Just because I need his help to give Belle her hand back, does not mean he gets away with his crimes. There will be a reckoning," he promised. "Let him come to this world, in a body like mine. He will find it quite different to when he left it those hundreds of years ago. All I have to do is make an anonymous call to Interpol or Scotland Yard once I am out of the country, and the manhunt will begin. I will take a perverse delight in following it on the news broadcasts."

* * *

The cottage was set back from the country lane, and a narrow gravel drive lead up to it. It was unoccupied at present, as it was for most of the year. A typical holiday home bought up by people who could afford the exorbitant prices estate agents charged these days. The new owners were English, and used the place infrequently during the summer months. Through the long cold winter months, it was allowed to stand unoccupied, whilst local people found good housing hard to come by.

The first petrol bomb flew through the air, smashing through the glass front living room window and exploding within. Flames lit up the interior, as a second bottle went through another of the windows, igniting the whole ground floor. The cottage was soon well ablaze, lighting up the night sky, and the arsonists stood smiling at their work, and patting each other on the back.

"Well done, lads. Wales for the Welsh, eh? Let the English keep to their own company, for they are not welcome here in this ancient land. Invaded many times, but never conquered," the bearded man swore.

"Aye, Daeffyd, you're right. Our own people can't afford to live decently, yet these parasites keep coming down here and buying up all the property. We'll burn 'em all out if need be," another promised.

The small group retreated off down the lane, taking a shortcut through the nearby woods, to where they had left their cars parked in a discreet lay-by, where they wouldn't be seen from the road.

*   *   *

It took over a week before Gabriel could organize the necessary travel documents and false passports he deemed necessary for the trip to Britain. It was mainly the medical documents that caused the most trouble. The transportation of human tissue, with regards to Belle's amputated hand in the portable cryogenic container. Gabriel took on the identity of a Doctor Jose Garcia. Belle became his patient, and Laura and Juliana naturally her mother and grandmother. Supposedly they were travelling to seek consultation with specialists in the UK, which was true enough, he supposed. Gabriel's acquaintances in the medical facility he subsidized in Cordoba helped with the necessary bona-fides necessary to get past British Customs & Immigration controls. Gabriel had used the last week to grow a small goatee beard, and with the application of a little bleach to grey part of his hair, it served to partially disguise his appearance to anyone who wasn't particularly looking for him. Glasses finished off his new look.

They arrived after a tiresome flight at Heathrow's Terminal 3. Traveling 1st Class was no guarantee against the presence of screaming unruly children. Gabriel had lost count of the number of times he had found one of the little brats sitting right behind him on numerous flights, irrespective of the class of ticket he was using at the time. Belle had glared at the troublesome tot, and he was glad she was sat with her mother to keep her temper in check.

A quick call at the Hertz Rental desk, and new credit cards hastily set-up and funded from a bank in the Caymans, matched to their new identities, assured them of two cars. Gabriel purchased some recent maps of the UK road-systems to check it hadn't changed much since his last trip here. He had visited the north-east of the country last year, but it had been over thirty years or more since he had last visited Wales. Laura drove behind Gabriel, with a copy of the map beside her, following his lead, as he headed north on the M25. Both of them had had suitable experience of driving all over the world, and so had little difficulty adapting to British road-systems. They would find suitable accommodation close to their destination, and discuss plans over dinner that evening once Gabriel had carried out some discreet surveillance of the site to ensure they would not be disturbed.

*   *   *

The M6 ran all the way up through Wales. Coming off the motorway system, the going was slower through the Black Mountains of southern Wales, yet the views compensated. They were in no rush after all. The familiar Brecon Beacons towered to the north of the M4, and soon they were skirting the westernmost slopes on their way up into Snowdonia. For once the sun was shining in Britain, and the drive north was pleasant indeed. Gabriel and Juliana were in the lead car, with Laura and Belle bringing up the rear. Juliana was having a hard time navigating from the road-maps, for she could not get her tongue around some of the convoluted Welsh/Celtic names, which amused Gabriel. In the other car, Laura and Belle were having similar difficulties, and glad they could just follow Gabriel's lead.

The drive was uneventful, and after a few hours, they eventually stopped outside a large hotel called The Tanronen Hotel, south of Beddgelet and just off the A498, which was a few miles south of their actual destination, and Gabriel left the three women to check in, whilst he took one of the cars to travel north past Llyn Dinas. After passing the lake, and before the river-crossing, he took a right fork onto an unmarked road, which lead east and south once more back to Cae Ddafydd, but he had no intention of going that far.

The forest was all around him after a few miles, and eventually he parked up in a lay-by, and took the small rucksack out of the boot of the car, and then changed his footwear, putting on a sturdy pair of Goretex boots. He would appear just as a casual rambler should anyone notice him. Checking his watch, and looking again at the ordnance survey map he had brought with him, he set off through the wood, enjoying the play of light through the trees, and the occasional birdsong.

Scarcely half an hour later, he found it. The dark stone altar lay within a natural clearing, surrounded by trees. The mighty oak still stood, looking down on the scene of so much bloodshed in times past. Beyond, Gabriel could see the faerie-circle, still unbroken after so many years, for local folklore still made people shy away from such things as these. It pulled at him, seeking to draw him closer, but Gabriel was content enough just to verify the existence of the place after so long. Those stones were partially moss-covered.

The clearing was pretty enough in the sunlight, but Gabriel knew from bitter memory how it looked in the full light of the moon. The memory was unpleasant. On that altar, the sky had been taken away from him.

Gabriel planned to give everybody tonight to get over their jetlag. It was always easier travelling east. They would begin the new crossing tomorrow afternoon if things were still quiet. Juliana, Belle and Laura would take it in turns to maintain a vigil by the faerie-circle, while he made the crossing and attempted to obtain Malevar's aid. Before then, he had a package to collect in Cardiff. He had phoned one of his many contacts to arrange delivery of some small weapons, easier than trying to bring anything through Customs. He had explained the sort of knives he wanted, and asked for a Beretta, eventually settling for a Glock and three clips of ammunition.

Britain was a strange society these days, with public ownership of firearms a carefully monitored affair, yet the criminal fraternity seemed to have easy access to guns, which put the generally law-abiding public at a decided disadvantage. The police force, as a rule, did not carry firearms either. A strange society indeed, Gabriel thought.

*   *   *

Upon his return from Cardiff in the early evening, he found that Laura had acquired a double-room for them both, and Juliana and Belle had adjacent single rooms. They joined the others for an evening meal in the restaurant on the ground floor.

Over a rich claret, Gabriel and his 'family' discussed their final strategies before putting their plans into action. "I picked up the weapons with no problems. I've used Harry before, and he's never let me down. I know what to expect over there this time, and Malevar will find me no easy mark if he tries anything," he assured them.

"I've never been here before," Juliana mused, "but I can sense a great affinity with the land, and there still seems to be traces of magick in the air, forgotten now, as civilization marches on," she sighed. "This was once a great land."

"If you look at the rise of civilization across the world, you can see that Britain dominated and advanced the world after the fall of the Roman Empire. They brought the world into the 20th Century, even if some countries did come kicking and screaming. America built on Britain's legacy," Laura admitted.

"The Romans built on the legacy of the Greeks, and the Egyptians. Depends how far back you want to go," said Belle. "There has usually always been one dominant civilization leading the way throughout the centuries."

"But what part did the realm of Faerie play in all this?" Gabriel mused. "We hear tales of mythical creatures the world over. Did they all originate there? Crossing over through portals like these faerie-circles? For such creatures are certainly not native to this world."

"Look to your own origins," warned Juliana, "for I sense this Malevar may have the answers you seek."

"I'll be sure to ask him. Don't worry on that score," smiled Gabriel.

"Let's get down to details, then. You cross over tomorrow," Laura stated, and Gabriel nodded. "Before you do, let's verify that Belle can also do so. If not, she'll need to use the belt. If that happens, then no one else can cross over once she's gone. You'd be on your own."

"I wouldn't let her come through unless I was certain I had things under control," affirmed Gabriel.

"Suppose things get out of hand and we need to come get you?" Laura cautioned.

"His castle is north of the woods, and I've told you how I got into the place," reminded Gabriel. Juliana held up her hand.

"If need be, I can open a doorway. I have done such before. Keeping it open will be the problem. Such things take a great effort, and I am old now," she admitted.

"Twenty four hours. That's all," insisted Laura. "Then one of us is coming after you," she insisted.

"You worry too much, Laura. I'll need a couple of days at the least," he insisted. Gabriel tried to reassure them. "I wouldn't consider this unless I thought it was possible."

"You don't have to do this, Dad." Belle reached out with the only hand she had, and Gabriel looked down at it, before reaching to cover it with his own.

"Family is precious, Belle. What's the expression? Blood is thicker than Water? More true than ever in our case. You and Laura are all that is left of my family, Belle. I would defend it with my life if I had to. This is just a little thing I have to do. Don't worry about it so much," he reassured her. "I still have allies over there, too, remember? If they're still alive, they will help me."

*　*　*

Later that night, Laura cuddled up to Gabriel in the big king-size bed. "You'd better come back in one piece, or I'll never forgive you," she promised, enjoying the feel of his naked body against hers, feeling him harden against her thigh.

"I'll never forgive myself. I don't want to lose you either, Laura. We've spent too much time apart. I want us to spend the rest of our lives together, for however long that lasts."

"I finally have a daughter, a child of my own. I'd give anything for her, even my own life, but not yours. I couldn't do that. I could never make that choice," she shivered, and Gabriel pulled her closer.

"Let's make our own magick.," he suggested, leaning forward to gently kiss the nape of her neck, enjoying the feel of her hardened nipples against his chest.

"Mmmmm," she moaned lightly. "You wanna do a little mattress-dancing? Why ah'm jest a lil' ol' Kintucky girl, sir. If my mother could only see me now?" she giggled, pressing herself harder against Gabriel's body, her hand sliding down his chest, and lower still beyond his stomach, till at last she gripped him, squeezing just hard enough to make him groan. "Why sir, whatever do we have here? And whatever shall we do with it?" she giggled, before sliding under the covers, and Gabriel groaned as she let him know just what she wanted to do with it.

*　*　*

Breakfast was held in general silence, and conversation was limited. Belle could see the flush on her mother's face, as she stole glances at Gabriel, and envied the intimacy between the two of them. Such relationships were rare. Laura was now 'chosen', and could share a long lifetime with Gabriel. None of Belle's paramours had been so gifted, and the relationships never lasted. Love was such a precious thing, so easily given, yet damned hard to hold onto. She didn't want to be responsible for ending her parents' relationship, yet Gabriel was determined to go through with this, despite the risks.

*   *   *

Shortly after ten, the four of them loaded up the two cars with rucksacks of food, thermos flasks of coffee, and Gabriel's own rucksack with the weapons the fence in Cardiff had procured for him. Gabriel and Juliana lead the way, and Laura and Belle followed. It was a short drive of less than twenty minutes to the wood, and they parked up in the same lay-by Gabriel had used the day before.

By daylight it looked just like any other wood, and they enjoyed the odd birdsong as they walked through the trees, seeking the heart of the wood itself. Finally, they came upon the clearing wherein lay the altar, and a strange silence descended upon them all, as though it was a special place. The woodland sounds were strangely muted within the clearing. Juliana nodded as she looked at the cold marked stones. "A place of power," she confirmed. "Much blood has been shed here." She looked up at the huge overshadowing oak tree defiantly, as if sizing it up as a potential enemy.

"So this is the place," Laura mused. She recalled the story of Gabriel's emasculation.

"Yes." Gabriel confirmed. "This is the place. My wings were taken away from me on that altar." Laura put out a hand, and gripped his arm affectionately. Juliana went across to the grey cold slab, and put her hand on it, and then immediately snatched back her hand, as though in disgust.

"Is that the faerie-circle?" Belle asked, walking around the clearing to the far side, which a ring of stone was set into the grass. Gabriel held up a hand, cautioning.

"Just approach them slowly, till we know for sure what will happen. I felt a strange feeling in the pit of my stomach when I went through. I put it down to that foul-tasting soup the druid had us drink."

Belle stepped forward gingerly, one slow step at a time, as she approached the innocuous looking circle of stones. She paused suddenly, and then took one more step. "Wow, I can feel it," she admitted. "Like a funny tickle in my tummy." One more step.

"Belle, that's close enough," warned Laura. Belle stopped, and turned around.

"Okay. It just seemed to draw me closer. Kinda weird," she admitted, moving back from the stones.

"A gateway." Juliana spoke. "There are many such in the world. A crossroads of sorts, whereby certain people, with the right keys, can cross between worlds." She walked across to it, and stepped within the stones, her eyes going suddenly wide, and grey hair suddenly alive with static electricity as it rose up around her head. "You can feel the earth-magick in this land, and this is one of the focal points," she confirmed, before stepping out of the faerie-circle once more.

Laura moved forward, and she too stepped inside the stone circle. She stood there for a few moments, listening, feeling for what she knew not. "I feel nothing," she admitted.

"Nor should you, child," chuckled Juliana. "You were born of ordinary parents. You have a gift, but you have not yet been taught how to use it. Once you learn that gift, you will come to recognize power when you come across it. But not now."

At a distance through the trees, a lone figure paused as he heard voices coming from the direction of the clearing. Putting down his rucksack, the man crept quietly forward, from tree to tree, till he could catch sight of the strangers within the clearing. As a poacher, his woodcraft was excellent, and he moved without a sound. No twigs snapped under his feet, and none of the four strangers knew they were being spied upon.

This was a sacred place, shunned by the local populace. Only the followers of the shining ones frequented this clearing, for it was listed on no map, and no outsiders should be aware of its existence.

He watched as the man kissed the blonde woman, and hugged the other two, before stepping forward into the faerie-circle. He stood there for a moment, turning to face the three women, before his outline slowly began to lose shape, as if fading though a fog. Then it vanished from sight altogether. The man gasped. This was sacrilege indeed. Wildwood must be told!

Chapter Nine

Gabriel stood there, disoriented and dizzy for a few moments, as he sought to get his bearings. Concentrating, he listened for the expected whispering in the back of his mind, but it was no longer there. He stepped out of the stone circle into a different world, one which he hardly recognized from his previous visit. The wood was no more!

Blackened tree trunks were all that was left of a once mighty forest. No leafy foliage overhead. Some trees had fallen, and lay there rotting and broken on the ground. A lone crow could be seen flying overhead as Gabriel looked up in disbelief at the catastrophe that had happened to the wood. This was a place of silence and foreboding now. What vegetation remained was slowly rotting, and unpleasant smells were everywhere. No woodland sounds of animals or birds could he heard. Malevar had had his revenge upon the wood and its people for helping him and Lucifer escape.

Unfastening his rucksack, Gabriel took the weapons from within, leaving the belt, amulet and scepter inside. He strapped the two throwing knives and their sheaths to his forearms. The Glock fitted in a shoulder-holster under his arm. He checked it for ease of use, sliding it free of the oiled leather holster. Satisfied, he climbed one of the shattered trunks to get his bearings, horrified at the devastation he saw wreaked across the landscape. The entire wood as far as he could see was a blackened mass of shattered and broken trees. Dropping back to earth, he set off towards the north. This would not be as easy as he had thought.

*   *   *

Back in the human world, Belle and Laura had marveled at the way Gabriel had simply faded from sight, though Juliana merely nodded, having had some experience in such portals. "How will we know when to expect him back?" Belle asked.

"We won't," answered Juliana. "We will need to maintain a vigil here for him around the clock. I don't foresee anything happening immediately, so we will start tomorrow. Eight hours each, with one of us relieving the others in turn. We'll use the cell-phones to contact each other if we have any sort of contact from him."

"Hopefully he'll come back to take Belle across with him. Don't you dare go near that ring of stones by yourself, young lady!" Laura insisted.

"I'm not that reckless, Mother. I'll bide my time, though I am curious about it. Having heard so much about it, I do want to see it for myself. But not *by* myself. I promise," she reassured her.

*   *   *

An agitated man called into the craft shop in Plas Gwynant, Wildwood Sculptures & Crafts. It was a local shop, for local people, though often frequented by tourists in the more popular months of the year. He could barely maintain his composure as he waited for the tourists to vacate the shop, leaving himself and the proprietor Daeffyd Wildwood, to talk in private.

"There are people in the wood. At the sacred grove," he announced. Wildwood was unconcerned.

"There are always ramblers walking around at this time of year, Aidrian. You can go back and prepare the altar for the ceremony later this afternoon. There is plenty of time," he tried to reassure his friend.

"No, Davey. You don't understand. One of them went into the ring of stones, and then he disappeared," he revealed, and this time Wildwood's eyes opened wide.

"What? Disappeared, you say?"

"Yes, Davey. Disappeared. Vanished, as I watched. There were three women with him, and not one of them looked surprised at him fading from view like that either," he revealed. "I saw their cars parked off the road, and I made a note of their license numbers," he offered.

"Good, Adrian. Good. This needs some thought." He scratched his white beard. "Some serious thought." He shook his head, trying to order his thoughts. "Find out who these people are. They must be staying locally. Then go out to the grove once more, and check if they are still there. Do NOT prepare the altar for now, for I want no visible signs that the place is still in use, till we find what these people are about. Arrange for some of the others to keep a watch on the place from a distance. I'll brook no interference with the ceremony, but we need to draw no unwelcome attentions to our religious beliefs. Druids are suffered, not revered, these days. Our rituals looked upon as nothing more than pagan ceremonies. Society looks upon us as cranks and eccentrics, but at least we fare better than we did under the Romans," he reflected, sadly.

Aidrian left to organize some of Wildwood's followers, leaving the Druid himself to ponder the significance of the strangers in the grove, and in particular, the stranger who had disappeared from within the circle of stones. Could it be? Aidrian was not known to exaggerate.

Angels and elves were the only beings ever able to cross over at will. No elves these days, so that left only one possibility. There still remained angels alive in the world. He had thought he had seen the last of their kind nearly 1500 years ago. Wingless obviously, but some still walked the earth.

*   *   *

The three women went back to the hotel for lunch, knowing there was nothing to do till tomorrow. Juliana intended on getting an early night's sleep, for she wanted to take the first watch in the early hours of the morning, before dawn. Laura would take over from her at midday, and Belle would take the midnight shift, till relieved by Juliana again at 4am. That seemed the fairest way of organizing the time periods. Juliana would drive out and then Laura would bring the second car out. Juliana was not too happy driving in this country, so it was better she had the road as deserted as possible, in case she started forgetting which side of the road she was supposed to be on.

Laura went up to her room to check on the portable refrigeration unit which they had plugged into the mains socket. It showed no fluctuation in temperature. The maid had not touched the unit, as instructed, though she had made up the room. Laura smiled wistfully at the big king-size bed she had shared with Gabriel last night. She wanted him back in that bed, or one like it. Any horizontal surface, really. She hoped Gabriel had been right about the risk factor in all this.

*   *   *

Outside in the hotel car-park, a small furtive figure checked off the license plates against the numbers he had written in biro on the back of his hand. They matched. Satisfied, he went into the hotel and up to the reception desk. "Excuse me," he said to the receptionist. "You should have a message for Davies. W. Davies?" he enquired, to get the receptionist to turn away from the desk and check the letter drops. Quickly, he perused the signing-in register, noting the names of the man and three women who had checked in last night, as well as the rooms they had been allocated. It was all noted before the receptionist turned back to the desk.

"I'm sorry, sir. But we have no messages for anyone of that name." he explained.

"Ohhhh. That's strange," the man said, looking puzzled. "I was sure it was today I was expecting it. I'd better check again. Thanks so much for your help," he smiled, reassuringly, before turning away.

"My pleasure sir. I'll keep any eye out for anything with that name on it."

"Thank you again," he smiled, as he left the hotel. He was already digesting the information. A doctor, a nurse, and mother and daughter. What could such a strange group want in Wales? Why were they nosing around the local woods?

One of the group was a waiter at this hotel, but he didn't come on duty till the evening shift. He would have to be primed, and asked to snoop around further. He knew Wildwood well. The wiley old man missed not a trick. He would not move against them till he was sure of his facts.

*   *   *

That evening, Juliana collected a packed meal to take with her early the next morning when she left to take up her vigil in the woods. She packed it in her rucksack, alongside a thermos flask, another small flask of brandy to ward off any night-chills, and a powerful hand-torch. Belle and Laura came down to the dining-room for dinner without her, leaving her to get an early night's rest.

Juliana's absence annoyed Thomas Dowie, who worked as a waiter in the hotel. He had been a member of Wildwood's following for three years, and had been charged with finding out as much as he could about the new guests at the hotel. He could only assume the older woman had retired to her room for an early night, but he hid a sly smile as he served the two remaining women with their meal, and drugged wine. He would search their rooms while they slept soundly.

The dark one was quite striking, though he was oddly taken aback at the sight of her stump when she started eating using one hand. Not unusual among Americans, who found the correct use of a knife and fork difficult to grasp, but the lack of a hand somehow made it stand out more noticeably. She had a slight Italian accent, which he couldn't account for. Passports left at the desk had been US.

He could see the resemblance between the two women, though it was hard to credit that they were mother and daughter, for their ages looked very similar. She too was a beauty, and he hoped she slept well, chuckling to himself.

*　　*　　*

The two women retired for the night at about ten o'clock, and Dowie went off duty at midnight. It was then that he sought out the upper floors of the hotel. All employees had a pass-key which allowed them to open any of the room doors in case of emergency. He used it quickly and silently, cracking the door open and listening intently for any noise from within the darkened room. There was none, and so he slipped inside, closing the door quickly behind him.

Standing there, with his back to the door, he looked down at Belle sleeping soundly in the bed. So beautiful, so helpless. He couldn't help but chuckle to himself. The drugged wine would keep her out for hours yet, and so Thomas began to rummage through her luggage, wardrobes and drawers. Belle had taken no precautions with her belongings, not expecting to have any need for such actions, and so Thomas had no problems in examining every one of her possessions. There was nothing untoward, except for a duplicate set of passport documentation, in a different name. A mystery in itself. "Who are you, darling?" he asked the sleeping woman, as he perused both passports. "There's something funny about you, for sure." He took a few photos with the camera he had brought along with him, zooming in carefully to get the additional passport details.

He put the passport back where he had found it, making sure nothing looked out of place, and then he went over to the bed. He touched Belle's arm lightly, nudging it, without reaction. Her long dark hair lay tousled under one shoulder, the blankets pulled up over her chest. Chuckling, he pulled the blankets down, wanting to look at her.

Belle wore a short nightgown, translucent, and rucked up about her thighs as she slept. Thomas leaned down to cup one of her breasts, chuckling as his fingers squeezed the soft flesh. His hand jiggled the firm mound lightly, as he felt himself getting hard. Belle slept on through the familiarity. "Very nice, love," he complimented, and then ran his hand down over her body, shoving it more roughly between her legs and cupping the mound of her crotch, feeling the rough pubic hairs within the tiny gusset of her briefs. "You're a right beauty, and no mistake," he chuckled. Thomas replaced the sheets back over her body. Best not chance fate, he decided.

As silently as he entered, he left the room, using his passkey to lock the door behind him. He then moved down the corridor to the room occupied by the 'mother'. Again, he listened carefully at the partially opened door before entering, but this occupant was just as much out of it as the previous one.

Laura lay slightly on her side, with the sheets partially rolled down, her long blonde hair loose on the pillow. Thomas started to search the room, and paused to study the cryogenic container plugged into the mains. It felt cold to the touch, and he cracked it open to peer momentarily inside, recoiling in a sudden fit of revulsion at the human hand he found within. "Ugghhh," he grimaced, and quickly sealed the container again. At least the find confirmed part of their story, though still no excuse for them poking around in the woods. He continued his search, lingering over Laura's choice silk underwear. He found a second passport here too. Definitely something fishy going on with these people. Certainly more than ordinary tourists.

Wildwood had contacts to investigate their identities further. He made a careful mental note of the names, wishing he could actually take the passports, but that wasn't possible without revealing his presence in their rooms. The photos would have to do, he decided, rattling off a few more shots, and taking one of the cryogenic container for good measure.

Turning, he looked again at the 'mother' asleep in the bed. He wondered how she matched up to her 'daughter', and so he pulled the sheets down from her body just as he had done with Belle. This job had its perks from time to time, he chuckled to himself as he admired the woman's body. Very nice. A natural blonde too, by the look of her, but just to make sure, his finger hooked in the elastic of her briefs, and he chuckled as he began to pull them away from her sleek belly.

He grinned as the blonde forest was revealed. Laura liked to grow it wild, unlike her daughter's well trimmed bush. This close, he could smell her musky aroma, and he leaned closer still, savoring the smell.

Wildwood's ceremony in the woods often made used of unsuspecting ramblers, and he was sure both these women would end up participating in the ceremony. Getting rid of the bodies afterwards would present little difficulty. They had done it often enough before.

*   *   *

Gabriel navigated the dark woods with care. This no longer felt like the vibrant land he remembered from his last visit. In daylight, it felt as foreboding as it had seemed at night previously. No isolated pockets of darkness any more. It was all darkness, except where the fallen tree-trunks let in isolated rays of sunlight.

The flowing stream was still there, though it no longer flowed with anything like water within it, for a noxious green foul-smelling substance now oozed slowly along its bed. No water-elemental existed within any more. Gabriel looked around for a fallen tree-trunk on which to cross, for he did not wish to wade through such poison.

All the time he kept hoping for the faintest of whispers in his head that would prove some of the faerie-folk had survived, but if any did, they were maintaining a deathly silence, or they were too far away.

Brin's cottage when he came to it, was burned to the ground. Of the elf himself, there was no sign. The site looked to have been deserted for many years.

How did Malevar affect such devastation on such a widespread scale? Gabriel found it puzzling. What strange magicks or alien technology could have caused this? A noise in the distance made him quickly whirl about. It came from behind him. He didn't know what had caused the noise, and he had no desire to find out. He pushed on quickly northwards.

A few minutes later, he heard another noise. Again, it came from behind, and sounded a little closer than before. Someone or something had picked up his trail and was following him. He surged forward with greater speed, trying to be as quiet as he possibly could, seeking a place to turn and make a stand.

Eventually, he came to a small hillock, where a couple of fallen dead tree-trunks offered a brief hiding-place from a distance. Gabriel slid into the gap behind the tree-trunks, waiting to catch a glimpse of his pursuer before using the high ground to his advantage in any combat.

As the slight sounds became louder, closer, Gabriel caught sight of it through the trees. It was a hobgoblin, more bestial by far than anything he had previously seen. They must have been breeding amongst themselves once originally created by Malevar. Surely even he would not create something as hideous as this. Almost of a height with Gabriel, it was twice as broad, stooping low to follow Gabriel's trail. Its face looked like a squashed version of a wild boar, with large tusks protruding from its lower lip, either side of a short snout. Greying flesh looked slightly decomposed. Brief, ragged furs covered most of its body, and it carried a crude axe made of stone lashed to a wooden club, in one hand. Looking behind it, Gabriel was glad he could see no further pursuit. A lone hunter had chanced across his trail, and followed up on it. Still, one such creature was going to be difficult enough.

Before slipping into his hiding place, Gabriel had first circled the foot of the knoll, so that the hobgoblin followed his tracks right beneath his hiding-place. He did not want to risk using the gun, in case the sound drew more pursuit, so that meant the knives only against the creature's stone axe and raw strength. Not the sort of odds Gabriel would have preferred. He slipped the two knives out of their arm-sheaths, hefting them lightly in each palm as he waited for the right moment.

He launched himself through the air just as the creature started to pass by, the brief sound of his movement alerting the mighty beast enough so that he whirled as Gabriel dropped towards him. He bellowed in anger as one of Gabriel's knives stabbed home in his shoulder, but his movement meant Gabriel missed with the second knife, and he rolled quickly aside as the stone axe was swung towards him. The creature was badly wounded, with the knife sticking out of his back, but still dangerous, and it came at him savagely, roaring its hatred and swinging that deadly axe, causing Gabriel to dodge behind a tree, which shook wildly as the axe thudded against its blackened bark.

Gabriel braced himself, holding the knife low, as the beast came at him again, waiting for it to raise the axe once more, and then he dived forward, rolling against the thing's legs, hopefully too close for it to swing the axe effectively, as he sliced at the back of one of it's knees. The hobgoblin squealed loudly once more as Gabriel severed the tendons behind the knee, and it fell heavily.

It rolled over, fearfully swinging the axe once again, but this time Gabriel quickly fell on the arm holding the axe down against it's body. The remaining knife plunged into the thing's throat, as Gabriel then rolled clear, watching and waiting for the thing to die, as blood spurted from it's throat.

It took less than a minute, but it seemed a lot longer, as the thing squealed weakly, gasping for air. When finally it was still, Gabriel retrieved his knives, cleaned and re-sheathed them. He then set about leading a false trail to the east, before doubling back and heading north once more, as fast as he could do so in silence.

*   *   *

Darkness brought its own terrors to the weird new world Gabriel now explored. The woodland sounds that started to be heard once the sun went down and the moon rose were like nothing he had heard before, with horrible screeching and wailing echoing through the night-air. He tried not to contemplate what horrible things were making such sounds, and he prayed he would not come across such.

He forced himself on, ever north, pausing only briefly to snack on the packed lunch he had brought from the hotel, to keep himself alert.

It was still dark when Gabriel came into sight of the great river, and by the moon's light, he estimated he was upstream of the city he had visited previously. He followed the river downstream, finally catching sight of the place just before dawn. It was eerily silent, and mostly turned to rubble. Nothing remained of Malevar's castle save remnants of the outer walls. The blast-radius, for that was what it looked like, had taken all the nearby dwelling places and raised them to the ground. Only a few ramshackle hovels remained on the southern edges of what remained on the city. Gabriel made his way carefully towards them, curious to see if any sort of life remained in the ruins.

As he got closer, and the skies lightened, he saw traces of smoke coming from some of the dwellings. He headed for those places, and as the sun rose, he saw elves wandering about their early morning chores and ablutions, fetching water from the river. Gabriel did not disguise his presence, and merely stood there in plain view, observing what remained of a once thriving society. It had regressed over the last few hundred years, instead of advancing as he would have expected. What disaster had occurred here to cause this?

Some of the elves noticed Gabriel, and regarded him warily, though he made no threatening moves towards them. They began conversing amongst themselves, and rushed to converse with others. "A human! A human!" went the cry between themselves as word of his arrival spread. Gabriel could still understand the dialect, which had changed little over the years since his last visit.

Soon, a small deputation had gathered, all male, though Gabriel detected other eyes peering out from the windows and walls of their houses. "I am Eradh, I speak for the people. Who are you, and what do you want here? No human has been seen in these lands since the Great Cataclysm which destroyed this city in my youth. From whence do you come?" the elder asked.

"I come from the same world the other humans came from." Gabriel replied. "I have been here before, yet this talk of a Cataclysm is unknown to me. When last I was here, this was still a thriving city, and the castle still stood tall. Now it is all but destroyed. What happened here?" he asked.

"Humans do not live long lives such as we. How can this be that you remember the days of my youth?" Eradh asked him.

"I am not an 'ordinary' human. My kind were sought after by the Grey Priest Malevar, and all killed, save myself." He saw their eyes widen at his explanation.

"I remember the winged ones," exclaimed one of the other older villagers. "You are wingless, yet you have the manner of one such. The same bones in your face."

"I came here before to try and find my people, and finding of their fate, I tried to kill Malevar. I failed, but managed to escape back to my own world. Now I come here seeking him again, and find this devastation. What happened here?" he asked.

Eradh spoke once more. "Malevar lost control of his magicks," he said simply. "After many years of oppression, and seeing him lay waste to the countryside with his poisons and his creatures, we folk rose up and hurled ourselves at him and his army. Fierce they were, but we were many in number in those days. Elves, faeries and woodland spirits all gathered together to attack him, and we killed many of his goblins and hobgoblins. Then, in revenge, Malevar turned some of his machines on the city itself, blasting and burning as we sought to tear down the very stones from his castle. Some of our leaders cornered him in his high towers, and just when it seemed we had won the battle, something went wrong with his machines, and the sky itself was ablaze and filled with thunder and lightning. The city was destroyed in a heartbeat, and only those on the outskirts survived," he recounted sadly. "At least that was what we thought at the time. For Malevar himself survived, and although he and the last of his retainers fled to the mountains in the west, he spread his curse on the land once more. This land is dying now as he poisons our rivers and streams. Since his capture of the Faerie-Queen, the use of earth-magic has ceased, and what faeries remain, hide themselves away in the far north, forbidden contact with the elven folk."

This news saddened Gabriel. Glad in a way that Malevar was still alive, yet how could he now deal with him to aid Belle? Malevar was certain to be hostile towards him, and even if he was willing to help, Gabriel still knew deep in his heart that he wanted to kill him. Such a tyrant should not be allowed to live.

Eradh and his followers made Gabriel welcome in what remained of their city, and he joined them for a hot meal. Small game still existed north of the river, and fish of a fashion still populated the rivers, though some showed strange lesions and deformities these days. He ate his fill, and accepted a couple of goblets of a heady wine, and then they showed him to a pallet where he could catch up on a few hours' sleep.

*　　*　　*

By midday, after conversing once more with Eradh, Gabriel had made his mind up to be away, getting directions on the whereabouts of the faerie-folk. They were forbidden all contact with the elves on pain of death to their Queen, but Gabriel hoped that as he was now the only human in this land, they would still talk to him. "They have seen no humans in many a year, and will doubtless treat you with suspicion," Eradh warned him, as he showed Gabriel a shallow place to ford the river, downstream of the city, and bade then him farewell.

Gabriel forded thigh-deep in the fast-flowing waters, and paused briefly to try and dry out his boots and trousers once across the other side. Then, trusting to the hike to dry them out fully, he set out northward in search of the faerie-folk. A plan was developing in his mind as he strode forth. He could not leave things the way they were here, even if Malevar did help him with Belle. But before he could develop it further, he needed to know exactly what the situation was, and what allies he could rely on.

The countryside north of the river was sparse and rocky. It was mid afternoon before the faintest trace of a whisper made Gabriel's head snap back, and he 'listened' intently for more of the faerie-talk. The further north he travelled, the more whispers he heard, till at length he tried to focus and thought really hard about the voices, trying to answer in a crude untrained way.

Suddenly, the whispers stopped once more, as if somehow they had sensed him. Despite further attempts by Gabriel, the whispers did not return, but he kept going anyway. As directed by Eradh, Gabriel turned his attention on the hillsides, till at last he saw the cave entrance which lead into the old abandoned mine, which the faerie-folk had now turned into their new home, having been forced to abandon the forests.

To all purposes it looked like any such abandoned cave entrance, till one looked carefully at the overgrown ferns and vegetation decorating the cave entrance, which glowed with a strange silvery luminescence, which had obviously come from the wings of the faerie-folk themselves. Gabriel began to enter, when he was suddenly stopped in his tracks by a very firm voice speaking directly into his mind.

"You are not welcome here. Leave us and we will leave you."

Gabriel tried to respond, filling his mind with who he was, and his reasons for being here. He got no reply, but decided to enter anyway. Brushing back the fronds of vegetation, he stooped to enter the cave entrance. Dark within, he stopped to take the torch out of his rucksack, and switch it on. Cautious, he went forward, following the shaft deeper into the bowels of the earth.

Some two hundred yards and the shaft began to twist and turn, going ever downwards, and soon Gabriel found he did not need the torch, for luminescent algae clung to some of the walls and rocks. Gabriel switched the torch off and put it in his pocket. He continued on, following his instincts as forks appeared in the tunnel.

Soon Gabriel noticed an even brighter light on one of the rocks, as he approached. It was the luminous wings of one of the faerie-folk, white and threaded with silver, calmly awaiting him. It showed no signs of flight at his approach, and it 'spoke' as Gabriel neared. "My name is Agron," he announced, verbally, using a dialect strangely similar to that used by the elves, though more sibilant. It was obviously how they communicated with the elves themselves and not their normal tongue. "None of us know you, human. But you are known to us by legend, if you are who you say you are. Our Queen Pfil spoke of you, but sadly she is no longer here with us."

"Pfil?" exclaimed Gabriel in surprise. "Pfil is now your Queen?" his mind flashed back to the beautiful young faerie he remembered from his previous visit. Like a Disney Tinkerbell come to life, her memory had remained with him all these years.

"Yes, Pfil has been our Queen for many years, since her father was killed in the battle against Malevar. Yet now Pfil is his captive in the mountains to the west, hostage to ensure we do not move against the Grey Priest," he explained. "Come, our Elders wish to see you, and ascertain how it is you understand our mind-speak, however crudely."

He fluttered up off the stone outcropping, and Gabriel followed him as he flew off down the passageway.

The man-made tunnels soon opened up into natural underground grottoes, where precious gemstones, still embedded in the rocky floor and walls reflected the luminescence of the algae to create a wondrous optical assault on Gabriel's senses. More faeries flew about, some obviously curious as to his presence here. Gabriel was careful as he walked, not to accidentally walk into any of the numerous fluttering creatures.

At length, in one of the larger chambers, many of the faeries were already gathered, and three such awaited him together on a rocky plinth. They were clothed in more ornate versions of the spider-silk that the other faeries festooned themselves with. Their wings varied in colour.

"I am Malon," the eldest greybeard introduced himself, his black and yellow threaded wings opened and closed, slowly and rhythmically. "Kel and Vindomar here," he indicated his two companions, "form a ruling council in our Queen's absence. We have heard her speak of you, if it is indeed you of which she spoke. We would hear from your own words the truth of this," he explained. Carefully taking a seat on one of the many large rock foundations, Gabriel then recounted the tale of his earlier visit to this realm, and his subsequent flight back to his own world. The three elders looked sternly at each other, conversing in low tones that Gabriel could not hear, as he told his tale.

Kel spoke. His wings were purple, and threaded with blue. "That was the start of our doom," he recalled sadly. "Because faerie and elf united against his forces at that time, Malevar redoubled his efforts against us. Subjugating the elves was only the start. Earth-magic he saw as a threat, and tried to destroy it by poisoning the wood we called home. His toxins filled our streams, and his creatures started many great fires to destroy the green of our land. More and more abominations roamed the wood, slaughtering what they found of the normal woodland creatures, and anything else they came across."

"We rebelled," Vindomar went on, blue wings, thread with green, were faded in places, revealing his age. "Factions of the elves joined with us again, and we took the fight to Malevar's own castle. Our King Ragnar died that day, as the castle was destroyed in a huge cataclysm which destroyed their city. In the aftermath, as Ragnar's daughter Pfil rallied the swarms, Malevar took refuge in the mountains of the west, with what remained of his army. We didn't know that he had survived for many years, till he came out of the west once more and caught us by surprise. Then our Queen was taken, and we could not move against him for fear of her life. He could not destroy us utterly, but he has rendered us helpless against him," he explained. "Pfil is the last of the Royal Line, never having married. The swarms would never rally behind anyone not of Royal Blood."

Gradually, as Gabriel had listened to the three elders, he became aware that the light inside this chamber was increasing. Looking around, he found that many more faeries had quietly fluttered in, their own luminescence was being reflected by the many gemstones that still littered or were embedded in the walls and floors.

*   *   *

Laura awoke with a sore head, and a sour taste in her mouth, moaning at the hangover she felt. Too much wine, she thought instantly.

She joined Belle for breakfast, to find that she too was suffering from a hangover. "Good wine, eh?" she consoled, as the two women ordered. It was nine thirty, and Laura was due to relieve Juliana at midday. Belle would have the rest of the day to amuse herself, maybe do a bit of sightseeing before taking her turn at surveillance that evening.

After breakfast, Laura used her cell-phone to call Juliana. "Morning Juliana. Everything okay at your end?" she asked.

"Beautiful out here," Juliana replied. "Wish I'd worn warmer clothes though. It was cold early on, and I feel it more acutely these days in these old bones of mine. Nothing happening out here so far. Too early I think. Best bring some music to listen to when you come out," she advised.

"Okay. See you at lunchtime. Bye." Laura put the phone away. "What are you going to do in the meantime?" she asked Belle. Her daughter shrugged.

"I might go into Portmeiron. It's nearby, isn't it?" Laura nodded in confirmation. "I'll take a look around, fill in a bit of time. The usual tourist thing, you know. Keep up appearances and all that. Always wondered what the place was like. I used to love that old series The Prisoner, even dubbed in Italian."

"Make sure you're back to relieve me by eight tonight."

"Yeah, lucky me! I get the midnight shift."

"Watch out for the werewolves and ghosties," Laura joked.

"They'd better watch out for me. I'll probably be a little pissed-off by then if any do decide to make an appearance," she chuckled. "How long do you think this is going to last?" she asked. "When do you think Dad will show up again?"

"From what he told us before, probably sometime tomorrow. The ring of stones doesn't take him directly to Malevar's castle remember. It's at least half a day's journey, then the same back, on foot."

"Let's hope he's reading Malevar right. That guy doesn't sound too trustworthy to me, assuming he's still alive. Anything could have happened in the last few hundreds of years."

Laura nodded. "We just have to keep our fingers crossed for now." she admitted. "I'm sure your Dad knows what he's doing."

"Let's hope so," Belle agreed, lost in thought.

"Don't worry. He'll be okay," she reached out to put a hand on Belle's shoulder.

"Oh it's not that," she smiled in return. "I suppose I'm just curious to go with him. He painted such a picture of that world/dimension, whatever the hell it is. I can't wait to experience it for myself."

"This world is hard enough to understand and survive in," Laura reminded.

*   *   *

Laura took Juliana a fresh flask of coffee when she went to relieve her. The wood was quiet and full of the normal woodland sounds and birdcalls. The morning sun was starting to warm the place up as it filtered through the trees. The odd squirrel dodged about from tree to tree, jumping between the branches. After fifteen minutes of girl-talk, Juliana drove back to the hotel, and met up with Belle. Juliana needed a hot bath to freshen up and then a light nap, and so Belle took the car to drive into Portmeiron. Even with the automatic transmission, it was still difficult for Belle to drive with one hand, and if a policeman were to stop her, she would probably be arrested, for the car had no special features designed to help her.

The roads were a challenge, being quite narrow and twisty till she caught the motorway once more. Then it became easier as she neared the city itself. She parked in one of the outlying car-parks, just to the north of the city-centre. Making a point of locking the vehicle, she wandered off into the busy streets to check out the shops.

Fashions were slightly different here, stylish enough, though nothing to compare with the haute couture of Rome and the other continental cities she was familiar with. Belle was really amazed at the prices. The British public really were being royally screwed by their government. Consulting one of the little tourist street-maps, Belle explored the city, finding a nice little bistro bar in which to have a late lunch. The meal was good and reasonably priced, washed down with a half bottle of an acceptable Merlot. Refreshed, she set out once more, choosing a more circuitous route to enjoy the architecture of the strange buildings she had first seen on television many years ago.

The giant chessboard was still there, and people were still taking part in the games. She bought an ice cream while she watched for a while, enjoying the sun.

*　　*　　*

Gabriel listened intently as the faerie elder continued his history of the unsuccessful rebellion again the Grey Priest. "When Malevar took refuge in the western mountains, he found a network of caves, which his hobgoblins enlarged for him. What he had managed to salvage from the destruction of his castle, they transported there, and set up for him. He is not as powerful as he once was, though his influence reaches far. Some say he is dying, but if so, he takes a long time to die," Vindomar explained. "His death is long overdue, and is the only thing that will bring back some stability to this land."

"I seek Malevar's aid for my daughter, but do not think me callous or unmoved by your plight. If I can get his help, once my dealings with him are done, I will do what I can to help you overthrow him. Perhaps while I visit his new fortress, I will learn something that may help to bring about his downfall, even find and release your Queen if it is possible," Gabriel explained.

"If the Queen were released, then we could oppose him more openly. As it is we can only do nothing whilst his creatures roam the land unchallenged," Kel explained. "I have pleaded with the tyrant on many occasions to free our noble Queen, but to no avail. I get only assurances that our Queen still lives, but must remain a prisoner in Malevar's mountain retreat."

"I sense a kinship with you, outlander," Malon spoke. "You understand our mind-speak after a fashion, and have some crude inherent skill in speaking back to us. We must investigate this further, and perhaps teach you how to better use this skill, that you may learn how to communicate with us over great distances," he suggested. Gabriel nodded in agreement.

The faerie-folk brought Gabriel some food, mushrooms and berries which they had gathered from the woods that still existed north of the river, and they showed him where an underground stream still flowed with untainted water deep in back of one of the caves. After he was rested, some of the other faeries came to him, and began helping him to practice the mind-speak which seemed to be inherent in their race, and strangely inherent in Gabriel also.

The trick of it came quite easily to Gabriel. Once they explained it fully, it was as though someone had just turned a switch in his mind, and it seemed natural to him the same way as the ordinary speech with which he had communicated for hundreds of years. Like a radio, his mind just needed to be tuned to the right frequency to broadcast and receive.

*   *   *

With added directions from Malon, Gabriel set out to the west, the next morning. He could see the blue-grey peaks in the distance, almost a full day's march away. Every few miles, Gabriel tried out his newfound talent, and was amazed how easily he could communicate with faeries still back in their underground caverns.

As he marched onwards, he pondered the affinity he had with creatures of this world. He could mind-speak like the faeries, and his body could attune its inner vibrations as the elves did to cross between their worlds. What did this mean? Why was he so unique? Malevar had hinted at answers when last they met. Did he know, truly? He had many questions about his own origins, such as why there had only ever been male Angels? That was why human females had often been 'visited' by his kind. What did Malevar indeed know of Gabriel's origins?

*   *   *

The setting sun revealed dark shadows among the peaks of the western mountains as Gabriel followed the well-worn path up into the high passes, following the water course which he had been told would lead him to Malevar's new retreat.

He saw the waterfall from a distance, the cascading waters pooling into a man-made dam, with a rough wooden waterwheel. Metal cylinders attached to the waterwheel had thick conduits leading back into the moutainside. Malevar was using crude hydroelectric power to supply his new laboratories, as he had done before.

Gabriel saw the entrance cut deep into the mountainside, and the two huge hobgoblins, bigger than the one he had fought, and more intelligent looking, standing guard just inside it, looking out onto the wooden drawbridge that spanned the rushing waters in the gorge below. Gabriel took his time examining the place. One way in, except for thc windows cut high above right into the rocky face of the crag itself. Just how extensive where the inner caverns and passageways anyway, he mused? Was there another way out? No way to tell without getting in there, and he knew the high windows would be his best chance of avoiding those hobgoblins. Hunkering down behind a large boulder, out of sight of the entrance, Gabriel tuned his mind and tried to contact the faerie Queen.

"Pfil?" his mind reached out.

"Who speaks?" came the instantaneous reply. "Leave now, before the tyrant discovers you. I wish to look no more upon the broken bodies of my people. Find another Queen. I am lost to you." Gabriel sighed as he remembered the honeysweet voice, though it was now older, and obviously strained. She had been captive by Malevar for many years, if what Malon had told him was true. That she had survived for so long spoke well of her character.

"My name is Gabriel. Do you remember me?" he 'spoke' in reply.

"The human? No, not human." Her voice now betrayed a change in her. "I remember you and one other, oh those many years ago, before my father died," she reminisced. "But why do you return?" she asked.

"On a quest," he truthfully explained. "I knew nothing of this land's troubles when I chose to come back here. I merely wanted to force Malevar to aid my daughter," he admitted. "But since I have learned of all that has happened here in my absence, I will try and aid your plight as well, if I may. Your own people are waiting for word of your safety," he revealed to her. "Even now, they rally support from the elven folk. Without you for a hostage, they would readily attack Malevar once again. Once I have his aid for my daughter, either voluntarily or forced, I will aid in that attack. He is evil, and his crimes should not go unpunished," Gabriel swore.

Pfil then used her mind-speak to reveal the inner layout of Malevar's fortress, as best she knew. "The lower levels house the Grey Priest's guards, where they keep me in a glass jar in plain sight, taunting me daily. They feed me scraps, but enough to survive. Malevar used his machines to open out and enlarge a natural series of caves, to make up the different levels of his new Keep. He has apartments in the higher levels, and places where he stores the remnants of his machines. I can hear their humming through the night as I try and sleep." He also understood where Pfil was kept prisoner, though he was unsure he could free her immediately. "Worry not, I have suffered here these many years without hope. Now you offer this to me, I can survive a while longer. I thank you, friend Gabriel, for hope is something I thought I would never know again in this awful place."

Gabriel then concentrated on the task in hand, though he was loathe to leave Pfil in her confinement. First things first, and that meant keeping Malevar alive long enough to help Belle. After that, Gabriel would take a great delight in putting him out of everyone's misery.

* * *

The darkening shadows made the climb easy. Strong muscles and sharp fingernails found easy purchase on the rough rock face, and he climbed up and diagonally, angling towards one of the darker, higher windows, following Pfil's directions, which revealed no one was within. Anyone looking up would see little, as he used what cover there was along with the growing darkness. It took but a few minutes for Gabriel to lever himself in through the window opening.

A store-room of sorts, as Gabriel looked around. Broken and burned machines and parts of machines littered the room. Salvaged from the sacking of his former castle in the city no doubt. Malevar was obviously using what he could to rebuild and re-equip his laboratories.

Parts of the room looked rough and half-finished, whilst others looked smooth as though cut with some industrial laser. Looking around now with his more educated mind, Gabriel still puzzled over the use of some of the apparatus, though others were easily discernible.

Generators, batteries, of strange design, true, but identifiable nevertheless. Racks of numerous jars of chemicals, labeled in a script Gabriel could not identify. The jars were carefully sealed with wooden stoppers.

Carefully, he opened the door, listening intently before opening it all the way and stepping out into the corridor. What power-source was powerful enough to cut this refuge out of solid rock, or at least carve out the passages between natural chambers within the honeycombed mountain? Malevar was still a force to be reckoned with, and if anything, his 'magicks' had increased since their last meeting.

Gabriel moved cautiously, wary of what he might find here, observing the strange constructs that Malevar filled his laboratory chambers with, some he recognized more readily now, though others were as much a mystery to him as they had been fifteen hundred years before.

Malevar was working late, he surmised, for the feint noises he heard from an adjacent chamber were not the clumsy manipulations of the goblins or hobgoblins. They were measured, and careful. Everything was as the mental map Pfil had described to him.

Suddenly he heard noises approaching from behind him, and hurriedly secreted himself behind a large metal bench, watching discreetly as one of the goblins carried a tray of food through to the next chamber. He could hear muttering of conversation, and then the Goblin returned, leaving the tray of food within. Malevar was planning on working through the night it seemed. That fit Gabriel's plans perfectly. He was not likely to be immediately disturbed by any of his retinue.

Withdrawing the jeweled scepter that he had purloined on his last visit, Gabriel regretted that neither he nor the scientists he had paid to examine it could make it work. Some sort of either force-field projector, or paralysis ray was how he remembered its effects. It would have served well to immobilize Malevar for this confrontation. He had brought it along merely as proof and a reminder that he still had the more-important vibro-belt, which Malevar needed to cross through the portal to the world of men once again, and also that indiscernible amulet, which he was sure was of some hidden value.

Slowly, he approached the opening to the next chamber, and very carefully peered around it. Malevar had his back to him, sat at one of his laboratory tables, meticulously eating the meal his servant had brought him. Gabriel thought for a second of pulling his gun, but Malevar would not know it's purpose unless he used it, and using it would gain him nothing if he had to kill him. Best leave it in its holster, and let Malevar think it of ornamental use only.

He started to take a first step into the chamber, when Malevar spoke. "You may put my scepter down on the table to your left. Then if you wish, I will order food for you. You must be hungry after so long a journey." Gabriel stood there astounded, and then Malevar slowly swiveled around in his seat, those huge black eyes of his looked upon him coldly.

Chapter Ten

Time had aged Malevar. Gabriel remembered him as a Grey, pale skin, yet smooth. Only the eyes were unchanged. His skin was now a leathery brown, and had long since lost its luster.

"Yes, time has not been as kind on me as it has been on you," he admitted. "You never did tell me your name before you set fire to my castle and escaped with my trinkets."

"My name is Gabriel."

"Is your friend with you this time?" Malevar asked. Gabriel slowly shook his head.

"Lucifer is dead. I am all that is left of my race, apart from my daughter." Malevar remained motionless, seemingly unmoved by Gabriel's statement, though indeed he was greatly interested in this admission.

"Allow me to have some food brought for you," he leaned his bald head to one side in question. When Gabriel showed no response, he raised a hand to his chest, touching a small gold medallion that hung around his neck, and he spoke in a language Gabriel did not understand. "Do not worry. I will not harm you. Time, if anything, has mellowed me. I am dying, you see," he gestured to his own body. "I sought escape from your human world because of the damage your atmosphere there was causing me, and yet history repeats itself here. My machines and inventions proved too much of a temptation to the inhabitants of this world as they did in your own, and the wars that have raged across this world have polluted the land just as they did in your own world."

"I came to ask your help," Gabriel admitted.

"Oh?" Malevar's mouth opened wide, though if it was a smile, Gabriel couldn't tell. "You ask my help after we parted on such ill terms, those many years ago? How strange. What reason did you have to think I would offer my aid? The return of that scepter there? Broken now, and useless," he commented.

"I still have your belt," Gabriel offered, "and the amulet I took from around your neck." Malevar remained silent for long moments.

"Do you have them with you?" he finally asked. Gabriel shook his head.

"I'm not that stupid. You tried to kill me last time."

"That was when I sought a body to try and return to your own world. Now my sickness has gone too far. I would not survive such an operation," he explained.

"Then you do not need the belt," Gabriel realized, hopes sinking.

"Oh, I still have a use for the belt," he assured him. "Not the use I intended, but a use nevertheless. I could not remain in your world, but perhaps after all this time, I could leave it at last. The power-supply in my ship should have regenerated by now, and I could at last leave your tainted world," he revealed. "The core was fractured when we first crash-landed on this world." Malevar explained. "We scavenged what we could to make a home of sorts on your world, whilst at the same time slowly doing what we could to repair our ship, but your technology was a long way behind ours. We set out to explore your world, in search of a civilization advanced enough to help us, and we found many strange races and creatures in our travels," he explained. "We took some for experimentation purposes, even before we found your atmosphere was slowly poisoning us. Eventually, a small island kingdom in an inland sea proved a magnet for us. At war with the Greeks, who sought to rule the waves, our aid was readily accepted by the inhabitants of that island, and I and my brothers ruled equally, as the humans treated us as Gods," Malevar recollected. "The Greeks were mighty, and many. Quite a naval power. Our tiny island kingdom could have not survived against them were it not for the technology we brought to bear on their behalf. We rained death down on every fleet they sent against us, but we were eventually brought low by treachery from within, as greedy humans sought to usurp our weapons and turn them against us. In the cataclysm that followed, the island was destroyed, and my brothers with it. I alone survived to retreat back to the crash site and continue work on my starship. Once I realized the length of time it would take for the power-source to recharge would be longer than my body could survive in your atmosphere, I began looking at a way of crossing over into the dimension used by the dark-elves, who came and went in the blinking of an eye, through vibratory rifts in the fabric of this universe, in certain parts of your world. Their bodies' inner vibrations could be adjusted to pass through these portals at will, and I began to build a device with which I could mimic those vibrations and pass through into their own world. That device was the belt you stole, one which I have not since been able to duplicate. At the same time, I began a genetic program to breed a body in which I could transplant my brain, and in which I could survive the pollutions of your own world."

Malevar was interrupted by his goblin servant, who eyed Gabriel warily as he entered the laboratory with a tray of food, hot steaming chicken and wild fruits. He put them down in front of Gabriel, and stepped away at a discreet gesture from Malevar.

"Would you prefer me to eat first?" he asked Gabriel, amusedly. Gabriel took an apple, preferring not to trust the prepared food. He bit into it, enjoying the freshness of it as Malevar continued his tale. "My race were advanced in the study of . . ." he held up an arm, lost for the right word. ". . . our bodies. We knew how they worked, how to replace faulty or lost limbs. Short of death itself, we could live forever. Our blood revitalizes our inner organs. We rarely succumb to disease. Yet our lungs, being smaller, could not handle the pollution in your world. We needed to experiment further with ourselves if we were to survive in your world. To do this, we experimented on all the races we found, human, animal, elf. We created many wonderful crossbreeds, which we released into your own world to study their behavior in your polluted air. We experimented on ourselves also, trying to alter our bodies to counteract the strange mix of chemicals that go to make up the atmosphere in your world. We used bits of ourselves in our experiments, studying which had the hardiest survival traits against which were the most compatible bodies for us to live on in. Your body, and those of your brother Angels were deemed the most successful of our creations," he revealed.

"I was *created*?" Gabriel asked, nonplussed at this unexpected turn of events.

"Oh, yes. Indeed. I am the closest thing to a father you will know," Malevar explained. Gabriel's worst fears were rapidly coming true. No father as such, no lost race of winged beings he could call family, just a laboratory experiment. "You were the product of genetic manipulation, using tissue samples from myself, humans, eagles and elves. Your blood was my blood, for longevity and self-revitalization, the eagle's lightweight bone-structure, human physiology, and the elves' inner physiognomy which allowed you to pass between the dimensional portals at will. Most of you were not genetically stable enough to act as hosts, and so I sought to capture as many as I could of your kind over the years, testing and finding them wanting. When I captured you, I found a perfect DNA match," he admitted. "Just a shame it is now too late for me," he gestured, conciliatorily.

"You think that excuses you the genocide of my race? Created or not, we had life. Once given, you had no right to take it away!" Gabriel's temper was up, and he found it was hard to control his emotions as he sought to let these revelations sink in.

"I was hardly the only one," Malevar excused himself. "The humans themselves hunted you down as freaks, even as they hunted down all our other creations," he defended his actions. "Such as you were not meant to live in their world. It was only your hardy biology that was meant to survive, not your race itself," he admitted.

"I survived." Gabriel glared defiantly at the strange brown-skinned creature that sat across from him. "Experiment or not, I survived."

"Your perseverance does you credit," Malevar nodded graciously, "but we digress. You returned to this world for a reason. Isn't it about time you told me what that reason was?" he asked.

"My daughter," Gabriel admitted. "Her hand was severed, and I need your help to re-attach it. Doctors in my world cannot overcome the regenerative properties of her blood to re-attach the hand. As you admit, you know more about my unique physiology than anyone else. If you can't help her, no one can. That's what I want, and in return, I give you back the belt that will enable you to cross through that portal into the world of men once more."

"I can do this," Malevar stated simply. "It is a relatively simple procedure. But you tried to kill me once before. How do I know you will keep your word, once this is done?" he asked, simply.

"My daughter will bring the belt and the amulet through the portal. Once the operation is over, I will return them to you," he offered, not wanting to say more, but Malevar pressed him.

"Your word, Gabriel. That you will offer me no harm if I help your daughter," he insisted. Gabriel was silent for many seconds, as he brooded on the vow he would make, the promise he had made to Pfil and her people.

"You have my word that I will not offer you violence. Once my daughter is healed, you shall have your possessions back." Gabriel finally promised, though his mind was already plotting his vengeance on the Grey Priest. Words are like weapons, and he was already preparing his strategy to attack, as Malevar would find out to his cost once Belle's hand was restored.

"Very well. The pact is made," announced Malevar. "I will make the necessary arrangements here in my laboratories, whilst you arrange for your daughter to attend me." If Gabriel could have recognized the strange contortions on the alien face in front of him, he would have recognized the sly smile, and perhaps realized that Malevar's short range telepathy made his mind an open book to him. Let Gabriel plot to doublecross him as he will. Malevar had his own plans for Gabriel.

"It will take a few days for me to arrange this. I have much travelling to do to return to the portal." Gabriel explained.

"I suggest you take care in your travels. This land is no longer as safe as it was," Malevar cautioned.

"Your doing, from what I hear?" Gabriel retorted.

"The rebellion was brought to my door. I ruled this land firmly but fairly until then. I used my powers well, but others wanted to usurp that power, and they reaped Armageddon. Such forces are not meant for human or elf to wield with impunity," he explained. "I will have my guards escort you out through the mountains. Then you may make your own way to the east. I will tell them to expect your return."

* * *

Gabriel headed East, away from the mountains, eager to rendezvous with the faerie-folk once more and tell them of their Queen's resolve. As he neared the faerie-refuge, he began hearing the whisperings in his mind, and the strange telepathic calls from one faerie to the other.

"He returns! He returns!" was the cry, and soon Gabriel was aware of colorful fluttering wings in the distance as many of them came to meet him, eager for news of their captive Queen.

They quickly lead him to where the Council of Elders awaited him, and Gabriel reassured them as to the health of their Queen. "Pfil is alive and in good spirits. She waits for the opportunity to revenge herself on Malevar for her ill-treatment."

Kel seemed eager to take the fight once again to the Grey Priest, but he urged caution. "Our people will rise up in a moment, but the blood-rush we followed last time proved our undoing. We need careful planning if we are to succeed against the tyrant, and free our Queen," he advised.

"I have a plan." Gabriel explained. "You will not fight this battle alone," he promised. "Let me explain . . . ."

Chapter Eleven

Belle made sure she wrapped up warm for the trip out to the wood. She had ordered hot coffee in the thermos, and some sandwiches and chocolate bars from the front-desk, to while away the night. An Ipod completed her 'survival-kit'. She took along a second thermos for Laura, who would doubtless be feeling the chill by now.

There was only the night-porter in attendance at reception as she went through the lobby of the hotel, and she left her key on the desk, before going out the front door. The small car-park was round the back of the hotel, and her car started first time. She waited a few minutes, getting comfortable to allow the heater the start to warm the car up, and switched on the heated rear screen to clear a bit of condensation. That done, she switched on the headlights, and drove slowly out onto the main road, turning right and driving through the town.

The road signs were easy enough to follow even in the dark. There was a full moon tonight, but it was shrouded in mist, casting an almost ethereal sheen on the landscape. Where it peered down between odd gaps in the mist, it looked decidedly pink and reddish, due to some atmospheric quirk no doubt.

Belle drove slowly, not wanting to risk an accident on these unfamiliar roads, and driving on for what was to her the wrong side of the road. It took her twenty minutes to reach the lay-by, where she parked her car. Tying the belt of her coat around her more tightly, she started off following the worn footpath deep into the woods, to where she knew Laura awaited her.

The going was easy enough, even in the scant moonlight, for the trees were not that thick with leaves. This was an old wood, she remembered from Gabriel's tales. Two thousand years old and more. The odd hoot of an owl, and a few odd noises didn't scare her, for she was used to the countryside.

Still, there was a certain feeling to it, the deeper she went into the woods, nearing the clearing with the shattered oak and the old altar. She heard the faint metallic click of the hammer being cocked on Laura's gun before the two women could see each other. "Sorry, Belle," Laura apologized, making the gun safe again and slipping it back into her pocket.

"No need. It's creepy out here," Belle admitted. "At least you'll get to sleep in a nice cozy warm bed tonight, while I'm freezing my ass off," she chuckled. "Here, I brought you an extra thermos. Hot coffee, Irish style," she grinned. Laura accepted it gratefully, managing a wry smile as she noticed the No 6 badge that Belle now sported on the lapel of her quilted jacket.

Laura chuckled as she took it and un-stoppered it. She could smell the whiskey the coffee was laced with, and poured herself a cup. "Mmmmm," she sighed contentedly, as she took a swig. "I could do with it," she admitted. "Bored silly out here. Haven't even been able to admire the night sky with the mist, though it might be starting to clear a bit now."

"I've brought an iPod to listen to a few tunes." Belle patted her pocket. "When do you think he's going to make an appearance?" she asked.

"Oh, tomorrow possibly. But no later than the day after if everything has gone well."

"And if it hasn't?" Belle asked.

"Well then, I think one of us will have to go look for him," she smiled grimly. "Don't worry. Your Dad can look after himself," she tried to reassure Belle.

"He didn't have to go."

"I know. But he wanted to go, so don't blame yourself." Laura soothed her daughter. She poured Belle a cup of the Irish coffee, and the two of them sat nursing their drinks as they looked up at the moon, now dark and visibly scarlet as it came out through the thinning mist.

"You get some weird shit in the sky in this country," Belle explained. "If the conditions are right, sometime you can even see the Northern Lights."

"Any UFO's?" Laura asked. Belle shrugged her shoulders. "Borrrrinnng," Laura laughed, then she yawned slightly. "Guess I'm getting tired. It's been a long evening," she admitted. Belle stifled a yawn too.

"It's infectious. I'm yawning now too," she laughed. "Have to keep awake all night. I'll really look forward to Juliana relieving me in the morning." Belle looked over at her mother, whose eyes were starting to close. "Hey, wake up sleepyhead. You'll spill your coffee," she warned. Laura's eyes opened again.

"Hmmm . . . what?" Laura found it hard to speak. She automatically raised the coffee to her mouth, and then paused, as Belle gasped. She held her own mug up to her nose, sniffing deeply.

"Don't drink any more. There's something in it other than whiskey!" she warned. Her nose caught the odor of something else in there, though by now it was affecting her too, and she couldn't identify it. Whatever it was, it was potent and fast-acting.

Laura dropped the mug, struggling to pull the gun back out of her pocket, but the hammer was caught in the lining, and her hands felt unbelievably clumsy. Belle staggered back against the altar itself, whirling at the sound of someone moving through the nearby shrubbery. Dropping her own mug, she pulled her torch from her pocket, and she shone it into the darkness, and two, three faces flitted past the thin beam of light.

"Good evening ladies!" a calm, elderly voice announced, and Laura and Belle turned towards it, Belle's torch revealing an old weathered bearded face. "Daeffyd Wildwood, at your service!" he smiled thinly.

Belle turned once more as Laura collapsed on the ground beside her, and then her own limbs began to grow heavier, and heavier, till at last her knees gave out, and she fell herself to the ground. The torch fell and rolled to a stop by the base of the altar. Wildwood picked it up, and switched it off. Around him, his followers came out from the darkness of the surrounding wood, to fill the clearing. Some of them carried oil-lamps, which they now lit.

* * *

"Two sacrifices instead of one!" Wildwood mused. "Prepare them both," he ordered, and shrugged off his coat, revealing his pristine white robes beneath, a sickle shaped knife was hooked in his corded belt. He knelt down over the two women, sniffing the very air above their bodies, taking a great interest in Belle. "This one has the blood!" he announced. "The blonde too, to a lesser degree, But this one is strong with it." His eyes gleamed wildly in the moonlight. "Stranger and stranger," his mind whirled.

The men with him lifted the unconscious women, carrying them over to one side of the clearing, where they began stripping the clothes from their bodies, chuckling and laughing amongst themselves as they did so, enjoying their work. They ran their hands over the two helpless bodies as more and more flesh was uncovered. They looked forward to these ceremonies.

Wildwood himself was lost in thought as the rest of his men prepared the altar for the ceremony to come. His followers had only reported to him the interest of these women and their other two friends in the clearing. Now he found that they possessed the blood, *the* blood. The same blood that had kept him alive for well over 1500 years. What did it all mean?

He had not seen the man himself. Could it have been one of *them*? What of the other woman? Who else knew of this clearing's existence, it's purpose? Who else could have crossed over? He turned to one of his men. "Caleb, return to my shop in the town. Bring empty bottles, jars, jugs, whatever you find. Make sure they're clean. I must have containers," he mused.

"But the ceremony . . . ." he protested.

"It will wait!" Wildwood assured him. "We won't start until your return, I promise you."

Caleb cursed his luck as he made his way back to where they had parked their cars. Wildwood might delay the ceremony, but they'd be fucking the arses off those two hot bitches while he was running errands, and he'd be missing out on all the fun. What did Wildwood want the containers for anyway, he mused?

It had been over a year since their last human sacrifice. Many tourists went missing in Wales, but Wildwood and his followers were only responsible for one a year, not wanting to risk any outside police investigations. The local butcher, another of Wildwood's flock, took care of the bodies, carving and chopping them up, finally grinding their remains for pigswill. That black foreign exchange student they'd taken last year had been a hot little thing and no mistake, Caleb remembered. But that blonde looked even hotter, and he wanted to slip her a length before Wildwood cut her open.

Finally getting to the car, he climbed inside, started the engine, and drove off back towards the town, as fast as the road would allow. Containers, indeed.

*   *   *

Back in the clearing, both Belle and Laura were now naked, and Wildwood's small group of followers knew the drill. One of them took out a hypodermic from a small medical bag, and filled it with solution from a small bottle. He stuck the needle into Laura's thigh, and slowly pressed the plunger down. Then he repeated the process with Belle. A powerful aphrodisiac, shared between them, as they hadn't expected two birds for the price of one, but still enough to ensure their co-operation in the evening's fun n games.

Wildwood wasn't interested in the sex, but it helped recruit his followers, and ensured their silence once the evening's festivities reached their 'climax'. They got so hung up on the sex, that the actual sacrifice itself was the next logical progression, and once involved, none of them dare back out for fear of reprisals and implication by the others.

None of the previous sacrifices had provoked a response from the ancient deity who had helped his religion in the past, but these two had the *blood*, and that might be enough, provided he didn't take too much off them before he carried out the ceremony.

*   *   *

Caleb's car roared along the road, just past the hotel where Juliana stirred restlessly in her bed. It woke her up, and although she tried to get back to sleep, she couldn't. The car roared past again nearly ten minutes later, further disturbing her. She felt distinctly uneasy, and got out of bed. Slipping on a dressing gown, she went out into the corridor and knocked on the next door to Laura's room. There was no answer. She checked her watch. Laura should have been back an hour ago.

She went downstairs to the main desk, and although the night porter was helpful, he could not attest to Laura returning to the hotel.

Her key was there behind the desk. It had not been collected. Juliana went hurriedly back upstairs to get dressed. Something was wrong.

*   *   *

Caleb trudged through the dark woods, lugging along the plastic kitchen containers with the sealed lids that Wildwood had asked for. He could see the glow of the oil lamps in the distance, and then gradually the sounds of merriment, much merriment, coming from the clearing itself.

Wildwood examined the containers. Enough for three or four pints of blood. The flagon he'd taken off the angel had lasted over fifteen hundred years as he'd slowly eked it out, but it was almost dry. Four pints of the stuff would last him into the next millennium and beyond.

Wildwood checked his watch. The moon was on the wane, and the sacrifices must be completed as the sun rose. Belle was dragged away from the milling throng by Wildwood, who persuaded two of his men to hold her down on the altar. Laura was left to the not so tender mercies of the rest of them, who mauled and pawed at her as they waited for Wildwood to give the signal to commence. Two men had her sandwiched between them, their embraces holding her upright, forcing unwanted kisses on her as she struggled weakly, barely aware of what was happening.

Belle was held down on the altar as Wildwood used his knife to slice her wrist, and allow the hot blood to flow into the container. She moaned, threshing helplessly, though hardly feeling the hot slice of the knife. The drugs were still numbing her body. Wildwood needed to use the knife twice more, to keep the blood flowing, as the wound tried to heal itself, but at last all the containers were full, and he sealed them carefully. He put them safely to one side. The moon was gone now, and the first tinges of dawn were appearing over the treetops. Time for the ceremony to begin.

*   *   *

Juliana parked her car alongside Belle's. She felt the bonnet and found it cold. Her hand left an imprint in the early morning condensation. Belle had gotten here, but neither of the two women had left. Deciding against using the torch, she began to follow the faint path into the wood as the moon dipped down below the treetops.

*   *   *

"We will honor the Earth Mother and ask Janus, God of Portals, to open the three gates (Fire, Well, and Tree) for us so that our prayers and worship will be attended by the three Kindred—the Deities, the Ancestors, and the Nature Spirits," Wildwood began with a typical litany, in preparation of his invocation to Malevar the Dark Elf. He switched into Welsh, which most of the men there could follow, but some of the words were too ancient, and in a dialect that few modern historians could follow.

Juliana heard the wailing, ululating voice long before she caught sight of the clearing, for the oil lamps were now burning low in the dawn light. A male voice. She took the Webley pistol from her pocket, carrying it low. Old she might be, but far from infirm. She remembered her firearms training from her days fighting the junta in Argentina.

Juliana slowed cautiously as she heard Wildwood's strange unearthly chanting echo through the nighted wood. Behind it came the coarse guttoral laughter of his followers, all excited and aroused by the ceremony. Sex and death, a synopsis of Life itself.

Juliana had been privy to, and had herself participated in, similar ceremonies in her life, pandering to man's most primeval impulses. The old magic was always the strongest. Sex magic had it's own power. The sex was mainly used as a lure to the unwary, but it had it's own distinct magic, and once the unwary found themselves participants in such rites, they were hooked, unable to deny and unable to denounce the profane acts they had participated in.

She recognized the particular invocation Wildwood was using, and hastened her speed through the wood, finger cocking the hammer of the pistol. The owner of the strange chanting voice was obviously no stranger to the arcane arts.

In the clearing, Wildwood was finishing his ceremony. He could feel the night air charged with energy under the pale moon. He raised his arms to the mighty oak tree as he prepared to finish the rite.

Caleb and the others ran their hands over the two naked women, holding them up between them so they wouldn't fall down in their drugged states. They could hardly wait for the ceremony's conclusion. He wanted the blonde one first, and he pulled her roughly against him, running his hands down her back to grip her buttocks as he pressed his hard erection against her belly. The ceremony was always concluded with sex, an old-fashioned gangbang before the woman was ritually slain. Tonight would be the first such double-slaying he had participated in. Twice as much pussy to go around, he chuckled to himself as the blonde struggled weakly in his arms.

Wildwood's chanting was increasing in pitch and fervour, when another voice interrupted.

"No!" cried Juliana, as she entered the clearing. She raised the Webley high, moving it back and forth to threaten all the men there. Wildwood was stood beneath the mighty oak. Laura and Belle were held by his followers on the other side of the altar. "This abomination has gone far enough. Let those women go," she ordered in a firm voice.

"Fuck me, it's Super-Gran!" joked one of the naked men, which sent the rest of the men howling with laughter. One of them sneered as they regarded her. "Piss off, luv. You're a bit too old for my type. I like em young," he joked, pulling Belle in front of him as cover from the pistol.

"Old woman," Wildwood turned to speak to her. "You meddle in things you don't understand. Leave now, while you still can." he warned.

"Don't understand? You call upon Janus, who was ever a two-faced deceitful god. I know of deities much older than him. You know not of what you speak. Heed me now, for I give no further warning." As Juliana's attention was held by Wildwood, whose wild red eyes held her own, his men began slowly moving around the altar towards her.

"Well, stay and watch, you old bitch!" laughed one of the men as he lay Laura down on the cold stone altar and spread her legs. "Perhaps if you get wet enough watching us screw these two, we'll give you a cock of your own to play with later," he sneered, and positioned himself between Laura's legs, thrusting into her, buttocks jerking rhythmically as he began to penetrate her.

The Webley roared, and a chunk of the man's left buttock was blown away as he screamed and fell back rolling around on the ground.

Wildwood seized the moment, as Juliana had turned the gun away, and he leapt at her, the crescent-shaped blade gleaming in the moonlight as he brought it down, and felt it bite deep beneath her shoulder.

Juliana screamed in pain, the gun dropping from her hand, and she fell to the ground as Wildwood collided with her. "You were warned, old woman. Time to pay the price!" he gloated, leaning over her with the bloody blade still in his hand.

"You too were warned," Juliana spoke in a pained voice, which seemed to change pitch in mid-sentence. "You know nothing of the powers I wield. Feel them now!" her mouth moved strangely, more strange even than the sounds which were coming from it. Wildwood froze as the hairs of his head and beard began to move as though caught by a breeze.

The breeze intensified, and now Juliana's eyes were as red and as wild as his own, if Juliana she still was. All her energy and venom were now directed at Wildwood, who jerked spasmodically, the knife dropping from his hand. Wounded and bloodied, she forced herself to her feet, directing her anger at the ancient druid.

Caleb and the others stood watching, speechless, apart from the poor wretch with only half an arse, who still squealed pitifully from the ground and whimpered helplessly as he was slowly bleeding to death. Things had taken a turn for the worse, and the old woman was far more than she appeared to be.

Laura lay prone on the altar, whilst Belle was struggling to her feet from where she had been dropped unceremoniously on the ground as Wildwood had attacked Juliana.

Witch and Druid now stood facing each other, and although nothing was being said, it was obvious to all watching that a tremendous battle was taking place, a psychic struggle for supremacy.

Caleb and the others had seen some strange things since hooking up with Wildwood, but nothing like this. The very air crackled between them as they stood facing each other. Blood was still running freely from Juliana's shoulder wound, and the old woman brought her fingers up to soak them in it. She raised her hand, using bloodied fingers to draw strange sigils in the air, like children with sparklers on Bonfire Night. Somehow the blood droplets stayed there in mid-air, forming indefinable shapes.

Wildwood was trying to speak, but only Juliana's voice could be heard, if Juliana's voice it still was, for it spoke in no tongue any of the men had ever heard. Finally there was silence. Wildwood and Juliana remained motionless, staring at each other as his underlings looked on. "Die!" was the single word uttered by Juliana, and as she said it, Wildwood's body flew through the air as though caught up in a hurricane, and it slammed back into the mighty trunk of the oak-tree with power enough to pulverize every bone in the Druid's body. The men looked on, horrified, as the limp corpse slowly slid to the ground, oozing blood from every pore. The outline of his body was imprinted in blood in the trunk of the tree. "Worship the wood, and die by it!" Juliana spoke one final time, in recognizable English, before the nerves of Wildwood's followers broke.

"Fuck it, lads. Run for it," cried one of the men, as Juliana stooped to pick up the revolver once more, and then struggled to keep her feet. The men rushed wildly about, gathering up their clothes, and vanishing into the woods in all directions. The wounded man was half-carried, still screaming and whimpering, as his fellows were quick to put this clearing of death behind them. The Druid's body lay where it had fallen.

In pain, Juliana went over to the altar, where Belle was coming out of her drugged stupor and attending to her mother. She gathered up the two women's clothes, and brought them over to them. They needed to leave this place. Wildwood's men would be back once they had regained their courage.

She felt the wound, wincing as her fingers explored. Not fatal, but she was losing blood at a greater rate than she could afford. She needed to get to a hospital.

Belle helped Laura as she recovered from the effects of the drug, her own experiences and expertise taught her the best way to fight off the effects. Soon the two of them were coherent, and able to dress themselves. Together the three of them made their way back to their parked cars. "I'm too weak to drive," was the last thing Juliana said, before she collapsed into unconsciousness.

Laura drove as Belle helped stem the bleeding, her driving erratic and painfully slow as the effects of the drug still raged through her system. At last, they got Juliana to the hospital in Portmeiron, explaining that they had found the woman lying by the side of the road, the apparent victim of a vicious mugging. They gave their hotel details and agreed to give a short statement to the police, hoping that their own physical states were not identified with drug-abuse.

Nearly an hour later, the two women felt more with it after a few strong cups of coffee from a vending machine, and a doctor updated them on Juliana's condition. The wound was not serious, and a transfusion had cleared the blood-loss. She just needed a few days rest and watchful care, and she would then be allowed to leave the hospital.

Belle managed a few words with Juliana in her hospital bed, advising her of the story they had used to get her admitted. They wanted as little problems from the police as possible, so had said the old woman was the victim of a mugging.

*   *   *

When Gabriel returned from the faerie-ring, he found no one there to greet him. All trace of the previous night's happening had been erased. Wildwood's followers had indeed returned to the clearing, and removed the Druid's body. They wanted no truck with the police either.

Making his way back to where they had normally left their cars, Gabriel found one of the vehicles still there, with the keys still in the ignition. He drove the car back to the hotel, where Belle and Laura were recovering from their ordeal, and quickly filled him in on what had happened to them.

He hastily made a phone-call to a man called Jim Maddox, whom the two women gathered was connected with the British Security Services, from the one-sided conversation they were privy to, and by the time the three of them returned to Portmeiron Hospital to visit Juliana, there was a young man sitting outside her room. He stood up as they approached, and they could tell by his bearing that he was no ordinary civilian, despite his unkempt clothing.

"Maddox told me to expect you. I got pulled off an exercise on the Beacons," he explained. Gabriel was all too familiar with that range, having gone up and down it a number of times during his own stint with the Regiment. "Another two of the lads will be joining me," he assured him. "We'll operate a round the clock operation to ensure her safety. You must know the old man pretty well to get such a fast reaction out of him," he probed, offering his hand, which Gabriel took and shook accordingly. "Name's Turnbull. Just call me Nick."

"Let's just say Jim and I go back a ways," he smiled. "Thanks for coming, Nick." Then he and the two women went into the room where Juliana was sleeping.

"Who was that young man?" Laura asked. "Who's Maddox anyway?"

"Says his name is Nick Turnbull, and he is SAS. He'll be one of their best, too, or Jim wouldn't have sent him. Maddox is ex, Green Slime now," he smirked. "Acts as liaison with the government's anti-terrorism units across Europe. He owes me a few favors. He can still pull a few strings," Gabriel explained.

"Didn't you used to have connections with some of those terror groups yourself?" Belle asked. "I thought you operated against us once with ETA?" she asked.

"Jim's one of the few people in the Intelligence community that I trust, and he trusts me. I explained my involvement with ETA was a one-off and extremely personal. As you know, the rest of those alleged atrocities were trumped up by Solomon to blacken my name and make it difficult for me to operate. Jim accepts my word on this. Even so, I'm still on Interpol's wanted list and that of the United Kingdom. Jim will keep this unofficial if he can, and if he can't then I'm sure he'll do his best to warn me of what's coming down."

Juliana's eyes finally opened at the sound of their voices, and she managed a weak smile. Laura and Belle each took one of their hands. "There's life in me yet, child. Fear not." She squeezed Laura's hand.

"Those horrible men," Laura started.

"Hush, child. They now know better than to pick on an old defenceless woman and her 'family'," she smiled. Gabriel chuckled at the remark.

"You? Defenceless?" he grinned. "That's a laugh."

"The next time I have my stick, my son, I am going to hit you so much harder with it," she promised with a menacing smile. Now it was Belle and Laura's turn to laugh.

Chapter Twelve

"Okay, here's what's going to happen," explained Gabriel. "Malevar is expecting me and Belle to show up back there at his mountain stronghold. I'm to bring the belt and amulet with me, but he knows I wouldn't just hand them over until he helps Belle, so the faeries have agreed to hang onto them until such time as I retrieve them from them. As long as Malevar is true to his word, I'll be true to mine. I won't fight him, which means that's your job Laura, with a little help, as I have no intention of leaving Pfil in his clutches."

"My job? Hang on a minute, if I use the belt to cross over into his world, I'll need it to get back. You and Belle might be able to cross over at will, but I can't," Laura pointed out. "Handing it over to Malevar doesn't sound too clever to me," she argued.

"I'm not actually going to hand it over. The attack will take place as soon as Belle's hand is restored, once I give the signal, and *before* I can collect it and hand it over. The elves themselves might be able to help you cross over, too, from what I understand. Physical contact with one of them makes your internal vibrations match theirs, and should enable you to cross over as long as you remain in contact. But like I said, I don't intend for him to get the belt. I gave my word, but the faeries didn't give theirs, and they want their Queen back!" he chuckled. "Malevar is in for a surprise!"

"How are faeries and elves going to attack that stronghold?" asked Belle. "The goblins and hobgoblins sound too big and fearsome for something the sizes of those elves, and the faeries themselves will be like insects against them."

"A little bit of help from 20th Century technology will go a long way. My contact in Cardiff should be able to rustle up enough hardware to even things up a little. Even so, I'll have to be careful with what I ask for, something the elves will be able to handle. Grenades and such. You'll have to handle anything larger than that, Laura," he pointed out.

"I'm handy enough with most small-arms, some explosives," she admitted.

"An all-out war isn't what I'm planning for, just a short decisive strike," Gabriel explained. "Once Malevar's forces get the surprise of their lives, I don't expect them to hang about. They'll run for the hills," he stated. "The elves may be smaller, but give them some modern weapons, and with the benefit of their gift of teleportation, they'll make a pretty effective strike force. In and out before the goblins know what's happening to them. I just need to make sure Pfil is freed before that attack starts."

"Will he really be able to attach my hand?" Belle asked, wanting reassurance that it was possible. Gabriel smiled, and put his hand on hers.

"If anyone can do it, then its Malevar," he nodded. "But I still don't trust the old bastard, that's why your mother here is coming along as backup."

"And I kick ass as good as anyone!" Laura confirmed, with a confident grin.

*　　*　　*

Laura took the metal belt from her luggage, to all purposes just another decorative belt in her wardrobe, it's inner circuitry hidden except to the most sophisticated x-ray devices. She put it on, and operated the switch on the buckle as Gabriel had showed her. She felt the faint buzzing almost immediately, though apart from that, nothing else seemed to happen. "Are you sure this will work?" she asked. Gabriel nodded.

"It worked for him, so it should work for you too." Then as Laura switched it off and removed it from around her waist, Gabriel used the phone to call his arms dealer in Cardiff. "Hello? Harry, it's Gabriel. Listen, that list I gave you the other day, how much of it can you get me?"

"It's a tall order, Gabe. Stuff like that doesn't grow on trees," his dealer complained.

"How about the priority items? The small, portable stuff. I need them tonight. I can have the money wired into your account before the banks are closed."

"I know you're good for it, Gabe. Money's not the problem, just availability on such short notice. I don't deal in miracles, man.

The grenades and small arms I can get, maybe one or two LAWS, but that's about it by tonight."

"Okay, it'll have to do," Gabriel confirmed. "Where and when do we meet?"

"We don't." Harry was blunt. "Park up in the King's Arms' car park between seven and eight tonight. Leave the boot of your car open. I'll be waiting. I'll put the stuff into your boot while you pop inside for a drink. Eight o'clock, you can drive away. Just make sure none of this stuff turns up in the hands of the police. They have ways of tracing this stuff back, despite the precautions I take."

"Don't worry, Harry. Where I'm taking this little lot, you can rest assured you'll never see any of them again," he promised, and hung up.

* * *

In her bedroom, Belle was quietly looking at the portable refrigeration unit that contained her severed hand. It still looked fresh, packed in the crushed ice. Once they unplugged it from the electrical supply, the internal battery was only good for between three to four days, so they couldn't dawdle on the way to Malevar's Retreat. She and her father would have to make good time to get there before the battery ran down. That meant Laura would have to stay behind and train up the elves in the use of the weapons that they would bring over into their world. The timing was awkward, for they had no idea how long it would take Malevar to fulfill his promise. Laura would be at least a day behind them, maybe longer.

She looked at the stump of her right wrist, the flesh all smooth where it had healed over. It didn't cause her any discomfort, but she just felt oddly unbalanced by the loss of the limb, still occasionally reaching for things with a hand which was no longer there, and cursing at her own stupidity, her temper flaring up suddenly out of nowhere.

Was it possible to reattach it? She didn't dare build her hopes up in case they were dashed cruelly once more. She wasn't used to relying on other people, but this once, she would have to.

*   *   *

The three of them drove into Cardiff early that night, and parked as agreed. Gabriel spotted Harry's car parked close by, but both he and the arms dealer ignored each other, as he led the two women into the pub.

They took a table, and ordered drinks and a meal, as had most of the other guests. The atmosphere was only slightly strained, as the tension was getting to the two women. Halfway through the meal, while Laura phoned the hospital to check on Juliana, Gabriel excused himself, and nipped out to the car park. Being careful he was not being watched, he quickly checked the boot of his car, grinning at the ordnance that was now inside, and weighing down the suspension of the car. He quickly closed the boot, and locked it, then going back inside to rejoin the two women and finish off his meal. He said nothing, just nodded silently.

An early night was called for, and then they would make the crossing in the early hours of the morning. It was a long drive back in the dark, and they wouldn't make it back to their hotel till near midnight.

*   *   *

Laura nestled securely in Gabriel's arms in the comfy wide hotel bed, one leg thrown possessively over his own. She loved this man, and he loved her. Both of them loved their daughter, and they would do anything, dare anything to keep her safe. Despite Gabriel's assurance, she was terrified of the thought of what she was going to do tomorrow. Gabriel talked about it so mundanely, yet she was somehow going to cross over into a different dimension, a different world. The mere idea of it was hard to comprehend.

Gabriel kissed her gently, and as she turned her mouth to meet his, a tentative tongue probed her lips. Moaning softly, Laura responded, her own tongue sensuously caressing his, in an oral ballet. She pressed against him, hungrily, feeling his body respond and harden against her. She put a hand down between them to grasp him and caress his hardening length, and Gabriel groaned, moving against her. Laura lost herself in the moment. Tomorrow was tomorrow. Tonight was for now.

Chapter Thirteen

The three of them scouted the wood thoroughly in the early hours just after dawn, but there was no sign this time of any interference from Wildwood's followers. There was no sign of anything untoward. The druid-worshippers had removed all trace of their activities. All three carried rucksacks and side-arms slung in shoulder-holsters. In Belle's rucksack was the portable and still cold refrigeration unit. Gabriel and Laura each had one LAWS rocket launcher slung over their shoulders. They looked ready to start a war.

"No need to be nervous," Gabriel tried to reassure the two women as they approached the faerie circle. Laura gave him a withering look, but allowed him to grip her arm as he did Belle's. "Switch on the belt, Laura," he indicated, and Laura activated the belt-buckle. He led them gently forwards, and together they stepped inside the circle. "Just breathe normally, and stand still," he advised.

Belle was hyperventilating. Laura remained more controlled, but twitchy just the same. She could feel the belt's vibrations running smoothly through her body, and as she concentrated, she found her sight becoming dim, as though a sudden fog had sprung up out of nowhere.

"Gabriel," she gripped his hand tighter.

"It's normal. Don't worry about it," he smiled, and then checked Belle to see how she was reacting. Her eyes were wide in wonder at the experience she was now going through. Her body tingled all over. It was as if her skin had become so sensitive and she could feel every fiber of the clothing she wore.

Vision faded altogether, before starting to clear as slowly as it had dimmed, and, without moving, they suddenly found themselves in another world. "Oh my God!" exclaimed Laura.

"You can switch off the belt now," Gabriel pointed out, as she got her bearings. Laura did so, marveling at her new location.

"It was daylight in our world, and now its night here." remarked Belle, slowly turning to take in the wood. The circle of stones was still here, but no altar, and the trees were different, closer together where they still stood. Many were fallen or rotted away as if struck by some unknown blight. There was still a fine earthy smell in the air, which she found intoxicating.

"Nice, isn't it? Takes a bit of getting used to at first," admitted Gabriel, pleased the two of them were coming to terms with the experience. "Take your time," he advised.

Belle giggled, and then so did her mother, the two of them feeling more alive somehow. They felt giddy, as though at high altitude. An owl hooted in the distance, and other night-time sounds could be heard. A strange wailing was suddenly heard across the treetops, as if from some night-time bird, and both the women looked to Gabriel for reassurance.

"Not something I've heard before," he admitted. "These woods aren't as safe as they used to be. We have no choice but to go on and get through them as quickly as we can. Stay close by me." He lead off through the trees, his keen eyes searching for the trail he had used on previous visits. Belle followed close behind, and Laura took the rear position, keeping their daughter between them.

Gabriel led off at a keen pace, alert and ready for any threat. They kept a tight formation, and moved in silence, watching for Gabriel's hand-signals which both the women now could use and understand.

After an hour or so, the three of them ducked down behind a fallen tree, as Gabriel cautioned them to silence, and as they held their breath, they heard the sounds of something heavy stalking through the woods close by. Gabriel and Laura had their guns drawn, ready for use, but the footsteps gradually faded into the distance, and they resumed their journey northwards, without knowing what it was that had just passed them by. Perhaps it was better that way.

*　　*　　*

Dawn came eventually, as they found their way to a section of the wood where leaves still covered some of the trees, and warm sunlight filtered down through the thicker canopy. It made the going easier, and by mid morning, the foliage was thinning out more noticeably as they approached the edges of the wood. They rested by a small stream which Gabriel declared fit to drink from, and they did, taking off their rucksacks which were getting heavier by the mile.

The mighty river was heard before it was seen, and Gabriel led them along its banks towards the east, where the city lay. At last, they saw it stretching out before them, with the ruins of Malevar's castle falling into the river itself. They saw some of the tiny elves in the distance, who quickly ran off as the three humans got closer.

All of a sudden, the air in front of them seemed to shimmer, and Eradh appeared, with a welcoming smile. Belle screamed in sudden surprise. "Shit!" was Laura's greeting, cursing automatically in surprise as she stepped back at the sight of the diminutive figure that appeared from nowhere suddenly in front of her. Small, and of normal proportions, dressed in a simple red smock. The sight of him was like viewing someone through a telescope.

"Welcome, Gabriel. Welcome, my friend," he beamed, arms out wide in greeting. Laura and Belle looked non-plussed, not understanding most of what he said, for the dialect he spoke in was not known in modern times, although recognizable as Celtic. Gabriel was chuckling as the two women got over their surprise at seeing for themselves the teleportation ability that these people had. "I have been busy, rounding up some volunteers to aid you in your fight against the tyrant. Sadly, not as many as I had hoped," he started to apologize, "but if your plan works, then they should be sufficient."

"It's good to see you, too, Eradh. As I promised, I have brought back help. This is Belle and Laura," he introduced the two women, in the same stilted language. Eradh bowed in greeting, recognizing Belle as Gabriel's daughter from the stump at her wrist. "We have brought some weapons from our world, which we will teach your people to use against Malevar. Laura here will teach them, while Belle and I go on ahead to seek Malevar's aid in restoring her hand. Once that is done, the attack may commence." Eradh nodded in agreement.

"Very well. Come, you must rest from your journey. My people have prepared a small feast in your honor. They await us." he insisted.

The three humans felt obligated to go along with his wishes, and followed as he lead them deeper into the city. Laura and Belle followed along, struggling to get their minds around the elves' language. It had its roots in Celtic and Gaelic, some of the words were similar, though some of the pronunciation seemed strange until you made the correct mental adjustment. They found it easier the more they listened to the tiny curious folk talking around them.

*   *   *

The 'small' feast turned out to be not quite so small after all, as over forty of the elves, townspeople and dignitaries all insisted on being there. Gabriel and the two women were well received as their possible saviors. Tiresome though it was, the three of them made the best of it. The food, fruit and wine were well appreciated.

After the meal, some of the other elves were presented to Gabriel, Belle and Laura by Eradh. "These brave men have volunteered to join the attack on Malevar. They are the bravest of our men-folk," he proudly announced. "We have Grandar, Josh, Magon, Brombi, Dale, and Arval." The six elves stood proudly, chests out, accepting the elder's compliments.

Gabriel nodded to the six elves in greeting. Not a lot, but enough. With their teleporting powers, and the weapons he had brought, they would be effective enough once he disabled the generators around Malevar's Retreat so that the elves could then use their teleportation powers.

Grandar was the spokesman, and obviously looked upon as leader of the strange looking group of elves. He looked to be given the deference due a natural born leader, as he stepped forward to make introductions. If he were human, he would look about mid forties, with short brown hair, and a devilishly pointed short beard. His clothing was typical of the elves, brown leather trousers, though his short sleeved hemp shirt was green to blend in more with the forest. Laura understood this distinguished the hunters from the rest of their tribe. He wore a peaked leather cap, decorated with a single bird feather, as did the others, though their feathers were all different, plucked from different birds, and of different colored plumage. Laura had no idea what this meant. Some sort of ranking amongst the elves?

Dale was clean shaven, and looked older, a few grey hairs appearing on his otherwise brown head of hair. In truth, it was difficult to guess the ages of this strange small race of people. He stood a little taller than Grandar, though not by much.

Brombi was the youngest looking of the bunch, and the tallest. Skinny, though not quite emaciated. He had a natural smirk on his face, which bore a few freckles to emphasize his relative youth. His mop of unkempt blond hair suited him.

Arval was shorter, with a slight paunch, and looked of the same age as Grandar, though his own beard was more full, and black as coal, as was his thinning hair.

Josh was bald, though still had a short ginger beard. He wore a constant smile, and gave an air of trust and assurance, that was somehow lacking in the other elves.

Magon was the stoutest of the six, with a chest like a barrel, but even though looking physically stronger than Grandar and the others, he was mild-mannered, and gave Grandar the respect that was his due, as the best hunter of the tribe. Clean shaven, his long dark hair was unkempt, and his dark eyes glowered moodily from under bushy eyebrows. Laura's first impression was that he either a deep thinker, or had a lot on his mind.

Leaving Laura to introduce herself to the six elves, Gabriel took Belle to one side. "While your mother stays behind to train these little guys with the weapons we've brought, you and I will head on north to meet up with the faerie-folk. They cannot aid us while their Queen is held by Malevar, so we devised a way of getting her out of there. It means one of them will have to change places with Pfil, whilst the attack takes place. I hope they've found someone brave enough to risk their own life for their Queen. I can't act overtly against Malevar, because I gave my word. But I can help smuggle a couple of the faeries inside that mountain, and let them free their own Queen. Then it's going to be up to your mother," he admitted.

* * *

The six elves looked up at the imposing sight of Laura with misgivings. Brave men all, they wanted to take the fight to the tyrant, but having to take orders from a woman? A human woman at that?

Human women had only been brought into this world for one reason, a life of servitude, either on the farms, or in the city-brothels, where the novelty of sex with a female giantess proved quite popular amongst their menfolk.

Their enthusiasm was thus dampened somewhat, as Laura started giving out orders like she expected them to be obeyed, in the pidgin version of their language that was improving surprisingly fast the more she used it. She had a keen ear. Laura looked nothing like the docile frightened humans that some of them still remembered from the old regime under Malevar. They followed her out of the city, and along the riverbank to a deserted length of shoreline.

Curious, they gathered around as Laura began taking out the weapons and firearms from the first of the rucksacks. They had never seen or handled modern weapons such as these, and Laura knew she had a job on her hands to train them to use them effectively in such a short time.

*　　*　　*

As Belle and Gabriel repacked their rucksacks and crossed the river upstream from the city, they heard the gunfire in the distance, as Laura had obviously started her training. A little later, they heard the sound of an explosion, and Gabriel hoped that none of the little elves would blow themselves up with those grenades.

Soon, the noises faded as they progressed through the thinner woods north of the river, striding out into the grasslands as they continued on. Belle grew more and more aware of the refrigeration unit in her backpack, the further north they went. She had checked the battery after the feast, and it still registered 80%. So close now to their goal, she didn't want anything to happen to her only chance of re-attaching the hand.

The wind picked up later in the day, whipping up a lot of dust and slowing them down somewhat. Holding their hands over their mouths, and squinting against the strong wind, they kept up their pace.

*　　*　　*

Darkness fell as they continued north, the going easy through the plains and valleys. Before too long, Gabriel felt the first fluttering in the back of his mind. Belle was shaking her head, just as Gabriel had done on his first visit to this land. Blood of his blood, she was hearing the faint whisperings of the faerie folk's mental communication without realizing what it was, and trying to dismiss it as she would an intrusive insect fluttering too close to her ear.

Gabriel communicated with them in silence, alerting them to their arrival, and before long both he and Belle could see what looked like fireflies hovering in the distance, and getting closer.

"Ohhhh . . . ." exclaimed Belle, as she saw them for what they were, tiny faeries with luminous wings. "Ohhh, how pretty."

"They've come to welcome us and show us the way to their caves," Gabriel explained. "We need to go over the final touches of the plan before we continue on by ourselves. Timing is going to be crucial. I just hope your mother can get those elves trained enough in time to join the attack. To protect himself against any unwelcome visit by the teleporting elves, Malevar has used his knowledge of their biology to ensure that the generators he used to power his equipment operated at frequencies which can disrupt the elves' internal ability to teleport. They can't teleport inside unless we take out the generators first. The faeries won't do that until their Queen is free," he explained. "So it all hinges on freeing Pfil. Then with the faeries help, the elves can do some major damage to his defenses. Once Malevar keeps his word, I will have to leave you with him while I supposedly get the belt and amulet back from the faeries. That is when the attack will occur. You'll need to keep your head down and get out of the way once it starts. I'll get one of the elves to help you escape," he assured her.

"Just give me a gun, and I can look after myself. I'm no sheltered angel, remember?"

"I know, I'd just rather not kill *that* many people," he joked, trying to keep the mood light. Together, they followed the glowing faeries as they lead them off into the hills, and eventually to the entrance to their caves.

Belle marveled at the interior once she had descended down into the lower realms, luminous gemstones were embedded in the very walls and scattered all over the place. "It's gorgeous." She soon found herself surrounded by inquisitive faeries, fluttering around her like butterflies, and she giggled delightedly. Gabriel smiled. It was good to hear the sound of her laughter once more.

"They will take you to some of the rear chambers, where food has been prepared for you. Fruit and lichen. No meat I'm afraid, but it's quite tasty. I'll join you after I speak to the elders." Gabriel assured her. The faeries were plucking at Belle's clothing, pulling her towards them, chattering animatedly, and she laughed as she allowed them to guide her deeper into the jewel-encrusted caves.

Vindomar himself came to meet Gabriel, and guided him to where the other two elders, Kel and Malon were also waiting. "Greetings Gabriel. We have not been idle while we have awaited your return." Kel assured him. "Malevar suspects nothing. I made my usual visit two days ago to plead for the Queen's return, and promised him our continued fealty. I noticed nothing unusual. His attitude was the same as it ever was, assuring me of her safety, but unwilling to release her." Gabriel nodded.

"Which of your people will be going with me?" Gabriel asked.

Malon spoke, frowning. "Melann, and Jarta will accompany you," he said, fingering his long beard.

"And the third?" Gabriel asked. "Have you found someone willing to swap places with the Queen? Malevar has to think she is still in his power, till we can launch the attack proper."

The three elders looked at each other, the mood darkening, as Vindomar replied. "One of our people was killed yesterday. A young female was collecting honey when she was attacked by a wasp."

"This is sad news, indeed," said Kel, "but perhaps fortuitous in that now we have a body to leave in place of our live Queen. We need sacrifice no more of our people," he proposed. Gabriel could see the three had discussed this at length. He had some idea of the reverence to which the faerie-folk gave their dead, and to offer this idea spoke a lot for the love they held for their Queen.

"So be it, then," he agreed, and removed his pack. He took out of it the metal belt which Laura had used to cross between worlds, and laid it across a small boulder. The three elders eyed it warily. He removed the amulet from around his neck. "As agreed with Malevar, I leave this belt and amulet here with you for safekeeping. Once he restores my daughter's hand, I will return for them. By that time, hopefully my wife and the elves will have arrived with weapons from my own world, which will help in the battle to come. The generators must be disabled before the elves can teleport inside the fortress and do some serious damage."

"We will not let you down, Gabriel," Malon assured him. "The rift between elf and faerie has gone on too long. Perhaps between us now we can rid ourselves of the grey one finally."

"Once Pfil is returned to us, we will attack with every means at our disposal. We will destroy or disable those generators you talk about," Vindomar assured him.

∗   ∗   ∗

Gabriel then joined Belle, where he found her washing her socks in an underground stream. "How did your war-council go?" she asked, wringing the water out of the socks, and laying them out on a rock to dry. "I've been learning their mind-speak. It's wonderful to be able to do that. It just sort of clicked all of a sudden, and then it was amazing. I can hear them just in my head. Sometimes it's all babble, as though they're all talking at once, but when one of them 'speaks' directly to me, I can understand them." She was obviously enervated by the sudden telepathic powers she now found herself with. Gabriel nodded, remembering his own feelings when he had suddenly learned to communicate with the faerie mind-speak.

He joined her, feeling hungry. The temperature down here was pleasant enough, and the mossy ground wasn't cold. He sat down on a small smooth stone, and picked at the selection of fruit, taking a handful of berries which he raised to his mouth one by one as he talked. "It went well enough. Getting Pfil out will be risky, but Malevar won't be expecting that. Once she is back with her people, they join up with your mother and the elves to launch a two-pronged attack on Malevar's fortress. Just keep your head down once the action starts."

"I will," Belle assured him.

"Okay then, better settle down and get some rest. We leave first thing in the morning." Gabriel found a clear spot on the ground, and used his rucksack for a pillow. He settled down and closed his eyes.

Belle opened her own rucksack, and looked at the regrigeration unit, checking the battery. It was now down to 43%. Another day's travelling would be needed to get to the mountains. She hoped there would be no delays.

* * *

In a dark corner of the caves, Kel flew silently and unnoticed up towards the surface. Out into the night sky and west he flew, to alight on a small rock escarpment, where he waited, watching the stars.

At the appointed time, he heard a faint squeak high up in the air, and a dark flitting shape plummeted down towards him. Ordinarily, any faerie would have taken flight immediately at the threat of an attack by one of these nocturnal bats, almost invisible in the darkness, but Kel was familiar with this one.

The bat, grey and ugly thing that it was, and much larger than himself, alighted on the rock a short distance away, it's leathery wings outstretched to balance where it's claws could achieve no secure purchase. Quickly now, for Kel knew the importance of speed lest he be discovered, he took the parchment scroll from his sleeve, and secured it in the small leather pouch that was attached to one of the bat's legs.

Once this was done, he stepped back as the bat readied itself for flight once more, and those leathery wings flapped, forcing it up into the night sky, squeaking once more as it turned to the west, and then was gone from sight.

Chapter Fourteen

Malevar smiled as the bat flitted in through one of the few natural openings in the stone of the mountain.

He had used laser cutting beams to re-shape the naturally honeycombed rock of the mountain into a fortress, designing rooms where the natural shape of the rock would permit. It looked haphazard, but after many years living here, Malevar knew his way around and navigated the different levels with ease. Some of his goblin retainers, being larger, often had more trouble.

The bat dropped down onto the table, where Malevar had left some dead moths and insects for it to devour. He unfastened the small leather container from its leg, and opened it, reading the tiny fey script which he had taught himself many centuries ago.

He commended Gabriel for his strategy. It might even have worked, but not now. Let them come. He could even have afforded to play fair with the Angel, for he had spoken the truth about his need for the belt. His ship would be recharged now after so many centuries, and safe behind an impenetrable force-shield. Of course, the cryogenic units would still have to be repaired, else he would not survive the long journey through space.

Still, far better that his experiments had borne fruit. His devices were much refined over the past centuries, and no longer relied upon the crude brain surgery he had first intended for Gabriel. A perfect DNA match was no longer a necessity. Over the long years, he had refined his techniques, even experimenting on himself with the DNA extracts of some of the captured faeries themselves, improving his own latent powers of telepathy so that he could now 'listen-in' on the thoughts of others, and even influence those of lesser intelligence. Once he had Gabriel in his clutches, and the belt returned, then Gabriel was not long for this world or any other!

It had taken many centuries with the crude technology at his disposal, but at last he had been able to duplicate the psychic imprinting machines that he and his brethren had used to transfer their essence into their new cloned bodies. Malevar would use this method of psychic imprinting to transfer his very essence into Gabriel's body. He did not know if Gabriel would survive such a psychic shock, but from then on, albeit in Gabriel's body, Malevar would live on, every thought, every movement, would be Malevar's not Gabriel's. The perfect revenge!

Pfil would remain in captivity, and Kel would rule in her stead, as he had effectively done since betraying her to him those many years ago, keeping the faeries in check. As long as the generators were not destroyed, those damn troublesome elves could not teleport into his retreat. Outside in the mountain pass, either his goblins or his explosives would destroy them.

Once in Gabriel's body, he would have the freedom to cross back and forth into the human world. He would seek out his repaired craft, however long it took, whilst maintaining a safe refuge here in the land of Faerie should it be required.

*   *   *

Later, on the riverbank once more, Laura found the hostility was making her lose her temper. She had demonstrated the awesome destructive powers of the grenades to the little men, but was insistent they practiced with stones, as they needed to conserve the explosives for the attack. The elves felt rather foolish mimicking her actions of "One thousand, two thousand, three thousand, throw!"

Only two of them were strong enough to use the pistols without the recoil knocking them over, so she kept the Uzi for herself.

Grandar, Josh, Magon, Brombi, Dale, and Arval were proud elves, used to ordering women around, not the other way around. As big as she was, she was just a woman, and a human woman at that.

Grandar was obviously the ringleader, respected by the rest of them, and they seemed to follow his lead. "We've thrown enough stones in our time, woman. Why do we need to keep throwing more?" Laura turned to regard him, hands on her hips.

"Because if you don't get rid of the grenade within three seconds of removing the safety pin, what happened to that blasted tree-stump over there will happen to you," she warned.

"We don't need this foolishness," he insisted. "We can just teleport inside, leave these 'grenades', and teleport back."

"Suppose the generators stay switched on?" she insisted. "You wouldn't be able to. Hence the need to practice throwing the things. You're just complaining because you can't throw as far as the others," she smiled defiantly, which enraged the proud Grandar.

"How dare you insult me?" Grandar's face reddened, whilst one or two of the others were trying not to laugh, recognizing that Laura's observation was correct. "I am the best hunter and tracker in our city. Why do we need a woman, let alone a human, to fight our battles for us?" he turned to his men for verbal assistance, and to a man they backed him up, agreeing with him.

"You need me because I have more experience than you. I'm familiar with these weapons, whereas you are not. And you'll do as I say, because if you don't, I'll kick your scrawny little ass!" she threatened, deliberately.

"What?" Grandar was livid. "It's time you were put in your place, woman," he snarled, and in the blink of an eye he disappeared. The next second, he reappeared just in front of her, grinning broadly as he reached up between her legs and gripped her crotch.

As Laura gasped, and swung her fist down to hit him, he disappeared again, teleporting about five yards away, and now holding her cam-trousers, much to the amusement of the other five elves. He grinned broadly at her, as he tossed them on the floor. "That's right, woman. What I touch, goes with me when I shift."

Laura's hands automatically went down to try and cover herself by tugging down her vest, but it wasn't much use. Her embarrassment was plain to see by her reddened cheeks. Goading Grandar into this fight might not have been such a good idea.

She had wanted to see how effective they could be at using their teleportation skills in a combat situation, for Gabriel's telling of his first encounter with the elf Brin had left questions, such as why the elf had been hiding from the boar instead of just simply teleporting away. She had her ideas, and wanted to put them into practice in this staged combat, but Grandar had already proved this might prove more embarrassing to her than to him.

Grandar disappeared again, and it was only the reactions of the other five elves that told her where he was. As she whirled around, she felt her vest being tugged, and then he was gone, and so was her vest. She stood there now in just combat boots, socks, and skimpy underwear. All six elves were laughing merrily.

Grandar tossed the vest on top of her trousers. "Very nice," he complimented her on her body, leering openly. "In this world a woman's place is on her back!" he grinned, and disappeared once more.

A kick to the back of her knees, dropped Laura to the ground, as Grandar pulled her back by her long hair, and a rough hand grabbed for her bra. As her fingers clutched at thin air, Grandar reappeared again a few yards away, waving the silken garment to and fro, much to the amusement of his fellows. "Nice tits!" he grinned. Laura cursed, and got back to her feet once more, all modesty forgotten as the rest of the elves leered and made crude comments. They were enjoying the contest. "Now lets have those pants off," grinned Grandar, who promptly disappeared again.

Laura whirled around quickly, pivoting on one foot, as she flung her leg back and out in a roundhouse kick, expecting the elf to reappear behind her as he had done before. The kick caught Grandar fully in the midsection, as he reappeared, knocking the wind out of him, and sending him rolling away in the sand of the riverbank. She was after him like a flash, not wanting to give him any time to recover, the rest of them yelling out a warning as he scrambled frantically to his feet.

Into the water he went, trying to put some distance between them, but Laura splashed after him. The other elves were cheering at the unexpected twist in the combat. Grandar was well-liked, but overly boastful of his abilities.

She closed him down quickly, lunging for him as they rolled about in the fast-flowing waters. He kicked, and punched, and she found him hard to keep hold of, but as long as she had him off balanced and stressed-out, he didn't teleport away. She'd been right about that.

"Now, you little bastard, it's my turn!" she snarled, as she grabbed him by the throat and forced him under the water. Grandar threshed wildly, and his nails dug into her wrists as she held him under, all his struggles for naught against her greater body-weight. Bubbles came out of his mouth as he tried to breathe but couldn't. He was drowning.

The other elves stopped their cheering as they thought she really was going to drown him, but eventually she pulled him up, gasping and spluttering for air, all the fight now out of him as she half-dragged him up onto the riverbank once more.

The fight had served its purpose. It had put Grandar in his place, and she had verified her theory about the elves' teleporting abilities. Stress and physical pain somehow prevented them from teleporting.

She dropped Grandar on the ground, where he rolled over onto his back, still gasping for air, and glad to be still alive. Laura was breathing hard herself from the exertion, her near nude body dripping wet, and she suddenly realized just how transparent the water had made her briefs, as she saw the grinning faces of the other five elves.

She went over to her discarded clothes, and began to pull them back on once more, trying to maintain her dignity, as the elves tended their beaten comrade.

Dressed once more, she tried to ring out the moisture from her hair as Grandar got slowly to his feet. "You're good, Grandar. But in my world, I am a warrior too." She tried to compliment him and help him regain some of his pride in front of his fellow elves. "I'm bigger than you, and I have fighting skills that you have never seen before. If you allow me, I can teach you these skills, and make you all much better fighters."

Grandar simply stared at her, a new respect in his eyes. He said nothing, just simply nodded, and then Laura turned away to head back into the city for something to eat, leaving him to lick his wounds and discuss the events with the rest of them. Hopefully, they would be easier to handle from now on.

* * *

The training continued into the afternoon, with all six of the elves paying a lot more attention to Laura's demonstrations. Grandar and Dale practiced also with the pistols, and proved accurate enough at close quarters. Beyond that, they certainly wouldn't win any marksmanship awards, but Laura expected any fight to be close up, almost hand to hand, and those pistols would give the goblins something to think about.

She used a stick to draw up a rough floor plan of Malevar's retreat, as described to her by Gabriel, from what he had seen. But Josh pointed out another limitation of their teleporting abilities that she knew nothing about. The fact that unless they knew a place, they could only 'port to a place they could see. As none of them had been in Malevar's mountain fortress before, they would have to invade the place by a series of lighting fast 'ports, using line of sight. Once in, they could instantly get back out again, but the actual penetration of the place would not be as quick as she had thought.

"That makes Grandar and Dale the two that make the initial assault, using the pistols to fight off any resistance you meet along the way," she pointed out, and Grandar responded with a grunt, throwing his chest out as though he expected nothing less than to lead the assault. "The rest of you can follow them in, once they take care of any resistance. I'll keep the outer guards busy with these," she patted the LAWS.

*   *   *

As evening approached, Laura began packing away all the munitions herself. She would carry one rucksack, and Grandar another. The rest of the grenades would be evenly split up between the rest of the elves. She advised them to pack some provisions, and get a good night's sleep, as she wanted to leave at first light the next day. She didn't know how long it would take Malevar to fulfill his promise regarding Belle's hand, but she wanted to be available whenever Gabriel gave the GO signal.

Chapter Fifteen

awn saw Laura rousing the elves from their beds, with only few complaints. They were keen to take the battle to Malevar, but none had the same sense of urgency as Laura herself.

They made good time, heading north out of the woods, and out onto the grasslands. Laura used the elves as scouts, having them 'port ahead as far as they could see, in different directions, reporting back at intervals. With the strong winds whipping up the dust, visibility was down to only a few hundred yards. The elves' ability to port fascinated Laura, and although they preferred to teleport within line of sight, Grandar confirmed they could teleport to a place they couldn't see, as long as they knew them in their minds, though the further this was, the more strenuous they found the experience. The obvious danger was that their mental vision needed to match the actual location. If anything didn't match that mental vision, they might end up trying to materialize inside a solid object, and that would mean death.

*   *   *

The first setback occurred a few hours into the march, when Brombi came back, looking agitated. "Hobgoblins!" he warned. "A hunting-party heads our way. They didn't see me. Do we fight?" he asked, reaching into his satchel for one of the grenades.

"No," said Laura, much to the dismay of the six elves. "We need the grenades for the assault, and besides, unless we can kill all of them, one might escape to warn Malevar. We'd best avoid them. Let's divert east towards those hills, and keep to the higher ground till they pass by. Then we can resume our original journey."

Muttering discontentedly, the elves relented, as much as they wanted to see some action, they saw the sense in her strategy. Together, they peeled right, and began trudging up the rougher ground towards the hills.

Overhead, dark clouds were gathering, and a few ominous rumblings could be heard from time to time. The storm finally broke as they were working their way through a narrow defile, and it wasn't long before the rain was running in rivulets down the steep sides.

*   *   *

Laura was soaked from the rain, her clothes heavy, wet and chafing on her skin as she forced herself on. The elves were suffering similarly, but they didn't complain. They needed to find some kind of shelter till the storm passed, and they regained their strength.

No sign of any cave of suitable size presented itself, but at one point, an overhang provided a sheltered area, which was dry in close to the face of the rock, and Laura and the elves sheltered there.

She bid the elves search about for kindling wood, whilst she searched through her rucksack for a lighter and firelighters, which were part of her survival-kit. When the wood finally arrived, after much foraging, Laura piled the branches and scrub over the firelighters, and used the lighter to ignite them. With a little tending, flames rose up, giving out their warmth. The smoke would be hard to spot in this downpour, and the twisting defile would serve to block any light from the flames.

Surprisingly, there was a surplus of wood, and Laura piled it up near to the fire, and then she began to undress as the elves watched amusedly. "Do you want to stay wet, or get your clothes dry?" she said, draping her shirt over the wood so the flames from the fire could start to dry it. She took off her boots, and unfastened her pants, and took them off too. She sat close to the fire in her damp underwear, as one by one each of the elves removed most of their clothing and did the same, doing their best to get warm by the fire. She took out of the rucksack a change of clothing, though no sense putting it on until her pants and bra were dried out a bit.

She kept the Uzi close by, making sure it was kept dry, and was pleased to see Grandar and Dale do the same with their pistols, showing them a marked respect after having practiced with them and seeing the devastating effects they could cause (provided they hit their targets).

Arval and Magon took out some flagons of strong brandy from their satchels, and took a swig before handing them round. Laura accepted gratefully, taking a good slug and feeling the fiery liquid burn all the way down into her stomach. Good stuff, heavily spiced with something or other, and certainly had the desired effect. Very strong stuff.

Laura accepted further swigs as the flagons were handed round again and again, and the strong liquor soon warmed her up and made her feel quite tipsy. The crackling of the flames was mesmerizing, and Laura just sat there staring into them, feeling a warm rosy glow inside of her. Steam rose slowly from her damp clothing.

Outside the shelter of the overhanging rock, the rain continued to pour, and the dark skies continued to hide the sun. She didn't know where the Hobgoblins were sheltering, but she hoped they were suffering. It looked liked they were here for a while.

*　　*　　*

By nightfall, the fire had dried out their clothing, and Laura damped it down, lest its glow be seen from afar by unfriendly eyes. They camped there for the night, with Laura and Grandar taking first watch, whilst the others got some sleep. Dale and Brombi relieved them a few hours later.

Just after dawn, and after eating some of their provisions, they set on their way again, letting the elves check out the nearby countryside. The storm had blown away, and the winds had died down. They made good time getting back down onto the plains and continued their way north.

Later that morning, Magon reported seeing another Hobgoblin hunting party, and they made haste to continue on their way before they were forced to make another detour.

"I don't like this," admitted Grandar. "This far out on the plains, there is nothing to hunt."

"Perhaps they hunt for us?" suggested Dale, which caused worrying looks to pass between them all. "They cannot help but notice your tracks," he informed Laura. "The wind has died down now, and there is no way of covering them. We leave little impression on the ground, but you are so much bigger and heavier than us. Those boots of yours leave deep tracks which are easy to follow." Laura thought long and hard. Something had alerted Malevar's forces. Either they had been seen leaving the city, or a spy had passed on the information. Grandar was right, she felt. The party of Hobgoblins was after them.

"Okay then, we can run but we can't hide. Sooner or later they'll catch up to us, so we'd better deal with the problem while we have the advantage. Start 'porting in all directions. We need to find a good place to ambush them. Sucker them in, then take them out. We can't afford to let any of them escape, so this going to be your baptism of fire, gentlemen."

The grinning elves were only too pleased at the thought of some action, and one by one, they popped out of sight, reappearing at intervals to report on their findings. Arval had found a rocky gorge, with steep sides, and only one way in or out, to the Hobgoblins anyway. The elves need simply watch from on high and then 'port in and out at will.

Laura lead the small band in the direction Arval had indicated, making sure her tracks were easy to follow for a while. Then once she saw the place in the distance, she told the elves to 'port the rest of the way. As it was her tracks that were leading the Hobgoblins after them, she was going to act as bait. A single human would seemingly present little threat, whereas they would be more cautious if they thought elves were involved.

There was still a mile to go to the gorge when she heard the cries behind her, as one of the Hobgoblins spotted her. She whirled around, seeing the party approaching. She turned and started to run. They were close, perhaps too close. She had to get them into the gorge where the elves stood more chance of attacking them successfully.

The sounds of pursuit were getting closer. So was the gorge, but not close enough. Laura's heart hammered inside her chest as she forced herself to run as fast as she could, but the weight of her pack was slowing her down. She was panting and gasping for breath, almost stumbling as a large wooden club whistled past her head.

She could hear their guttoral voices now as they enjoyed the chase, close behind her. She wasn't going to make it. Only a few hundred yards, but it might as well have been a mile. For half a second she thought of dropping the pack for greater speed, and then the decision was taken out of her hands as something hit her in the back, and she fell.

Laura rolled as she hit the ground, grazing her knee, and feeling the pain in her back from whatever had hit her. They were on her before she could regain her feet, one of them casually backhanding her across the face, hard enough to draw blood as Laura dropped to the floor dazed.

"Human sow!" one of them cackled, and drew back his foot to kick her in the stomach. She saw it coming and rolled with the blow, but it still knocked the wind out of her. She scrambled to her knees as a large gnarled hand reached for her. She pulled the commando knife from her thigh-sheath, and sliced at the hand as it came at her, the hobgoblin squealed in pain as his blood was spilled, but her token show of resistance didn't last long as another of them slammed into her and she went down hard, losing total consciousness. Everything went black.

*　　*　　*

From on high, Grandar and the rest of the elves were watching the events with concern. Hobgoblins were cannibals normally, but these were obviously after more than food. They wouldn't kill her straight away. The human woman had proved herself a good fighter, but against one hobgoblin she would be hard-pressed. A group of eight like this, and she stood no chance.

Out in the open, using the grenades was not an option, without risking killing the woman also. The two guns were all they had, as well as their own knives. Unless she could lead them into the gorge, this was going to get messy very quickly.

*　　*　　*

The bestial humanoids laughed cruelly as they rolled Laura over, pulling the rucksack off her back. One of them used his large fingers to fumble at the catches. Some food, and some metal stones, and some sort of metal club, were strewn carelessly on the ground, and the hobgoblin cursed as he found nothing of seeming value.

Another of them ripped open her shirt, pausing in much amusement at the sight of Laura's bra, which was something he had never seen before on a woman's breasts, and he poked and prodded them much to the amusement of the rest of them all. Laura groaned as she began to regain consciousness.

She opened her eyes to see the subhuman creatures all gathered around her, one of them standing over her as he played with her breasts. Cruel eyes looked down on her, and she knew there was no reasoning with these creatures. She spotted the contents of her pack strewn on the ground, including the Uzi, but too far away for her to reach.

With a snap of his fingers, the bra ripped apart, and Laura's breasts spilled free to even more guttoral grunts of laughter. She tried to cover herself but the creature batted her arms to one side, and continued to amuse himself at her expense. "Pretty human!" he taunted her.

The brute was nearly eight feet tall, and built like a brick shit-house. Bestial in nature and appearance, but basically still a male, and when Laura swung her foot up between his legs, he reacted the same way men did in her own world.

Screaming in pain, he fell over, clutching his aching balls, allowing Laura to quickly regain her feet. She dove for the Uzi as the rest of them tried to grab her. She freed the safety catch, aimed and fired all in one movement as she rolled away from them, and the gun chattered in her hand, spitting leaden death in the direction she chose.

The first hobgoblin's brains splattered the rest of them as they suddenly paused in shock. Laura shot a second, before the rest of them charged her.

Another bullet took out one of the other hobgoblins, as Grandar made his appearance, firing the pistol with both hands as Laura had taught him. Then Dale 'ported in, to shoot a fourth. As the creatures whirled to deal with this new threat, Laura shot another two of them in the back, and Grandar and Dale calmly shot the remaining creatures. Laura got to her feet, regaining her breath, whilst the two elves grinned at the effectiveness of the weapons they had been given. "I'm glad you two arrived when you did," she admitted.

"Our pleasure," smiled Dale, leering at her bare breasts. Laura scowled, pulling the torn halves of her shirt together. Men! They were the same in one world as in the other.

Gathering up the contents of her pack, Laura put on a spare shirt, and used the old one as a makeshift bag, wrapping up the grenades and food, using the sleeves to tie it closed, and then popped it back inside the rucksack which was still serviceable.

They left the bodies of the hobgoblins were they lay, and continued their journey north.

Chapter Sixteen

Gabriel and Belle were hailed by the hobgoblin guards as they approached through the narrow gorge. Belle shuddered as they got closer and she got a good look at them. Huge beasts with deformed features and limbs. Some of them more like animals than anything remotely human. "It's alright. We're expected," Gabriel assured her, as he informed the guards.

They nodded, snarling in disgust at the sight of the two humans, but they stood aside to let Gabriel and Belle cross the drawbridge over the fast-flowing water. They passed out of the light of day, and into the murky gloom of the castle. Belle almost shuddered as the warmth of the sun went off her shoulders. Gabriel took her arm to guide her.

The goblin retainers they passed gave them no trouble, and in one darkened alcove, he paused briefly to open up his shirt, and two faeries climbed uncomfortably out of his clothing, pulling the dead body of their comrade along with them.

It had been an extremely arduous confinement for Melann, and Jarta. The dead faerie Evys was known to them, though her appearance had been changed since her death to shape and colour her hair more like their memories of their captive Queen. If this deception were to work, then Malevar must believe Pfil to be still in his power. When the hobgoblins realized she was dead, they would not think to look for her escaping.

Already they were sending out their mental calls to their Queen. Gabriel could 'hear' them. With a blur of pink and yellow gossamer wings, the two faeries flew off, carrying their dead comrade with them, keeping to the heights and the dark shadows, where they could remain out of sight of Malevar's underlings.

Gabriel and Belle walked on, through the twisting corridors, till one of Malevar's goblin retainers bid them follow him, and he escorted them to where Malevar awaited them in his laboratory.

He was busy adjusting some instruments attached to a large glass tank, which was filled with a translucent blue liquid. He turned as they entered, and Belle got her first look at him. Inwardly, she cringed. His alien physique was even more disturbing than the repulsive goblins that fetched and carried for him. Outwardly she showed no sign of her inner feelings, but Malevar stared at her long and hard, as though he could read her thoughts, but then that was silly, Belle thought, not knowing that that was exactly what Malevar was doing. He withdrew his thoughts from her mind at the first traces of alarm. New to mind-speak, she was already gifted in it's use.

He turned and briefly did the same with Gabriel, before he spoke, careful not to delve too deeply or too long in Gabriel's mind as he knew from previous contact, that he had the faerie-gift also, and might detect him if he maintained the contact for more than a few seconds. Still it was long enough to tell him what he wanted to know.

"I have instructed my retainers to prepare food after your journey. We shall begin the procedure tonight," he explained. "The mixture of chemicals in this tank will have reached optimum temperature by then, and the subject will need to be immersed sufficiently for her body to absorb enough of the chemicals to inhibit the healing-factor long enough for the operation to be performed."

"You mean you want me to climb in that tank?" Belle asked.

"Not just climb into it. I want you fully submerged. The amniotic fluid is oxygen enriched enough for your lungs to process it. You will not drown, I assure you."

"Deep sea divers use something similar in our world, when the pressure is too great for their lungs to breathe normal oxygen," Gabriel assured her. "You'll be okay."

"So I just sort of float in there all night?" Belle asked. "Like a flotation-chamber?"

"I will administer a sedative, so that you will be unconscious. You will know nothing about it until you wake up afterwards, all being well, with both your hands. I take it you did bring the severed hand with you?" he asked. Belle shrugged off the pack, and opened it to reveal the portable refrigeration unit. The battery indicator was flashing now, power down to 15%. She handed it over and Malevar put it on a table, examining it most carefully. "Very well. It seems to be preserved sufficiently. I don't think it will take too long to re-attach, though I advise not using the hand normally for a few days, till your healing factor starts up again and everything knits together once more." he confirmed. "Please, go with my servants and refresh yourselves. We will begin the procedure this evening, and then by tomorrow, you will keep your part of the bargain, friend Gabriel."

"Very well. Once Belle recovers from the procedure, I'll go back and bring you the amulet and belt," he agreed. Malevar returned to his study of the portable refrigeration unit whilst one of his retainers came to show Gabriel and Belle to a small lavishly furnished room, where food had been laid out for them.

They both sat down and began picking at the food. Fresh cooked meat, probably wild boar, some grilled fish, and berries from the forest. "Can we trust him?" Belle asked her father.

"About as far as I could throw him," admitted Gabriel. "We don't have much choice for the moment. As long as he carries out the operation on you before the shit hits the fan. I'll only give the go ahead for the attack once that is done. I just hope nothing goes wrong with the rest of our plans. Melann and Jarta have to free Pfil themselves if we are to get the faeries to aid the attack."

*   *   *

The two faeries flew slowly and cautiously towards the wing of the fortress where Pfil was being imprisoned. It was heavily manned with Malevar's hobgoblins, and even keeping to the heights and the shadows, they decided they needed to wait for darkness before making any attempt to free her.

153

They lowered the body of their fallen comrade Evys onto a high ledge, and settled down beside it to wait for nightfall.

*   *   *

In his laboratory, Malevar had finished admiring the human technology that was used in the construction of the portable refrigeration unit. Remarkable how much they had progressed over the last couple of millennia.

He checked the gauges of the amniotic tank. The fluid was almost ready. He would be true to his word in that regard. He would restore the woman's hand. Once he was in Gabriel's body, he would need a companion or consort. He had dallied enough with human women during his time as High Priest in Gabriel's world. He had made do with one or two of the human females the elves used to bring him, before they were used as breeding machines to generate his goblin and hobgoblin forces.

He now turned his attention to some of the other devices in his laboratory, namely the psychic-transference conduit between the two low tables, upon which both he and Gabriel would lay. His goblin assistants knew how to operate the device, for he had kept the controls simplified enough so that even their limited brains could operate the device safely. It was power-hungry, so he needed to ensure the batteries were fully charged. If a generator failed whilst the procedure were underway, the results could be catastrophic. Once attached and switched on, the contents of Malevar's brain would technically be uploaded to his computers, then downloaded into Gabriel's brain, overwriting every thought in Gabriel's head.

Kel would ensure that the amulet and vibratory belt would be delivered to one of his men. His personal guards were already alerted to the rescue attempt on the Faerie Queen, which was now doomed to failure. His hunting party may or may not have captured the elven allies, but he had taken secondary precautions by mining the adjacent slopes overlooking the entrance to his fortress. As for Gabriel himself, by this time tomorrow evening, Gabriel would be Malevar, and vice versa.

*   *   *

Later in the evening, after Belle and her father had rested, one of Malevar's goblins came to escort them back into the laboratory complex. Malevar was there himself to greet them, performing last minute checks on the solution.

He turned as they came in and then took a filled metal goblet from one of his workbenches. "This will make you sleep soundly. Once you take it, you may remove your clothes and climb into the tank. Just attempt to breathe normally. The liquid will feel strange, a lot less viscous than water. Your body will soon adjust, and you will sleep while your body absorbs the chemicals contained in it," he explained.

"When will you attempt to re-attach her hand?" Gabriel asked, his mind concerned with his own private timetable of events. It was hard for Malevar not to chuckle as he took another little 'peek' inside Gabriel's head.

"Tomorrow, while she is still sleeping. When she awakes, the limb will be attached, and as the effects of the fluid diminish and her healing-factor regenerates the necessary tissue, she will have full use of it within a week." Belle seemed thrilled by the news.

"That is good to hear," admitted Gabriel.

"You may watch the procedure if you wish," Malevar offered, but Gabriel shook his head. "The day after tomorrow, it should all be over." Malevar seemed confident.

Belle took the goblet, and downed the contents. It had a slightly salty taste from whatever chemicals it contained, but not too unpleasant. She began to undress, piling her clothes on one of the benches. When she was down to her underwear, Malevar showed her to a small set of steps at the rear of the tank, and she climbed up before swiveling over the lip of the tank and lowering herself into the warm chemicals, gasping as she slid beneath the surface.

Gabriel looked slightly concerned as Belle deliberately submerged herself, long black hair flowing wildly around her head, holding her breath at first, before opening her mouth and taking a first tentative inhalation of the fluid. She spasmed wildly, threshing about at first, at the unfamiliar feeling of liquid in her lungs. But so oxygen-rich was the fluid, that her body began to process it almost at once, and her wild movements slowed, her eyes widening in wonder, and she eventually gave a thumbs-up sign to Gabriel to show she was now okay, and 'breathing' if that's what you could call it, normally.

She hung there in the fluid, suspended amid the gently bubbling chemicals, long dark hair wafting gently about her face and head. Malevar began taking more readings, adjusting the temperature of the liquid to compensate for her body-temperature. He seemed satisfied.

As Gabriel watched, Belle's eyes slowly closed. The sleeping draught had worked, and now she would remain floating like that while the chemicals did their job. Malevar now turned to Gabriel. "Nothing to do now but wait, eh?" he smiled thinly, and escorted Gabriel out of the laboratory himself. "Come with me now if you would learn more of your past. It has been long since there was anyone who could appreciate my history." Malevar invited Gabriel into his own chambers, signaling to his retainers to leave a small meal for them both, and then leave them alone.

Chapter Seventeen

Gabriel picked at his food, enjoying the wine. He took a seat across the small table from the aged alien. "Tell me then, of how an alien from another world comes to mine, and then to this one."

"I have told you already of how my brothers and I came to this world. Not by design, but by necessity. It provided almost the right atmosphere, and gravitational mass." Malevar went on. "The accident to our craft needed repairs, which could not be done in the vacuum of space. The damage to our engines was worse than we supposed, though, and we soon realized it would take many of your years for our power cells to recharge themselves." He paused to take some of the fruit, breaking the berries off and slipping them into his narrow mouth one by one. "Leaving our craft secure behind an energy field, we took ourselves and some of our devices to an island kingdom, where the people thought us Gods from the sea. It was an easy matter to convince them thus, and so my brothers and I had ourselves an island to rule, an island already at war with Greece, and we used our devices to fight that war, which we did quite successfully. While some of us devoted ourselves to this battle, others began experimenting on the native life-forms of this planet, travelling about the globe by means of flying devices unheard of even in your present time, we visited every corner of your world. When we first saw one of the dark elves, we were amazed at the creatures' latent teleportation abilities. For a time, they eluded us, until eventually we found a way to capture one. From this one captive we learnt of the existence of this other

157

dimension, if it is such and not in fact a separate planet which their teleportation ability has taken us to, I still don't know. From what the creature told us, and demonstrated using very carefully controlled conditions, we managed to analyze the vibrations used to control the effect, however crudely."

Malevar ate and drank from the same table as Gabriel, though Gabriel watched what the Grey Priest ate and swallowed, and made sure his choices matched those of Malevar, bite for bite, and swallow for swallow, as he did not trust the strange little man.

"Dissection revealed internal variances in the aesophagus and lung-cavity which we could not duplicate, even surgically, amongst our own kind. It was one of our scientists that discovered impurities in your atmosphere were slowly poisoning us, and so we discussed our problem amongst ourselves, trying to decide upon a course of action. Close enough to our own atmosphere, the chemical mix was sufficient to breathe for a short term, but prolonged exposure damaged our lungs. Our craft was unusable. We used our genetic skills to experiment even more on your world's life-forms, in the hope of creating a suitable hybrid form into which we could transfer our psyches, or transplant our brains, which is a common enough procedure among my kind. This body you see before you is automatically cloned at birth, grown to maturity and placed in suspended animation. When one body dies out, we can transfer psyches or transplant our brains into a ready-made replacement body, with no fears of the body rejecting the brain. DNA matching must be almost perfect, and the general species of homo-sapiens we found unsuitable for such a procedure, hence the need for all the hybrids that we created."

Malevar smiled a strange smile to himself, that Gabriel could not recognize due to the differences in their physiology, as he watched Gabriel copying his movements and choices of food. Malevar had already taken an antidote to the drugs that were in the foodstuffs, so it would do Gabriel no good whatsoever.

"Lots of the legends of your world had their birth in our laboratories, both on land, in the sea, and in the air. We achieved the best results once we captured the elf, and mixing DNA from his unique physiology with that of humans and eagles, we created the Elohim, you and your brother angels. You were meant to be suitable vessels for transference for me and my brothers. Sadly the cataclysm came before this could be effected, and you and the rest of our hybrid experiments were loosed into a strange new world, one made even stranger by your own admittance to it. Those war-mongering islanders were not content with merely defending their shores from the Greeks, they wanted to rule the inland sea, and they overpowered some of my brothers to operate our devices themselves."

Gabriel leaned forward, intrigued by Malevar's tale.

"Of course, they had no idea what they were doing, and they overloaded some of the power-cells, which had a devastating effect. It resulted in a chain reaction which destroyed the island and everyone on it save myself. Desperate, I salvaged what I could from my laboratory and used the last remaining flyer to return to my craft. I was at a loss to know what to do now. All our experiments had been lost to us. I knew I could not survive your atmosphere for much longer. In an act of desperation, I flew to the land where we had encountered the dark elves, and used the vibration-belt to cross over into their world, taking with me enough devices to ensure my mastery over their race. Later, once the subjugation was complete, and they became my slaves and servants, I sent them back over into your world to bring more of my supplies through, to enable my existence in their world to be a little more comfortable. Years later, when I became aware that you and your little band had survived, and now occupied that same island, I made contact with the heathen Druids who beseeched my aid to capture your kind, and send you through into this world. Only you, Gabriel, were a near perfect DNA match for myself."

"Then it's just as well your transplantation device was destroyed in your old castle," Gabriel said somberly. Malevar chuckled.

"As I said, that is no longer my intention. Age changes your outlook and your perception of things. By now the power source in my original ship will be at full power once more, and it sits there behind a powerful force-field, unknown to your modern world, just waiting for me to reclaim it, and then the stars will be mine once more."

"How could such a thing remain hidden in my world?" Gabriel asked. "The human race might not be as advanced as your own kind, but they are certainly clever enough to find such an anomaly."

"Two miles beneath the ice of your southern polar region? I doubt it." Malevar smiled confidently. "That's where it crashed, and the heat from it's outer hull melted deep beneath the ice-cap, where we had no choice but to leave it until we had sufficient power to break free. We enabled the force-field to prevent the weight of the ice from crushing the hull. It remains there now, as the day we left it to seek a life for ourselves in your human world."

Malevar could see Gabriel's frustration as he sought to take it all in. "It must be terribly frustrating for you, at not being able to remember so far back. My own memory fails me too at times, but then I have lived so much longer than even you. This isn't even my original body." Malevar stated, looking down at himself. "The mind endures when the flesh is weak. Flesh can be replaced." He said, pointedly. "I remember the first day on your planet as though it were yesterday," he reminisced.

Chapter Eighteen

ire roared across the night sky like an angry dragon, and the people who saw its fiery tail ran indoors, fearful. Some made small sacrifices to their many gods, in case they had somehow displeased their deities.

Far to the south, this angry dragon roared, flying ever lower and away from the populated areas, altering it's flight as though by design. Over frozen seas and shelves of ice the creature roared, till at last it came to earth, burying itself deep within the ice, which cracked and split, and boiled immense clouds of steam long after the initial collision was over, and the snows had settled once more.

The once mighty starship finally came to a halt nearly two miles below the ice, its battered hull cooling and straining as the full weight of the ice began reforming around it. Within, automated systems were engaging, and life-pods were busily working to inject chemicals into the sleeping bodies of the crew, to bring them out of stasis.

Grey spindly limbs were slow to move, and lungs ached as they sucked in the atmosphere within the vessel. Interstellar travel could hardly be described as comfortable, and one had to endure the life-pods during the many long years between the galaxies. Even stasis couldn't put a halt to the ageing process completely, and clones of the crew were always kept in the laboratory complex in case of accidents or even death.

Body-parts could be replaced, and brains could be transplanted whole into the new host body in the worst cases, if psychic transference was not possible. Speed-growth could generate muscle and tissue within relatively short periods of time, but the brains themselves suffered from lack of conscious input. It was always preferable to discard such brains, unless it was found absolutely necessary to program them from an original damaged brain in a psychic-imprint, uploading consciousness from one brain and downloading it into the other. Automated machines could do such tasks quite simply.

Alarms sounded throughout the vessel, indicating an emergency to the awakening crew. Something untoward had happened during their sleep, and automated systems had cut in, preprogrammed to respond to just about any imaginable scenario. A hull breach had occurred for some reason, a small meteorite possibly, but regardless of size, the breach had serious consequences, releasing the pressurized atmosphere in at least two compartments in a large explosion of debris into outer space. Automated systems had analyzed the damage and responded by changing the flight-path of the ship, realizing that repairs were needed to complete their mission, and that repairs could not be carried out in space.

As the crew regained their senses, some of them began checking their computers to assess the damage. Others moved to carry out a physical inspection. Verbal communication was rarely used between themselves, as their inherent telepathic powers were of more use to keep in contact at a distance. Each knew their role in life and what was required of it by the others at any given time.

Malevar, and eight others were the ship's compliment, each a specialist in their own field, but competent to take on the duties of at least two other members of the crew in an emergency.

The star system was identified as being along their chosen route, and the ship's automated systems had sought out the nearest possible atmospheric match, finding it in the third planet from a G3 class star. The crash had left them buried beneath the ice of the southernmost continent.

Power was down, and it looked like the crash itself had damaged the generators. The outer space collision had ruptured the laboratory complex, and the clone bodies had been sucked out into space along with most of their medical equipment and all biological specimens. Re-growing replacements would not be easy unless they could restore the ship's power, and build replacement machinery and apparatus.

This was a serious situation they now found themselves in. Their communication equipment was useless within a planetary atmosphere, so assistance from their home-world or other exploratory craft was not possible. With the ship damaged the way it was, it wouldn't be moving from it's present location until they could restore power, but the damage was such that they had no way of doing so. They were marooned on this planet.

Over the next few days of their confinement, Malevar and the others completed their diagnostics of the ship's controls and power supplies. Sensor probes had revealed the volcanic activity in the area, and it was envisaged that this thermal energy could be used to trickle-charge their generators, once they managed to repair them, but this crude process would take hundreds of years. The time itself was not a problem, due to their naturally long life-spans, but the atmosphere of this planet wasn't totally suitable to their metabolisms, and unless they could re-grow the clones, they would need to avoid serious injury whilst they waited for their craft to become space-worthy once more.

They couldn't remain on board the craft in such close quarters for such a long time, and the life-pods wouldn't work without draining the power even more. Probes revealed that the surrounding landscape was unsuitable for habitation even should they manage to break free to the surface. Things looked grim indeed.

Malevar himself solved the first problem, as he and one of his fellow crewmembers adapted one of the small shuttle-craft's weaponry, so that it emitted reduced energy from it's pulse cannons just sufficient to shatter the ice in front of it's path to powder, and it's engines were powerful enough to force a way through to the surface.

The bleak hostile landscape offered little hope of refuge. White snow in every direction, and bitter driving winds blew from all directions. It was all Malevar and his fellows could do to stand amid the buffeting. The strange air felt heavy in their lungs. A refuge was needed. They must take what they could in a couple of the shuttle-craft and find a home for themselves on this alien world, until such time as they could repair their ship.

It was agreed that three of the shuttle-craft would be sent out to explore this strange world, whilst the rest of the crew remained on board to get started on repairs, and Malevar, Lladris and Tasnar were chosen to pilot them. Each set out in a different direction, flying as high as they could and using their craft's computers to scan far and wide.

Tasnar it was who reported back with signs of habitation and descriptions of the bipeds who lived on this planet. Malevar and Lladris had no such luck, and returned to their frozen ship to await Tasnar's return. When it came, he shocked them all by presenting them with a specimen of the planet's natural inhabitants, a large heavily boned individual who was in awe of his captors, and obviously fearful.

When he tried to resist, Tasnar used his scepter to shock him into paralysis once more, and Kedro and Vassath helped connect him up to one of the still-functioning computers, attaching the nodes to the creature's skull. With a little modification in programming, instead of his brain controlling the computer, the machine itself would reveal his language and all his knowledge of this world. In the process, the brain would perhaps be damaged irreparably, as his alien physiognomy was not designed to withstand the process, but the meat itself would provide sustenance of a sort until other food sources could be found on this world.

The information that was gleaned from the creature's brain gave the nine crewmen knowledge of the world they now found themselves in, or rather the known world as far as the creature himself knew. Such bipeds were scattered far and wide across the planet, yet pockets of more advanced civilizations were developing along a small inland sea near the equator of the planet.

Wars were constantly being fought amongst different bands of these bipeds, as they strived for dominance with each other. The language the savage used was verbal, and difficult to enunciate, but Gurup, Wef and the others all exercised long-dormant muscles in their throats and chests to speak it.

Tasnar and H'nnarl were sent back out to capture new specimens, and these too were connected up to their computers for a fresh insight. The strange new language was of help in controlling one of them, but the others spoke a different language, and this had to be deciphered and practiced also.

The dominant civilization called itself Greek, and was spread far and wide along that inland sea. It was currently at war with an island kingdom in the huge inland sea, and that island seemed to suit their needs, providing a secluded refuge, and was easily defended, far enough away from nearby land-masses and possible threats. It was decided then. Once repairs had been completed as best they could, they would use their shuttle-craft to leave the ship to recharge it's generators, and make their home amongst the inhabitants of the island, taking with them what weapons and equipment they would need to survive amongst this alien race of beings.

*   *   *

Gabriel found Malevar's tale fascinating, knowing what he did now of the world, and extra-terrestrial theories, and it seemed to fit the known history of the Mediterranean area. Was it Malevar's droning voice, or just the hour? Gabriel tried to stifle a yawn, not intending to appear rude to his host.

"You must be tired. I talk too much, but have had little opportunity for such conversation in this world, surrounded by so many intellectual inferiors," Malevar apologized. "Let me show you to your chambers and we can continue this conversation in the morning." Malevar got up and bade Gabriel to follow him, which he did, and the soft pillow beckoned invitingly, as Malevar left him to his rest.

Chapter Nineteen

It was dark now in Malevar's Keep, and from their place of concealment, Melann and Jarta could see the glass bell-jar in which their Queen was kept captive. It broke their hearts to see such a proud figure now reduced to captivity in this way. Only her own mental strength had helped her survive her captivity.

She looked in a much worse state than the dead body they had brought along with them. Naked and begrimed, long auburne hair now matted and unkempt, and her once proud wings had been shredded, perhaps irrevocably. She would not be able to fly with them, and that would make this escape attempt more difficult than they could imagine. Both faeries were having to re-think their strategy.

Pfil had been kept in this glass jar since her capture years before. Within it were the decayed remnants of scraps of food, and her own bodily wastes. The goblins flushed the jar with water only when they felt like it. The thin membrane covering the top of the jar was the only way in or out, and the walls of the jar to were too far apart, and the top too high for her to reach.

"Leave me and go." Pfil eventually 'spoke' to them, after discerning their plight. "I will think no less of you for having made the attempt so far. I want no more deaths on my conscience," Pfil made the mental plea.

"My lady, you are our Queen. The human Gabriel has helped us get this far, and we may never have such an opportunity again. It is now or never. We have not come so far to give in so easily," said Jarta.

The two faeries were studying the jar carefully from their position up in the rafters. It was too heavy for Pfil to move by herself, though the rubbery membrane that covered it's top could be forced by the two male faeries so that Pfil could crawl through. Once they put the dead body of Evys into the jar, they could push it off the bench to smash on the stone floor, leaving the goblins to think Pfil had somehow tipped over the jar, and perished when it smashed into the ground.

Evys had been clothed in similar garb to that which Pfil had been wearing when her people had last seen her, and Jarta was now stripping the body, as graciously as he could.

Melann remained on high, to begin the gruesome work of shredding the dead faerie's wings so that they would pass for the Queen's. Jarta flew down to alight on top of the bell-jar, and began passing the clothing through the tight opening in the membrane. Pfil accepted them gratefully, and hurriedly began to clothe herself once more.

Once she had done so, Jarta signaled to his friend Melann, and flew back up to help him carry the body of Evys down. The two faeries alighted on top of the jar, and eagerly began pulling at the membrane, forcing it open.

"Well, well, well." A deep guttural voice came from the doorway of the room. The two male faeries whirled to see three large hobgoblins between them and the doorway. "Jarta and Melann, is it? Now which is which, eh?" laughed one of the fearsome creatures.

"Milady, we are betrayed!" Melann cried out. No time now to force the membrane wide. "Jarta, do what you can!" with that, Melann soared into the air, pulling from his belt the tiny thorn dagger, which was the only weapon he carried. Fearlessly, he flew at the three hobgoblins, straight in the face of the first he flew, buzzing wings speeding him forward, and a bloody line appeared close to the thing's left eye as it cried out.

Jarta frantically tried to hack at the rubber membrane with his own dagger, as all need for subterfuge had now gone, but it would not cut so easily, and he eventually gave up the attempt. "Push milady! Push!" Jarta urged Pfil, as he pushed on the large jar. Inside her confinement, Pfil flung herself at the heavy unyielding wall of glass, and the weight of the two of them began to move the jar slightly. Again, and again, they flung themselves at it, hoping against hope that Melann could buy them enough time.

Melann knew it was hopeless, but he had to try, and he managed to scratch a second of the creatures. Thorn dagger it may be, but coated with snake-venom, it would incapacitate even such as they in time. But time was what they didn't have, and as he fluttered about, one meaty hand swatted him aside, and he slammed into the stone wall before falling to the floor.

"Foolish faeries!" laughed one of the creatures, as he stooped to pick up the fallen Melann. "Our spy Kel has betrayed you to us just as he betrayed your Queen." Laughing, he offered the limp body to one of his comrades, and as they grabbed one leg each, they ripped the body of the faerie into two, in a sudden shower of crimson. Melann didn't even have time to scream. The two tidbits were eagerly consumed, deformed teeth crunching the small bits of flesh and bone.

"Harder, my Queen! Harder!" urged Jarta. Pfil was stunned by the death of Melann, and the knowledge of her betrayer, Kel, who was one of her most trusted advisors. She flung herself at the glass, feeling it scrape and move towards the edge, crying aloud in her frustration.

At last, the three hobgoblins realized what Jarta was trying to do, but they moved too late to stop him, and the jar toppled over the edge, smashing noisily on the stone floor. An act of extreme desperation, which fortunately had resulted in Pfil being merely winded instead of cut and bleeding from the broken shards of glass. Jarta had only time for one glimpse of his freed Queen, before a cruel fist slammed down, smashing his body to a messy red pulp on the benchtop.

Pfil wanted to scream, but there was no time. If she hesitated for a second, they would catch her once more. She ran as fast as she could for the small crevice against the wall, where she had seen the odd rat come and go in search of food. Behind her she could hear the curses of the hobgoblins and the heavy pounding of feet as they moved to catch her.

A last sudden surge, and the scream finally came as she felt a blow to her back, but the clutching fingers merely pushed her forward, and she rolled into the crevice, frantically scrabbling on her hands and knees as she put distance between the opening and herself. Gnarled fingers were already trying to grasp for her, reaching deep into the crevice.

Panting for breath, she followed the natural course of the rat-hole as quickly as she could. She grasped the thorn dagger from Evys' tunic, fearful of the rat's return. She had to get out of here. Time was of the essence. Kel was the go-between, and it could only be him who had betrayed Gabriel's plans to Malevar. Mentally, she tried to reach him, to warn him, sending out an urgent call, but there was no response.

Behind her she could hear the curses and mumblings of the hobgoblins, frustrated by her escape, but would they tell Malevar? They had a dead body to show if they claimed she had been killed, but if Kel had betrayed the attempt, he may well have given details of how it was to be done. She had best assume the worst. For now, she was on her own.

*   *   *

Gabriel slept uneasily, his dreams disturbed. None of the faeries had thought to try and communicate with him directly, but their mental cries of distress were felt by his subconscious. The short shrill mental cry from Pfil had almost gotten through, disturbing him enough to awaken. He woke from a fitful sleep, feeling unusually lethargic. His limbs felt heavy, and his movements sluggish as he levered himself up off the bed that had been prepared for him.

He was finding it hard to focus, yet through squinting eyes, he made out a small slim shape across the room from him. Malevar!

"Try as you may, you won't get very far, Gabriel. The drug you ingested with your food has had too long to take hold," he laughed thinly. Gabriel swore as he struggled to stay upright.

"You treacherous . . . . bastard!" he staggered, holding onto the edge of the bed for balance.

"Speak not to me of treachery, for I know of your plans. They are all in ruins, even as we speak," Malevar boasted. "My guards will prevent any attempt to rescue the faerie Queen. Without her, Kel my ally will keep them in check. As for your elven friends, my hunting parties have been looking for them for the last couple of days. I daresay they are dead by now." He moved back as Gabriel tried to grab for him, his movements seemed to be in slow-motion as his vision blurred further. "Your daughter is safe enough for now, for I will go ahead and restore her hand. But I have other plans for you, my dear prodigal son!" Gabriel fell to the floor, his breaths short and shallow. As he looked up, everything seemed to be slowly spinning around. Malevar's face was the last thing he saw before he lost consciousness.

Chapter Twenty

The darkness wasn't quite absolute, as Pfil edged her way nervously along the small tunnel, part natural, and part made by the rodents themselves as they had foraged for food. Tiny cracks and openings occasionally let in small streams of light.

It had a horrible smell of urine, foul and disgusting, which Pfil tried to ignore, but it was all-pervading in such close quarters. There were other openings into one or two rooms, but Pfil was wary of crossing the vast expanse of floor, even in darkness. She had seen what had happened to her two loyal subjects. As long as the small tunnel went in the direction of the outer walls, she would follow it.

On and on she went, stumbling occasionally in the darkness over rough ground or the dead carapaces of previous food. She shuddered as she thought of being eaten by those rodents. She cried out suddenly as she walked into something in the dark, something furry and wet. Recoiling, she lashed out with her small dagger, but there was no response from whatever it was she stabbed. Controlling her fear, she let her eyes adjust to the gloom, and used her hands to verify the blockage in the tunnel. It seemed to be a mouse, albeit a dead one. Its throat had been ripped out, presumably by one of the larger rats in a dispute for food, and now it was food itself. A large part of the front of its body was missing. Pfil tried, but she couldn't squeeze past the body. The rat would be back for more, sooner or later, and so she retraced her steps. She had no choice but to leave the relative safety of the tunnel and make her way through the rest of the rooms till she could access an outer window.

She peered out from the security of the dark cleft for long minutes, watching and listening. The floor of the room seemed to go on forever. She would be exposed and in plain view to anyone who entered the room.

Nothing for it, Pfil quickly exited the crevice, flattening herself against the wall, as she edged around the room. There was more chance of her remaining unobserved if she kept to the walls. Unfortunately, something else had already observed Pfil.

High up in the roof of the chamber, was a grey mass of cobwebs. Husks of dried-out, devoured flies clung to places on the web. A bloated yellow and black spider hung there on its web, watching events below. The diminutive faerie was watchful of Malevar's retainers and guards, but paying little attention to threats closer to home. Slowly and silently, the spider began to spin out its web, lowering itself an inch at a time as Pfil's movements brought her within reach.

Pfil edged along the wall, listening, and watching the entrances to the room. The spider dropped silently from above, getting closer and closer to it's unsuspecting prey. It remained at a height until the last second, staying out of Pfil's view. Then it dropped suddenly, striking without warning, and Pfil screamed at the sudden shock of the attack, flailing against the many legs of the arachnid as it attempted to spin it's web around her.

She fell back, entangled in the silken thread, and buffeted by the many spiked legs. The thorn dagger flailed back and forth, cutting and tearing the threads before they became too cumbersome. The spider attacked once more, this time trying to use it's fangs to paralyse her, and Pfil tried to force two of it's legs back, keeping the fangs at a distance.

She kicked out at the bloated abdomen of the thing, and was rewarded by a gushy squelching sound as her foot ruptured the swollen sac. Despite the wound, the spider came forward once more, rearing up on it's back legs, jointed thorax tilting to get at her once more, and giving Pfil the opening she needed.

She slammed the point of the thorn dagger into the jointed thorax, ripping it to one side, and spilling ichor all over the floor. The spider shuddered, making an unearthly sound as Pfil dragged her dagger free.

Mortally wounded, the insect halted its attack, limping away from the victorious faerie. Pfil knelt, winded and gasping for breath.

Once she was sure the insect was vanquished, Pfil got to her feet, brushed off the remnants of the sticky webbing, and continued to edge around the walls, though more observant now. Into the next chamber, and there was a window cut into the outer wall. The only way to access it would be to climb the rough wall. It would not be easy. Outside the dark night was slowly lightening as dawn approached. She had to complete the climb before daylight, else she would surely be seen.

*   *   *

Malevar was in his laboratory wing, supervising his menials as they prepared the two 'humans' for the forthcoming surgery. Gabriel was strapped down on one of two adjoining benches, over which hung a strange plastic conduit, the ends of which connected in two shiny metallic skull-caps, which were also wired-into the large metal boxlike computer which stood behind both benches. He was well sedated, and would keep until Malevar carried out the surgery on Belle.

The unconscious female was lifted from the chemical bath by two of his goblin attendants, who carried her to the far side of the chamber, where other devices were on hand to assist with the surgery. She was laid down on another bench, and her wet undergarments cut away from her body, before they covered her with a thin sheet of flexible vellum-like material. Her right arm remained outside the sheet, and Malevar inspected it with care, pinching the healed flesh over the stump of her wrist.

Satisfied, he took the refrigeration unit, which now showed only 7% power remaining, and opened it to remove the actual hand which would need to warm to approximate body-temperature before it could be reattached, and he placed it by the bench, while he began preparations for the surgery, coating Belle's stump with a sterilizing agent.

Hours later, after checking the temperature of the severed limb, two of his servants helped him in the operation, assisting where required, though it was Malevar himself who carried out the actual surgery. Her stump was opened up with a small surgical laser, and quickly sprayed with more chemicals to reduce the blood-flow. It was a relatively simple matter to re-attach the hand itself, connecting nerves and tendons. Alien eyes and fingers were so much sharper and nimbler than human. Her very own healing-factor would complete the attachment, connecting bones and tissue, once the effects of the chemicals wore off.

By mid-morning, the operation was completed, and Malevar used a solvent adhesive of his own design to complete the attachment. A thin scar all the way around Belle's wrist was the only sign that any surgery had been carried out. The scar itself would diminish with time. He lifted the limp arm, inspecting his work, and nodding to himself in satisfaction. It had been many years since he had had the need to carry out such primitive techniques. Without the medical computers which remained on his hidden spacecraft, he had been forced to use much cruder methods than he had been used to. As the effect of the chemicals wore off, Belle would regain full use of the hand within a few days. All she needed now was rest, and she would sleep for the rest of the day.

Malevar now turned his thoughts to Gabriel. Power was the problem with the device to which Gabriel was now attached. It was a hungry machine and required all the power the batteries could store. Power was always a big problem in this world, and he could only utilize what water there was to create hydro-electric power for his machines. He needed to be sure therefore that the planned attack was disrupted before going ahead with the mind transference. He would leave himself vulnerable to attack while the procedure was occurring.

As he pondered the risk, one of his Hobgoblin guards entered to bring him the bad news of Pfil's escape. "I am sorry, my liege, but the faeries managed to smash the glass bell-jar, before we killed them, releasing her, and before we could recapture her, she took flight down a rat-hole where we could not follow her." He trembled as he gave a slightly false version of events.

"You stupid oafs! Forewarned and forearmed about the attempt, and still you let her escape," he raged. Malevar's temper was legendary, and the Hobgoblin feared for his life if Malevar suspected what had really happened. "Find her! She has no wings to fly away. If she gets free of these walls, she may still seek aid to help her escape back to her own people. This cannot be allowed to happen!" The hobgoblin scurried away to organize greater efforts in the search for the escaped faerie Queen, whilst Malevar cursed his luck, and the standard of his so-called helpers. If Pfil managed to escape, the faerie-folk would again be a force to be reckoned with, for harmonics wouldn't keep *them* out of his fortress.

The faerie Queen was a formidable adversary before her betrayal, marshalling her forces to attack Malevar's Hobgoblins at every turn. Small and innocuous they might be, but they could harry and infiltrate, using a variety of forest 'weapons' against them, from their thorn-daggers dipped in snake venom to a variety of spores and pollens which were alternately distracting and sometimes deadly to his forces. The forests had only been safe to travel once the proud faeries had been curtailed by her imprisonment.

Their telepathic skills had been studied most assiduously whilst Malevar had been experimenting over the years, injecting himself with faerie DNA in a successful attempt to boost his own natural powers, which had once only worked between members of his own species. The traitor Kel had given him more information, and he knew that Pfil could communicate with other species as well as her own. It was how he had trained the bat to do his bidding, and it was to that selfsame bat that now he went, and he stroked it's furry body as it hung from it's perch inside the little cage. Pfil could not be allowed to flee back to her people. It was doubtful she would gain free of the stronghold itself, but if she did somehow manage the impossible, then this bat would prove far swifter than any bird she might seek to summon to her aid.

*   *   *

Pfil was finding the climb difficult, having fallen twice to the hard stone floor. Only her frail tiny body-weight prevented the falls being fatal. Still she persevered: the open window beckoned and was her only chance of escape.

Three, four times, she had heard angry voices, and the sound of running feet. Magically, none of the searchers gave more than a cursory glance into the small room, looking down only to the floor when they did so, and not to the walls where she now clung desperately. Nearer, ever nearer, she inched upwards towards the sill of the window opening. Finally, she pulled herself up over the edge, and stood there, shielding her eyes from the bright light of day which she had not seen for many years.

The high rocky crags of the mountain pass reached up to the sky across from her, and far below, the thundering waters of the fast-flowing river ran down the gorge, providing power to the many strange devices in Malevar's fortress, as they passed through the generator house. The mighty water-wheel could be seen slowly turning through a slotted hole in the timber roof of the building which sat over the waters. The fresh-air she could feel against her body was most invigorating after all this time, and she breathed it in, filling her lungs.

Now was not a time for remorse, though she ached to just fling herself out onto that wind, but her wings were shredded and useless. Perhaps they would never grow back, but there were other wings out there, friendly wings to the faerie-folk, and as she crouched there, she cast her mind out into the ether, seeking contact.

*   *   *

Further to the East, Laura and her small party of elves were approaching the Faerie Caves. As they travelled, Laura began shaking her head, now and again. At first she thought there was some sort of balance problem with her inner ear, until she remembered what Gabriel had said he experienced when he first encountered the Faery folk.

The whispers grew stronger, and words were recognized. The more she listened, the more she understood. Laura tried to mentally reply to the strange mind-speak, and was pleased to feel some sort of response, after encountering a subdued silence for a few minutes.

"Are you the human Gabriel spoke about? Come to help us?" one voice asked. Laura answered mentally as best she could, and sensed an excitement in the many whispers which suddenly seemed to deafen her. Grandar's keen eyes picked out the first fluttering of faerie-wings in the distance, as their presence was noticed and a few of the more inquisitive ones came out to see the newcomers for themselves.

The tiny fluttering shapes began appearing in the distance, as the Elves laughed aloud, pointing, and Laura saw the tiny shapes getting larger as they approached.

Laura found she couldn't help but join in the laughter, as the multicolored winged faeries surrounded them, obviously pleased to see them, as much as the Elve were pleased to see the faeries.

"It has been many a year, since Elves and Faeries last communed like this," explained Arval.

First Elves, and now Faeries. Laura was suddenly finding all her childhood fantasies and folklore suddenly coming true. Little People, and Faery-Folk. They actually existed here, if no more in her own world. Today's mere legends did indeed have some basis in fact.

"You have arrived in good time," explained one of the faeries as he alighted on Laura's shoulder. "Gabriel has given us hope, and is even now helping to free our Queen. We are planning our assault on Malevar's Keep. Come join us, and we will prepare food for you, while the debate is underway." He spoke aloud, so that the Elves could hear him, though Laura heard his thoughts, too.

She found it strangely intriguing that the elves could not hear the mind-speak of the faeries, and yet she herself could do so. Gabriel and Lucifer had also understood them. Had Belle been able to do the same?

Word travelled back to the three Elders, and Kel just managed to suppress his feelings of surprise, as he had expected Malevar's hunting-parties to have captured or destroyed them by now. He went with Vindomar and Malon to meet the newly arrived 'allies', who were to aid in the supposed attack.

Laura was quick to get over her shock of actually seeing the faerie-folk for the first time. A pleasant delight came over her to find that figments of her childhood imagination actually existed, and after the shock of witnessing the elves and their teleportation powers, and then those fearsome hobgoblins, the shock element was wearing off somewhat.

Dry and dusty from the plains, Laura and the elves were quickly shown to a small underground stream, where they could refill their water-sacs, and assuage their thirsts. This they were doing when the three Elders came upon them. "Greetings from the folk of Faerie." Vindomar welcomed them. "It has been many years since such diverse races were gathered together in friendship. In common need," he added.

"Mayhap this time, our common cause meets with success, and the Grey Priest is finally slain," Grandar spoke, the rest of his fellows nodding and mumbling in agreement.

"Rest after your journey. My people will bring you fresh fruits. This evening we will meet in a war-council to discuss our strategy."

"What is there to discuss?" Kel disagreed. "It would appear as though the critical part of our plans has gone awry, for our Queen was supposed to have been returned to us. This has not happened, and we must assume that the plan has failed. Without her, we cannot risk going against Malevar." Many of the fluttering faeries were in agreement. Laura was disappointed to hear this news, which boded ill for Gabriel and their daughter who remained in Malevar's hands.

"Then we need a new strategy," she said, boldly. "Together we will find another way. We are all experienced warriors here. Together, we can do this," she put a brave face on things. Dale and Brombi backed her up.

"Tonight then," agreed Malon. "We will decide what can be done. Rest now." He and the other Elders left, deep in continued conversation, as Laura and the elves were left with a small contingent of fairies, who showed them to where fresh fruit had been gathered for them.

*   *   *

"Come to me," Pfil projected out across the sky. "All ye who have known the friendship of my race. My need is great. Come to me." A faint echo, or had she imagined it? Yes. "To me., to me. Come take me from this place on swift wings, for I would go home to my people after all these years in captivity," she pleaded.

Looking up into the skies, she scanned across the heavens, till at last there appeared the tiny black speck of fluttering wings, growing gradually bigger as the bird, a tiny sparrow, flitted and swooped closer, homing in on her mental call. She stepped back as the tiny bird alighted on the narrow sill, and it regarded her quizzically out of one large blinking eye. Pfil climbed eagerly onto its back, sitting between its wings and seeking a handhold in it's brown feathers.

"Up, now. Up into the sky, and eastward, for I have a kingdom to reclaim!" she spoke, and gripped tight as the tiny bird sprung aloft, wings beating to send both it and it's passenger aloft onto the swirling winds, which soon carried them high above the peaks.

Higher still, flew the bat, echo-sounding in patrol above Malevar's Keep as its master had ordered it to do. Pfil and the sparrow had hardly flown more than half a league when the bat's radar picked them out. It turned, following it's unsuspecting prey, and began to close on them.

*   *   *

Malevar followed the chase mentally, putting his mind in tune with that of the bat as it swooped lower, silent leathery wings gliding along the air-currents, and approaching its prey from behind. Lower and lower it swooped down, approaching the unsuspecting bird from behind. Closer and closer it came, claws drawing back and spreading in readiness for the attack.

*   *   *

It would have been a perfect kill, if Pfil's mental powers hadn't picked up the approach of the bat just in time. Turning on the bird's back, she saw the bat closing in for the kill, claws outstretched to rip her from the bird's back. Her fear paralyzed her for only a few seconds, before her mental commands had the bird twisting in mid-air, rolling them away from the sharp claws. Pfil's only chance was the greater maneuverability of the bird's feathery wings, for the bat, for all it's greater speed, was less able to change direction quickly.

Chattering in frustrated rage, the bat climbed for the heavens once more, seeking to dive at them with greater speed. Again, and again, it came at Pfil, who had the tiny sparrow working hard to keep clear. The brave bird was tiring rapidly from its exertions and it's extra burden. It could not keep the evasive actions up for much longer. She screamed as she was jerked around in her perch as one of the bat's claws caught on the shoulder of her tunic, ripping it as the bird plunged down and away.

No time left now. The bird was falling from the sky, exhausted. It was kill or be killed, and Pfil drew the thorn dagger from her belt. She turned, watching for the bat's next attack. It came swiftly, leathery wings flicking this way and that, then diving straight at her. Pfil screamed a savage war-cry as she flung herself from the bird's back in mid-air, straight at her attacker, letting the furry body slam in to hers as she clutched at it's fur with one hand, and stabbed the thorn dagger home into it's hide again and again in savage fury.

Screaming and screeching hideously, the bat tried to throw her off, rolling this way and that, as Pfil hung on. Again and again she used the dagger, and red blood spurted with each thrust as the poisoned blade bit deep. The snake venom coursed fast through the bat's body, stiffening arteries and the flapping wings labored to keep aloft. Then finally, those wings stiffened altogether, and bat and faerie plummeted down through the skies.

"To me, bird. To me, else I die!" Pfil screamed mentally to the labored sparrow as she fell through the air, throwing herself clear of the bat's falling body, and spreading her arms and legs to slow her fall, trying to give the bird time enough to get to her before the onrushing ground claimed her. She would not survive a fall from this height.

The sparrow's wings beat hard, using gravity to assist its flight as it raced Pfil to the ground. Pfil's shoulder muscles worked her shredded wings as though they might arrest her fall themselves, but they were too damaged. Whether they helped at all could be argued, but mere seconds before Pfil connected with the ground, the bird's feathered body was there to cushion the fall, and Pfil had the breath knocked out of her as she clutched at the welcome feathers with both hands, lungs gulping in great amounts of air as she realized how close she had come to certain death.

Pfil gasped for breath as she mentally turned the brave sparrow around and headed east once more. "On, bird. My people have sacrificed themselves for my freedom, and friends remain in peril. Let it not be for naught. Take me home!" she implored.

Chapter Twenty One

Back in his mountain fortress, Malevar was still recovering from the mental shock of the bat's death. He had been attuned to the bat's brain as Pfil had successfully attacked the beast, and the psychic shock of its death had stunned him. This sort of psychic feedback was new to him. If he hadn't severed mental contact in time, he may have shared in the beast's death. He cursed aloud at this latest setback.

No news from his hobgoblin patrols meant that the elves must have successfully joined up with the faeries, and now Pfil had escaped to rejoin them and reveal the traitor in their midst. The attack on his fortress would take place within a day, he expected. There was much to do in preparation. "Guards! Guards, to me. Hasten now!" he bellowed.

*   *   *

Laura sat down with the elves, now that they had refreshed themselves. "Can we succeed without the faeries' help?" she asked the six tiny men. "The weapons we have will aid greatly, but we are few in numbers, and you can't teleport in until those generators are disabled," she pointed out.

"We can do it," Grandar insisted. "My people can disappear within the shadows, and one of us can sneak inside if we distract the guards."

"I'll go," Dale quickly volunteered. "Not many can move as stealthily as I," he boasted, and even the pompous Grandar nodded in agreement. "Explain the workings of these 'generators' to me, and tell me how to disable them, and I'll see it is done," he promised.

"Even if you are successful, there are still only the seven of us. We are going to need some shock tactics to make Malevar's forces scatter. We can't possibly defeat them all, with such small numbers on our side," Laura admitted.

"We only need to clear the entranceway. Once inside the place, we can 'port as far as we can see in a heartbeat. In such close-quarters, with your weapons, even those ogres can be routed. Malevar cannot bring his entire forces to bear on us in one spot." Grandar pointed out. "That will be in our favor."

"We must locate Gabriel and Belle and ensure they are safe. The faerie Queen as well. How do we do this in time?" she asked. "We need aid from at least one of the faeries, to use their telepathic powers to locate the three of them. Will they help us while their Queen remains captive?" she mused.

"Surely they will see the wisdom in this?" argued Brombi.

"Perhaps not," Laura argued. "You have no monarch as such amongst your own kind, Brombi. In my world, many countries still have monarchs, Kings and Queens, and they are generally revered and respected. Malevar does not have such a strong hold over you as he does the faerie-folk."

"True, he leaves us to our own devices these days, but we still live in fear of his marauding hobgoblins and the other abominations which now infest our once-beautiful woods. No elf will wander abroad after dark, these days. Everyone lives in the cities now, where once we lived in isolated cabins and communities. There is safety in numbers," Josh admitted.

"The woods themselves are slow to heal from the Grey Priest's poisons, but heal they do, and we would reclaim them as our own," Grandar stated. "We cannot continue to live in fear."

* * *

As everyone gathered for the great debate, Laura had never imagined such a sight in her life, the large underground chamber was a wealth of color as faeries were everywhere, some clinging to the walls, others alighting on various rocks and protuberances. Their wings were all unique in their pigmentation and patterns. It seemed like the whole swarm now filled this chamber. Laura and the six elves sat cross-legged on the ground, ever careful of the numerous faeries around them, and wary they didn't accidentally harm any of them.

The three Elders held court on a flat rock, where Vindomar addressed everyone. "Our choice is plain." he began. "To suffer the continued threat to our Queen or to aid in her rescue."

"Attempted rescue," Kel interrupted. "There is no guarantee this attempt will succeed," he pointed out. "Already one such rescue attempt has obviously failed, else our beloved Queen would already be here with us. Who knows what Malevar will do to her after this?" he played to the many faeries whose wings fluttered nervously.

Malon argued. "Malevar will not harm her further. If she dies, his hold over us is gone, and he must realize this. He has tried to kill us off before, and found it nigh on impossible, thus he needs the Queen alive to exert a measure of control over us," he explained.

"He doesn't need to kill her," Kel explained. "I have not wanted to reveal this to our people, but in my meetings with her in Malevar's mountain fortress, I was aware that her Majesty had been subjected to various forms of ill-treatment," he disclosed, to much gasps of indignation from the faerie-folk. "Would you have her harmed further by these ill-advised attempts at rescue?"

"Pfil is the last of her line. Her father left no other heirs. She has been a good Queen since her father fell during the last battle against Malevar," Vindomar insisted. "We cannot leave her in Malevar's clutches."

"Yes. Ragnar fought and fell trying to oust Malevar," Kel went on. "But Malevar is still here. We couldn't defeat him, only make him retreat," he insisted. "Now an uneasy truce exists between the forces of darkness and our own. Would you cast all on the throw of a single dice like this? His forces are too powerful. Our Queen is lost to us. Perhaps it is time we elected a new monarch?" he suggested, to much outcry from the fluttering wings of the many faeries present in the chamber.

*   *   *

Pfil took the bird down when she was in sight of the low hills in the distance. It was exhausted from its long hectic flight, and she joined it in plucking berries from the bushes it landed in. Sweet nectar, the fruit moist and fleshy, and almost forgotten in her confinement.

She was tempted to use her mind-speak to contact her people now she was in range, but kept her thoughts well under control, still seething at the knowledge that Kel had betrayed her. Like all of the elders, they had argued with their Queen from time to time, all of them taking different viewpoints as a matter of course to make her consider all options to the lofty decisions she made as their monarch, but Kel had always argued the most vociferously. In retrospect, she should have recognized his arguments for his true beliefs.

He had obviously plotted against her for a long time, as mediator with Malevar, a task she could not readily stomach after the death of her father, he had been in an ideal position to be corrupted by Malevar, turned completely around and used to betray her.

She had only the vaguest idea of what was happening to her people from what the 'human' Gabriel had told her. Kel ruled in a Triumvirate with the two other elders who hopefully were still loyal to her. If they were, then all well and good she stood a chance. If not, then civil war might well follow among the faerie folk.

By now they would be aware that the plan to rescue her had apparently failed. Malevar knew differently, but was he still in contact with his turncoat? If so what sort of a welcome had he prepared for her?

Malevar had Gabriel and his daughter in his clutches, and Pfil had a debt of honor to fulfill. She would not leave them to the tyrant's mercies, for he had none. She must rouse her people to rise up against him one final time, and if the other human had brought the kind of weapons Gabriel had described, then this time they might succeed.

The berry had provided much needed sustenance, and quenched her thirst at the same time. The bird was likewise refreshed, and Pfil climbed onto it's back once more, urging it into the air. Onwards to the eastern hills.

*   *   *

The debate was gathering momentum. Kel steered the argument skillfully in the direction he wanted it to go. "Malevar continues to hold our Queen hostage, and has done so for years. She may even be dead as we speak." he held his hands up to quell the instant clamor his suggestion had caused. "Perhaps it is time we chose ourselves a new monarch? One who could lead his people to victory against the tyrant." He paused as more voices were raised in both astonishment and more than a little anger. "With the aid of the elves and the human weapons, this could be done, I am sure. We cannot allow ourselves to be intimidated forever. By choosing a new monarch, we sever ties with the past, with repression and intimidation. If we do indeed find our Queen alive when we storm Malevar's Keep, then of course, she becomes our Queen once more. If she is already dead, then a new lineage is already in place, and our people will endure, knowing they still have a wise head to rule them."

"Who do you suggest we elect as our new monarch?" asked Vindomar, guessing the way the speeches were going.

"Why, as the senior Elder here, I would propose myself of course," Kel smiled, adding just a touch of humility. Voices became raised throughout the large chamber, as Laura and the elves sat back, and held their peace, not wanting to comment on the way things were going.

Kel was a well-respected figure, and had led the council well in Pfil's absence if the truth be told. But all the truth could not be told, and must be withheld from the rest of his folk at all costs. Even Malevar had no idea of the extent of Kel's ambition, and both the Grey Priest and the Queen herself must die in the ensuing raid on his mountain keep.

"If the raid is to go ahead as planned, then there is no time to gather all our people from their many refuges across this land. We must decide tonight, by majority decision. I am sure the rest of our people will accept the logic in this. I will lead the raid on Malevar's Keep myself as King of the Faeries," he promised humbly, with hand on his chest, bowing slightly to those gathered in the chamber, many of whom knew him well, and respected him. If he could force through the vote now, with so many of his followers present, he would win. And during tomorrow's raid, he would ensure that both Malevar and the Queen met untimely ends to cement his new reign.

*   *   *

The debate was going back and forth, and Laura shifted uncomfortably, her backside starting to ache from sitting on the cold rock for so long. Dale and Brombi were whispering together in the corner, she noticed, and Grandar and the others soon joined in. Laura shifted over to see what the huddled conspiracy was all about.

"Well? You've obviously got some opinion of what's going on. Care to share it with me?" she asked. The elves looked none too pleased.

Grandar spoke for the other five elves. "We elves have never had a ruler as far back as we can remember. We lived independently and only gathered together for festivals and weddings and such. The towns only grew from fear of the wild beasts and Malevar's goblins raiding through the forests. Some of us have met Pfil, their Queen, and we found her a noble, and honourable Queen of her people. Her bloodline has ruled the faerie-folk since time began. What is proposed is tantamount to treason among her kind. True, she has lived in bondage in Malevar's Keep for many years now, but to abandon her to her fate like this, rankles me somewhat. Elves do not abandon each other! Each would give our own life to save another's. Not all the faerie folk feel the same way, obviously," he glowered.

Laura shrugged her shoulders. "Irrespective, if what you say is true or not, a fast resolution one way or the other is called for. We need their help to attack the Keep, and if electing a new King will get that help, then Hell, I'll vote for him myself. If Pfil still lives, then no harm done. If she's dead, then at least a ready-made successor will have already been chosen. It works for me, so get on with it, I say," she moralized.

Brombi butted in. "The reason the Triumvirate rules in the Queen's absence is because there is no successor to the Royal Bloodline, for Pfil has never married. No one person is deemed to be honest or noble enough to put their own agenda to one side, in favor of the greater good of her people. Power corrupts, and absolute power corrupts absolutely. Just look at Malevar. Pfil has never used her power to harm others, only to protect her people. Wise men they might be, but they are all statesmen, and never a one was born that could be trusted to be selfless." Some of the other elves nodded and muttered in agreement.

*   *   *

As the haranguing and arguing continued, the three Elders each took turns speaking to the assembly, arguing the pros and cons of putting this thing to a vote at this time. All of a sudden, the taller greybeard Vindomar went whiter than his beard, almost stumbling as his face suddenly dropped, and his eyes bulged wide.

"Vindomar, what's wrong?" asked Malon, and both he and Kel went to quickly support their fellow elder.

"It's nothing." Vindomar gasped, recovering himself, and looking from one to the other in surprise. "Excuse me, I must leave you for a few minutes. I feel unwell, and would rest," he explained, falteringly. "I will return momentarily after I have refreshed myself. Please continue without me for now." He turned and, wings fluttering, flew slowly, unsteadily out of the chamber.

A couple of the other fairies went to accompany Vindomar from the chamber, concerned about him, but Vindomar waved them away, and flew alone, more steadily now, through the myriad deserted tunnels of their refuge. Onward and upward he flew, towards the surface, his heart beating faster and irregularly in his chest. He wanted to believe so very badly. Had he imagined the voice in his head?

The light grew steadily brighter as he flew up one of the narrow fissures in the rock, and he shielded his eyes against the sun's glare as he finally felt the wind buffet him. He alighted on the irregular rock, looking slowly around him. Her silhouette was framed against the setting sun, and he gasped as she walked slowly toward him. "It's really me, Vin," a weak voice managed to speak. "You were the only one I could still trust." The voice was choked with emotion, and she stumbled to get the words out.

"Oh, my Lady!" Vindomar gasped, as he saw it was really her. "My poor Lady!" she half fell into his arms, sobbing with him, together, and they held each other like that for what seemed forever, his long arms cradling her, feeling her chest heaving against his as she cried with relief. He cried too at the feel of her shredded wings under his hands. What had been done to her was a crime that could not go unpunished.

*　　*　　*

In the council-chamber, the debate went on, and after nearly an hour's absence, Vindomar rejoined the other two elders as they began to organize a vote on Kel's motion. He waved away the attentions of some of the other faeries who were worried about his health. He still looked pale, but they mistook anger for ill-health. It was all he could do to hold himself in check after what he had learned, but control was paramount if this treason were to be nipped in the bud.

"Very well," announced Malon, taking control of the proceedings. "We will put this matter to the vote." All around the chamber, heads were nodding and tongues were wagging, except those of a select few with whom Vindomar was now rapidly communicating with mind-speak. They went rigid with the full knowledge of what he now revealed to them. Eyes flashed with a controlled anger. Slowly, cautiously, a small number of faeries began gradually moving together, till they were gathered in a group, making their way almost unnoticeably to the rear of the chamber. Only Laura's eyes followed them, for small details of things rarely escaped her, and had saved her life more than once. The faeries could certainly be considered small enough to qualify. What were they up to?

"All those in favor of electing a new monarch, raise your hands." As the three Elders looked around the room, many hands rose. Kel tried not to smile. He had enough followers in the chamber to carry this off. "All those against?" Malon announced, and another sea of hands reached into the air, though not quite as many as before. Malon took his time. He was not looking forward to life under King Kel, but he believed in democracy as well as the next man. If that was what his people wanted, then he would go along with it. "Well, it looks like we vote for our next monarch," he said with sadness.

"Hold!" interrupted Vindomar. "There is still one more vote left to cast." He stared accusingly at Kel as he pointed to the back of the chamber, and all eyes turned to follow his finger.

"And I, your *Queen*, vote no!" said Pfil, daughter of Ragnar, Queen of the Faeries, standing there in the blood-soaked rags she had worn since her escape, dirty, disheveled, and shredded wings hanging almost uselessly down her back. Yet on her head, once more, was the gold circlet crown of her father Ragnar. Despite her begrimed appearance, she stood every diminutive inch a Queen, defiant and proud, head held high. She was now surrounded by a small loyal cadre of Vindomar's most trusted retinue, ready to protect her with their lives at any threat from Kel's people.

The chamber was stunned into a deathly silence, as voices caught in the backs of throats. This was their Queen. Pfil, their *Queen*! A small handful of loyal faeries stood around her, their daggers already drawn to protect her from any rash attempt on her life by Kel's followers.

"This is a trick!" accused Kel, glaring directly at Vindomar, furious at the turn of events.

"No trick of mine, Traitor!" Vindomar laid the accusation before the assembly, and eyes turned this way and that, as Pfil and her close entourage made their way slowly across the floor of the chamber. The crowd parted to let them through, some of them weeping openly, male and female faeries alike, to see the damage done to her in her captivity. "You betrayed your Queen into captivity. You sided with Malevar against your own kind!" accused Vindomar.

"Lies! All of it lies! What is this? What trick are you playing, Vindomar? I have always been a loyal subject. I have worked faithlessly for my people. Majesty, I know not what happens here," he turned to Pfil as she ascended the platform awkwardly, climbing slowly now she was flightless.

"Kel, son of Brinagh, I have heard how you betrayed me and your own people. I have suffered greatly at his hands in the years in between, but now I stand before you as your accuser, and I will have my vengeance!" she swore. Kel's face reddened further as she denounced him in front of everybody. Even some of his own followers now cried him down, as Pfil's reappearance quickly carried the mood of the assembly. "Stand you back," she warned Vindomar and Malon. "I am my father's daughter, and I fight my own battles." The two men moved back, leaving her and Kel alone, the centre of attention now in the chamber. "I swore an oath in tears, the day my father died," Pfil said proudly. "I am your Queen till the day I die. I swear again now. This will not be that day!" Kel looked around him for support, but he could see little in the chamber anymore. He glared back defiantly at Pfil. If this was how it had to be, then so be it. "You want my crown, Kel? Come and take it!" she drew the thorn-dagger from her belt, holding it low. The blade was already red with dried blood, and she meant to use it.

Kel moved slowly, weighing her up. Pfil had been a mighty warrior-Queen in her day, but she had spent years in captivity. Weakened and now wingless, she had only a dagger to defend herself with. This might be the easiest way after all. No one could question his right to rule if he killed his predecessor in open combat, fair or not. He smiled cruelly. "Again, Majesty, I say this accusation is false, but if this is your will, and there is to be no other way to settle this?" He drew his own ceremonial knife, which was of silver, its blade more than twice the length of Pfil's own rustic weapon. He stepped forward towards her, hefting the longer length of shining silver lightly in his hand.

Everyone held their breath as the two began to slowly circle each other, eyes locked. Each was a skilled combatant, their prowess proven over many years and many conflicts. This combat would end in death, no quarter asked, none given. Such was the Faerie way.

Laura and the elves watched intently, aware that they were witnessing something special here. There had been no Rite of Combat held between a Faerie monarch and a would-be rival for centuries. Laura had experience of knives, and had watched Gabriel at work. Both Pfil and Kel looked equally accustomed to using their weapons.

Gradually, the silence gave way to hushed whispers, and then the first cry rang out as Kel leapt forward, outthrust arm slicing for Pfil's face with inhuman speed, and she dropped to her knees as the sharp silvered edge grazed her hair, turning the crouch into a forward roll, and slamming into Kel's lower legs to bring him down. Gossamer wings lifted Kel up into the air however, and he hovered above her, taunting her, as he bided his time. "Would that you could join me up here Majesty, 'twould be a memorable fight," he acknowledged, swooping low once more, and Pfil fended him off, the silver blade notching her own thorn dagger in the process."

The crowd roared as the battle quickened, with one then the other launching an attack with frightening speed. Kel had the skill, and the wings, but Pfil had the ferocity. Kel would have remained aloft, but felt obliged to at least give the pretense of a fair fight if he wanted to win the crowd over.

Hands and blades flashed back and forth, cut, thrust, slash, low, high, lower. Kel smiled as he left a bloodied streak across Pfil's left cheek, but the proud woman ignored the wound, closing to grapple with Kel, who was physically stronger and threw her back. He followed up quickly to end it, and Pfil half rolled, putting her boots into the older man's stomach to throw him over herself. He was too close to the wall to take flight, and slammed into the hard stone, winding himself. She followed up quickly, raised dagger descending towards his chest.

She screamed in frustrated rage, as once more, Kel parried her blade, using his body mass to force her back and give himself some breathing room. Laura's eyes could barely follow the two blades as they flashed back and forth. Kel's robe was now torn in three places, as Pfil had almost struck home, but none of the blows had penetrated flesh. Hands flew back and forth as though merely touching, stroking each other, pointing perhaps, but Laura soon recognized the artistry with which both combatants were using their deadly weapons.

Kel took to the air once more, gossamer wings beating furiously, as he planted a boot in Pfil's face, stunning her and knocking her back. The two rival sets of supporters cheered and groaned as the fight swung first one way and then the other. Pfil was tiring, the sweat running from her quite noticeably. It had been a long day, and she was still not recovered from her journey, or her ill-treatment at Malevar's hands. Kel smiled as he listened to her labored breathing.

He came at her again, swooping down from a safe height, slashing at her arm as she raised her dagger a moment too late, and she cried out, dropping the dagger. Grinning in triumph, Kel alighted, advancing on her quickly as she tried to quell the flow of blood from her arm. He raised the silver dagger high, and brought it down quickly as he rushed at her. The crowd went wild as they scented blood. Kel's arm rose and fell, yet Pfil rushed to meet him as he came at her, closing the gap too quickly for him to adjust the angle of his blow and his wrist met her shoulder as she head-butted him full in the face, breaking his nose as he cried out.

The crowd roared anew as blood flowed from Kel's face, and Pfil kicked out at his wrist, sending the silver blade flying across the floor. Now evenly matched again, the two combatants grappled together in the middle of the chamber as the faeries gathered around them, yelling and urging on one or the other. As Pfil grappled with the bigger man, she suddenly felt herself leaving the ground, as Kel's wings beat once more, taking both of them into the air. "Your bones will shatter when I drop you from the roof of this chamber," he snarled, still struggling with the wildcat Queen. She sank her teeth into his cheek savagely, and Kel roared with pain, feeling more hot blood flow, and Pfil used the opportunity to reach around and grab one of his wings where it joined his body, squeezing hard and painfully, bringing him back down to earth quickly, and she rolled away from him as they hit the ground hard.

Pfil was winded badly, though Kel had taken the brunt of the fall beneath her, and he staggered slowly to his feet. He rushed for his fallen knife. Pfil rushed for her lost dagger. Like two animals, they flew at each other one final time.

Pfil feinted one way, and then, throwing the dagger from one hand to the other, leapt to one side as Kel's arm seemed to reach out towards her, and she used a small stone, jumping up on it to get height to bounce off the wall at his unprotected side. The dagger bit deep, and Kel screamed as he felt the wound to his vitals.

He reached down to his side, feeling the raw flesh. Blood was running freely and darkly down his leg. Something vital had been severed, and he could already feel the fiery venom coursing through his body. Pfil stood there before him, legs spread, hunched over and breathing hard as she awaited his next move. "Who would have thought I'd end up killing myself?" he laughed weakly. "I taught you to use a blade too well, my Queen," he gasped, sinking to his knees in his own blood. The venom coursed through his system like fire, and then he fell forward to lie face down on the cold stone, lifeless at last.

"That you did, Kel. That you did," she acknowledged, saluting him with the bloody dagger.

Vindomar was quick to rush to Pfil's side, lest she collapse alongside Kel in exhaustion, holding her up, and her bloodied dagger high. "Your Queen, now and forevermore!" he saluted her, and the chamber rang to the sound of cheering from both her own supporters and those of the defeated rival and supposed traitor Kel. It could never be proved now, for the combat had made it academic. He was dead, and Pfil lived.

"Let Malevar tremble!" she announced, taking a deep gulp of air. "My vengeance is not yet complete! Three of my people died that I might be freed, and two humans remain captives of the tyrant. Send out the word to the rest of the swarms. Tomorrow we attack Malevar's Keep!"

Chapter Twenty Two

Malevar brooded, alone in his chambers. The death of the bat had proved that the faerie-Queen Pfil had completed her escape. No word from his hobgoblin patrols could only mean the human woman and the elves had now joined forces with the faeries. He could expect their attack at any time. Things were not going well. By morning, mid-morning at the latest, the batteries would have stored enough power to commence the psychic-imprinting on Gabriel. All other power could be directed towards repelling the forthcoming attack. If the generators went down, those damned elves could teleport in and out at will, and he would be helpless to stop them. Unless Kel could stop her, marshaled by a vengeful Queen, the faeries would be a force to be reckoned with, and it would only be a matter of time before they disabled those selfsame generators. The elves therefore would have to die before that happened, in the earliest stages of the attack.

If this could be achieved, then his own hobgoblins and goblin retainers could be trusted to handle the faerie swarms, whilst he surrendered himself to the psychic-imprinting. The process would take little more than an hour, but he needed to be secure during that hour. The machines took a lot of power, and were very delicate in their adjustment. If anything went wrong during the procedure, the results could be disastrous.

He called on his hobgoblin guards to re-check his perimeter defenses. "Are the explosive charges set as I instructed?" he asked Balog, the most senior of his security force, and the most intelligent.

"Yes, milord. Placed and armed. I saw to it myself," he affirmed. Malevar nodded in acknowledgement.

"Good. If they attack as planned, those annoying elves will be wiped out in one blow." Malevar had learned much of warfare whilst on this planet, from studying the Greeks, and later the way the elves and faeries used their powers. The faeries would spearhead the assault, attacking the water-wheel and seeking to disable his generators. Once the generators went down, the elves, with their teleportation powers were free to enter his Keep. It was the elves he needed to kill first. Without stronger backup, the faeries could be dealt with, this far from their natural forests. After Pfil's escape, he had now taken precautions to keep them out of his retreat, blocking off all the windows and openings effectively enough to prevent their entry.

He checked the controls for the explosive charges. Everything was wired in to one switch, and when that one switch was thrown, the higher reaches of the overlooking slopes would come crashing down on the slopes below, where he expected the elves to observe the assault by their allies, the faeries.

Malevar then left Balog to marshal his forces, and returned to the laboratory complex to check on his batteries. Almost fully charged, yet he would not submit himself to the procedure till he had taken care of those annoying elves.

Gabriel was still sedated on the table, and Malevar stroked his brow affectionately. A thin smile crossed his lips as he admired the human body he would soon inhabit. Leaving him, he next turned his attentions to the human female, who was now resting in a private locked chamber, recovering from the operation.

*   *   *

Malevar was surprised to see her already sat up in the bed, the sheets pulled up around her bare breasts as he entered. She was admiring her hand, turning it this way and that.

"It will feel a little strange at first, and I would recommend that you refrain from using it for a day or so, till everything knits back together. Your regenerative powers will slowly return, and the scar may disappear altogether."

"It's marvelous. I didn't think it was possible," Belle blurted out, her emotions were running away with her. "Where's my father?" she asked. "He should be here."

"Gabriel is on his way back to the faeries to collect my belongings. He, too, was very pleased with the operation's success. I daresay he will be in to see you later, when he returns. But for now, it is important that you rest, and let your body slowly heal. I will have some of my retainers prepare you a light meal. Sleep for now." He turned, and left the room. Belle heard the lock close as he left. She had already tried the door once as soon as she had awakened. Gabriel had warned her that Malevar could not be trusted. He had performed a miracle in re-attaching her hand, but his motives were far from selfless.

A quick search of the room revealed nothing out of the ordinary. The window was high up on the wall, covered in a thin metallic mesh, which looked recent, and was far too small for her to get through. The locked door was the only way in or out, and so she needed to bide her time. Her clothes were laid out on a small table. No sign of her underwear. A hole in the floor, revealing running water, served as a crude toilet, doubtless connected to some crude sewer system. She had used worse in her time, during her travels.

She would wait for now, and see if Gabriel did indeed come to visit her. If not, then she must seize whatever opportunity presented itself when one of those retainers came to bring her meal.

*   *   *

Laura marveled at the colorful spectacle as the faeries gathered to honor their restored Queen. Now rested and bathed, Pfil looked every diminutive inch the regal monarch, though her wounds and bandages were still visible. Three neighboring swarms had joined forces with her own, and more were on their way as backup, though would arrive too late to join in the initial attack.

Grandar and the other elves gathered their weapons and equipment. Laura carried the two LAWS rockets, slinging them together and hoisting them over her shoulder. "Twill be enough, lass. Don't worry," Grandar spoke, as if reading Laura's mind. "Faeries can kill you in any number of strange ways, despite their size, and Malevar's forces are relatively small in number, too."

"I hope you're right, Grandar," Laura muttered, under her breath, as she checked and re-checked her own weapons.

The strange army set off to the West by mid-morning, with Brombi acting as scout, and porting back and forth ahead of their march, to verify the lay of the land.

*   *   *

It was late afternoon by the time the western mountains came into view, and getting on towards dusk as the makeshift army took up their positions. The battle-plan was obvious. The elves must be held back in reserve until the generators were disabled, and likely vantage points high on the overlooking slopes were chosen for the elves to observe the initial assault by the faeries.

Pfil was determined to lead her forces herself, despite the lengthy protestations of Vindomar and Malon. "I am no figurehead. I lead by right. I ask no one to fight a battle I am not prepared to fight myself." Dismissing their advice, she toured her forces, mounted on her brave little sparrow, rallying all to her side. Everyone that saw her, had a lump in their throat, as they saw for themselves the shredded wings, yet despite the many injuries that Malevar had inflicted on her, she still led by example. Malevar had broken her body, but not her spirit.

"The lady's got balls, alright," admired Laura.

"Eh?" Grandar looked puzzled.

"Just a figure of speech. It means she's pretty tough for a woman." Grandar nodded in agreement.

"A pity she wasn't a wee bit bigger. I'd marry her myself," he chuckled. Laura laughed with him.

"Let's get to our positions. We attack just after dark, when they're settling down for the night. Your teleportation powers will be most effective then." Laura began climbing up to where some of the other elves were already waiting. Grandar teleported on ahead of her. The faerie swarms remained below, out of sight of the Keep's entrance and it's guards. They would wait for Laura to use one of the LAWS rockets before launching their own assault.

*   *   *

Still no sign of Gabriel, and Belle knew his concern for her would not allow him to be distracted by Malevar, so she knew something awry had happened. Time to take action herself.

She gathered the sheets up to her chin as the door slowly opened, and one of the goblin servants entered with a tray of food. The creature shuffled over to the bed, to lay the tray down, when Belle casually let the sheets fall back, revealing her bare breasts. The goblin's eyes moved to her chest, as expected, distracting him, as Belle's left hand darted for the knife on the tray, and she launched herself off the bed, burying the blade in the creature's chest. Taken by surprise, the goblin fell back under her assault, as it tried to fend her off. Belle slammed a knee up into the thing's crotch, and straddled his thighs as she brought the knife down again and again. Blood spurted freely as the thing flailed about, but the first blow was too near it's heart, and it died quickly. It was dead in less than a minute.

Panting heavily with the exertion, Belle stood up. Her body was covered with blood, and she went over to the toilet, using the sheet and water, she washed herself down, and then went to put on her clothes. Pausing only to wolf down some food, a few mouthfuls of meat and fruit, she went to the doorway, holding the knife in her good hand. She would try and favor her reattached right hand if she could, but getting out of here in one piece came first.

*   *   *

Laura took note of Malevar's defensive positions once she reached her observation post on the lower slopes. Four hobgoblins guarded the narrow drawbridge across the fast-flowing water. Upstream, a large wooden structure housed a big waterwheel, which turned slowly in the strong current. Behind the structure, she recognized thick power-conduits vanishing into the face of the mountain keep.

The narrow gorge was easily defended against a large land army, with only narrow access from the plains. Where the gorge led, further into the mountains, she didn't know. The river's source doubtless came from the snow-covered peaks she could see further to the west. The high slopes offered a protective barrier as far as she could see.

The sun was setting now over those peaks, and the gorge lay in shadow. She laid the two LAWS down beside her, and extended the first tube. The elves had been told what to expect, but all were curious to see her use the strange device. She had likened it to throwing a grenade a long distance, and the one grenade she had used during weapons training had impressed them all greatly. From various vantage points, in the slopes around her, Grandar, Dale, Brombi, Arval and the others were all watching her.

She took up the extended tube and brought it to her shoulder, sighting along the lenspiece. The waterwheel was her first priority, and she took aim carefully on where it's main axle projected through the wooden structure.

As she triggered the device, a long tongue of flame leaped out from the tube, and she was glad her hair was tied back in a single braid, even protected as she was by the face-shield. Elves and Hobgoblins alike marveled at the tongue of fire which licked out and down, and then the wooden structure, housing the mighty waterwheel, erupted in a savage explosion, filling the air with splintered wood and smoke and fire.

The elves cheered automatically, as the first blow was struck, and the hobgoblins below milled around in panic. Hearing the explosion, Pfil and her faerie forces began flying up into the gorge, eager to close with Malevar's retinue.

Laura took up the other LAWS, extending the tube. The wheel was still turning, albeit slowly and erratically. Some of the paddles were broken, and the axle was moving loosely. She triggered the second LAWS, and another trail of flame sped towards its target. The wheel finally tore itself apart in the second explosion, as the axle was shattered completely.

*   *   *

Inside the entrance to the keep, Balog was hurriedly trying to marshal his forces, and he ran to the switchboard where Malevar had wired up his explosive charges, and he threw the main switch, arming the devices.

*   *   *

High on the overlooking slopes, Arval's head suddenly turned at the flashing red light that had caught his attention. He ported over to it, and found a strange rectangular shaped device, with three colored jewels set into its face. The red jewel was flashing on and off, and he didn't know what to make of it.

As he pondered it's significance, the device exploded, killing him instantly, and bringing down a significant portion of the rock face. At other points in the slopes above, similar charges went off, setting off a chain of rock avalanches. The rest of the elves looked up to the heights above as the explosions went off. Josh, and then Magon vanished beneath a massive rockslide.

*   *   *

Laura was frozen as she turned to see the onrushing tide of rock and shale, her mind flashing back to a time before, in the catacombs beneath the Vatican. Fifty feet, twenty feet, ten feet. As she opened her mouth to scream, she felt a hand grab at her wrist, and then all went black.

*   *   *

Inside the Keep, the first two explosions were plainly heard by everyone within. Then came the tremendous roar as the upper slopes of the mountain pass came crushing down. Malevar confirmed with his hobgoblin lieutenant that the explosive charges had detonated, and then, satisfied, he returned to his laboratory complex to begin the psychic imprinting into his new host body. His men could be trusted with the clean-up work, and the now ineffective force remaining outside in the gorge.

The batteries were now fully charged, despite the water-wheel's destruction, and were more than sufficient to perform the operation. He switched to auxiliary power, and the lighting grew dim. All main power now diverted to operating his machinery. His goblin retainers were well-trained, and knew what to do. The machine itself was programmed to carry out the operation without outside help, but Malevar had informed them of possible problems and of what to do should such occur.

The skull-cap was already attached to Gabriel's head, and the plastic conduit lead back from it into the main body of the machine. A similar skull-cap awaited Malevar himself on an adjacent table where he would shortly take his place. It had taken centuries to build this complex piece of equipment and duplicate the intricate internal circuitry with the basic technology available in this world. He hadn't expected that Gabriel would reappear in this world, and had resigned himself to living on in another human body, to be purloined by the elves, or in one of the elves' bodies themselves. He was quite proud of the device, and his own achievement in producing it, single-handedly. Two test-trials with members of his goblin retinue had produced successful results, in swapping psyches back and forth between two of the goblins.

*   *   *

Belle skulked through the darkened corridors of the keep, having armed herself with a small short sword to replace the smaller knife she had used to kill the unfortunate goblin servant. She had heard the explosions outside and then the tremendous chain of explosions and loud roaring that had followed, and realized the attack on the keep had commenced. Shortly thereafter, lighting had dimmed, and Belle knew that her mother had succeeded in taking out the mighty waterwheel, the source of Malevar's hydro-electric power.

The assault would start from the main entrance to the keep, and so she moved deeper into Malevar's stronghold, seeking out the alien, and her father. Twice she hid when goblins came rushing past her. She wanted no conflict if she could help it. Finding her father was her first priority.

*   *   *

Laura found herself on her knees, senses swimming. Grandar was laid on the ground beside her. His eyes were rolling as he regained consciousness. Laura looked around her, through all the still settling dust. She was now on the floor of the gorge, almost out of sight of the keep's entrance. She was also naked. "I had a choice of grabbing you or your clothes. I couldn't port both." Grandar managed a weak laugh as he forced himself to sit up. "Took a bit out of me, too," he groaned, and then coughed.

She took in her surroundings, forgetting her nudity for the moment. The entire shape of the surrounding rock-face had changed due to the rockslide. "Was everyone else killed?" she asked, concernedly.

"Arval and Josh, certainly. I don't know about the others. If they live, they'll port back here before long, once they get their bearings. They might have ported in blind panic, and who knows where they might end up?" he explained.

The two of them turned to look down the gorge, where a strange buzzing could be heard growing in volume, and a colorful cloud of faerie-wings could be seen fast approaching. Pfil was leading her own people to war. "You'd better take cover for a few minutes. Let battle commence," Grandar spoke, and then disappeared. Laura took his advice, sheltering behind a large rock as the cloud of faeries passed over her. Her weapons were gone now. Naked and defenseless, she wouldn't be much use in the fight.

*　　*　　*

Pfil was mentally organizing her attack, moving the swarms to attack in waves as the hobgoblins came out to defend their keep. They had nets, but only crude hand-weapons against the more esoteric weapons in the faeries' arsenal. Blow-darts, tipped with a variety of poisons, pollen spores to disorient and cause severe itching, bio-electric discharges were possible from the male faeries, powerful enough to stun even a hobgoblin.

While some kept the hobgoblins busy at the main entrance, others were seeking egress through the carved windows, though she now found that Malevar had had netting installed over all of them, so that egress would prove more difficult. Now the generators were down, she was looking for assistance from the elves, but where were they?

*　　*　　*

Laura gasped as Grandar reappeared, suddenly, carrying her rucksack. "All I could find amongst the rocks. Your weapon is gone." Laura took the rucksack gratefully, and pulled out her spare shirt and another pair of denim shorts. Still slightly damp, but they'd do. No boots unfortunately, so she would have to remain barefoot. As she dressed, Grandar checked his pistol.

Suddenly, Brombi popped into view, followed by Dale. None of the other elves appeared. Sadly, they realized their fellows must have perished in the avalanche. "Time for mourning the dead later," Grandar announced. "We have a war to fight!" He led the way up the gorge, to where the faeries were already engaged in fighting the hobgoblins.

One after the other, the three elves disappeared from beside Laura, to reappear in the thick of the fighting ahead of her. Laura heard the pistols go off, once, twice. She ran forward to catch up, grabbing a fallen short sword from one of the wounded hobgoblins.

Chapter Twenty Three

Malevar trusted his hobgoblin guards to handle the faerie attack. He had taken precautions to cover all known points of egress into the Keep, and the netting would take some getting through. That left only the main entrance, and with no help from the elves, the faeries should not be able to breach his defenses. The loss of the waterwheel was a nuisance, but it could be replaced in time.

Time now for the completion of his dream, and see the world through new eyes, Gabriel's eyes. His attendants had finished all the preparations. Gabriel himself was now awake on the table, and straining at his bonds. The procedure required consciousness, and so he had been given a stimulant to counteract the drug in his system. "You bastard, Malevar! I knew you couldn't be trusted." Malevar chuckled.

"As I knew you could not be trusted, also. I think you'll realize, my preparations were more thorough than your own. Who knows, you might like the life you have left in this body, if I allow you to live." He moved away from the table, and finished programming the equipment himself, checking and rechecking all the settings before he surrendered himself to the final preparations. He laid himself down on the table adjacent to Gabriel while one of the goblins applied a conductive solution to his shaven skull, before fitting the skull-cap.

Malevar settled back comfortably. Having experienced this transference twice previously, when his body had suffered serious damage, resulting in the need for another clone-body, he knew what to expect. It was just like going to sleep and dreaming strange dreams.

Attendant goblins flipped switches as instructed, and he could hear the equipment warming up. As the electrical pulses stimulated his scalp, he began to feel drowsy.

*　　*　　*

Laura fought her way through the melee at the entrance to the Keep, helped by Grandar alongside her. The hobgoblins were kept busy by the industrious faeries swarming around them, Dale and Brombi stayed behind to aid the faeries, as they slowly made ground into the Keep. Behind them, Laura heard one of the grenades go off, and she hoped the faeries had pulled back before either Dale or Brombi had used the explosive device.

Laura needed to get inside fast, and Grandar lead the way, porting in short hops, occasionally using the gun to kill the odd goblin or hobgoblin whose path they crossed. She knew the way from Gabriel's description of the place, and directed Grandar, following quickly behind him. The fact that they had seen no sign of Malevar himself was worrying her. She had to find Gabriel and Belle.

They came upon the first dead body after a few minutes, and Grandar looked at Laura in puzzlement as he shrugged his shoulders. A second body was found a couple of chambers away. "Someone's been busy," mused Laura. Both bodies were still warm.

"Okay, so I'm untidy!" announced Belle, as she stepped out from behind the heavy wall-hanging. "Next time I'll stack the bodies up neatly."

Laura's eyes fastened on her daughter's wrist, once she got over the initial shock of seeing her. "Belle, it's a miracle! He actually did it?" Belle held it up, turning it this way and that. She nodded.

"Feels a bit sore, but it's useable. He obviously knows a lot more about my physiology than we do. I haven't seen Dad. I think Malevar is up to no good."

Laura nodded. "Let's find out," she said, and she led the way, with Belle and Grandar close behind her.

*　　*　　*

In the laboratory, both Gabriel and Malevar were now relaxed, eyes closed, in an almost dreamlike state. One of the goblin retainers threw a switch, and the machine began to hum in a low, almost subsonic tone. The hollow plastic conduit attached to the skullcap covering Malevar's cranium began to glow, starting from the skullcap itself, as if siphoning some sort of glowing green energy directly out of Malevar's skull.

The machine was slowly deprogramming Malevar's brain, the green glow an indication of progress. Once this was done and processed, the same would happen with Gabriel, before the download would begin into Gabriel's skull. Then, Gabriel's thought patterns would download into Malevar's skull, and the two psyches would effectively be swapped. Gabriel's body would be Malevar's new home.

*   *   *

"I can hear them." Belle suddenly stiffened. "They've broken through and are inside the Keep," she announced, hearing the faerie-speak in her mind. Behind them they heard another explosion as one more grenade went off.

They moved quickly along the corridor as Belle lead the way now. A goblin servant came out from one of the side rooms, and he had time to scream once before Belle ran him through with the short sword. "Quick now. That scream will have alerted them!" She ran forward, with Laura close behind her. Grandar followed, unsure of directions and so unable to teleport.

As they entered the laboratory complex, they took in the scene in front of them, with Gabriel and the alien strapped to adjacent tables, and the interconnecting devices between them. Three goblins were monitoring the progress of the device they were using, and two of them turned to deal with the threat from the two humans, whilst the third hung back.

Laura and Belle flew at their larger opponents, their short swords more than a match for the sheer physical size of the goblins. Both women showed no mercy to either of their assailants.

The third cowered behind the machinery. "Whatever that thing is, turn it off!" Belle ordered, gesturing with the bloodied blade. The poor creature was terrified.

"I don't know how. It's all supposed to work by itself." It pleaded.

"I know how to stop it!" Grandar smiled cruelly, before emptying the last bullets into the machinery itself, and both Belle and Laura were pleased to note that the machine powered down, though it began sparking and crackling where the bullets had torn through it's casing.

Malevar's body began to spasm on the operating table, though restrained by the leather straps. The bullet-riddled machine began to spark, and some flames and smoke began to appear from it's jointed edges. The plastic conduit to Malevar's skull tore away from the housing, and the green mist it contained began to spill out, heavier than air, to pool on the floor.

Laura was quick to unfasten Gabriel from the table and help him down. Belle stood over the goblin retainer, who remained fearful for his life. The green mist began moving, seemingly of it's own volition, as though it had purpose and direction. It was moving towards Gabriel. "What's happening?" Belle cried out.

"I don't know," he answered truthfully.

"Let's get out of here," Belle suggested, and as Gabriel came round slowly, the two women helped support him as they helped him from the room.

"No. Not yet." Gabriel managed to speak. He eyed the mist with suspicion, but it was moving slowly. On shaky legs he went over to one of the laboratory benches and found a stoppered vial, which he opened. He gave it to Belle, and motioned to the large tank of blue fluid in which she had been immersed. "We need a sample of that stuff to analyze. Maybe we can duplicate it. We might need it some day." Belle nodded, and went over to the tank, dipping the vial beneath the surface till it filled, and then she corked it up once more, secreting it within her shirt. Then, together, they left the laboratory.

Behind them, the goblin retainer stayed cowering in the corner, watching the green mist grow in size. Slowly, almost imperceptibly, it began to move this way and that, before it finally changed direction and began to move towards the nearest living object, the goblin himself.

A loud, eerie scream echoed down the corridor behind them, as Grandar and the two women helped Gabriel along. His strength was starting to return, and his senses were clearing. Gabriel as well as Belle could now hear the triumphant mental calls from the faeries who had routed Malevar's forces, slaying those who had stayed to fight, but allowing all who wished to flee to the far western mountains up the narrow gorge.

As they made their way out of the Keep, black smoke swirled overhead, pouring out of the upper windows near the laboratory complex, and a tremendous explosion blew out part of the rock face above them as they all ran to seek cover.

*   *   *

Pfil withdrew her swarms further down the gorge, regrouping as they waited for the humans to catch up, accompanied by the three elves.

"Our losses were light, thanks to the assistance of these brave elves," Pfil announced to her people.

"Malevar himself is dead. I killed him." Grandar took credit. "The Tyrant's reign is over!"

"Then let us go home. It is time the land was healed." Pfil said, sadly.

*   *   *

Two days later, as preparations were made and finally completed, Pfil and all of the faerie swarms accompanied Gabriel, Belle and Laura and the three elves southwards. This world had never seen such a sight as the very sky itself seemed to be composed of fluttering brightly colored wings. The time was come for renewal, to breathe life into the poisoned forests and woodlands once more.

*   *   *

Grandar, Dale, and Brombi were hailed as heroes upon their return to the city, and their fallen comrades were mourned as befitted their bravery. Faerie and elf joined in the festivities as Malevar's death was celebrated. Gabriel, Laura and Belle were caught up in the occasion, and couldn't escape if they'd wanted to. The merrymaking went on long into the night.

The next morning, it was time for farewells, and Pfil stood on Gabriel's offered hand as she spoke to him vocally, so that other not of her own race might be aware of her words. "We owe you a debt we cannot pay, so how then shall we pay it?" she mused, sadly. "Without you, this day would not have come about."

"Make this land what it once was, and perhaps once day I may visit it again," Gabriel promised. Pfil laughed with a mischievous twinkle, and she moved forward to kiss the tip of his nose.

"You are a noble man, friend Gabriel. I wish there were your like among my own kind, but alas . . ."

"Hands off, Queenie. He's spoken for." Laura warned in jest. Pfil turned to regard her.

"Then take great care of him, friend Laura," Pfil warned, with a flash of her eyes, and a quick toss of her short auburn locks, "for he is a special man indeed. A good man is hard to find, and even harder to hold onto." Then she turned to Gabriel once more. "I will hold you to your word. One day, we will meet again, you and I, in this world of mine, or in yours if it is still within my power."

Gabriel turned his head slightly, as though hearing something unspoken, and not meant for public consumption, but then Pfil alighted from his hand as he lowered her to the rocky outcrop where Vindomar and Malon awaited her.

The rest of the faerie swarms filled the trees, their multicolored wings appearing like brilliant leaves on all the nearby trees.

Grandar, Dale and Brombi, said their goodbyes to Laura, as she knelt to hug each of them in turn, and then she and Belle and Gabriel headed south, towards the faerie circle and home. Time to check on Juliana, and if she was well enough to travel, arrange flights back to Argentina.

Chapter Twenty Four

I t was good to see Belle in such good humor once more. She had taken to using the gym in the basement to work out and get back in trim. Her reattached hand was now fully healed, and the hairline scar was only noticeable if you were looking for it.

Manuel took Laura's jacket as she came back in from the garage. "And how is Mistress Juliana?" Manuel asked her. Laura smiled, pushing her sunglasses up above her forehead.

"Getting back into the old routine, Manuel. She's quite able to fend for herself now. Takes great exception if you try and help her around the place. She's still a bit weak on one side, so she carries that heavy pail in her other hand, but she's getting stronger. How's my daughter doing?" she changed the subject.

"Mistress Belle is coming along quite nicely, Madame. In good humor, and Master Gabriel is pleased with her progress. Her physiotherapy sessions have proved a complete success. She now has full movement in the hand, and all the ligaments and bones seemed to have knitted together correctly. The latest x-rays are in the Master's study if you wish to view them yourself."

"Maybe later, Manuel. Thank you." She watched Belle and Gabriel work out on the exercise mat, with each of them taking turns to wrestle with and throw the other in a limited contact combat. Both of them were going flat out, the moves and counters so fast that they wouldn't be apparent to anyone who wasn't an expert. Laura was, and they were a joy to watch.

After a while, when they had both worked up a good sweat, as if by mutual agreement, the two of them stripped down to the waist. Belle kept her bra on, but was otherwise bare above the waist. Gabriel went over to one of the benches and took two paint markers. He uncapped them both, and handed one to Belle. Moving apart, the two of them squatted down. Things were about to get very interesting, and Laura settled back to enjoy the spectacle.

A knife-fight without knives, master against pupil as it were, and Belle was no slouch herself. Gabriel, Laura knew, was a master without peer with a blade in his hands, but he had never faced off against his daughter before.

It was Belle who came in first, circling to the right, and then switching hands in mid-air as she turned and wheeled back on him. Her longer reach closed the distance in less than a second, and Gabriel flung himself to one side as the tip of the marker missed his skin by millimeters. Laura laughed, as she watched the blur of hands.

Slash, slash, reach, cut, point, slash, back, forward, again and again. It was hard to follow. This was a fight for the connoisseurs and Laura felt privileged to watch it. Gabriel was working hard against a more than skilful opponent. In fact she had never seen him work so hard. Back and forth they fought, hands moving more than their bodies, tracing intricate patterns in the air with the marker-tips as they fought for dominance.

Gabriel scored first, leaving a thin red line on Belle's cheek, which infuriated her, galvanizing her into a ferocious assault as Gabriel backpedaled to put distance between the two of them as she fought to close him down.

Gabriel took a hit on the arm, and then another across his midriff, in non-critical areas. Belle kept him within reach, though just, of her longer arms, and it was all Gabriel could do to defend against her attack. Making an attack of his own was now proving difficult.

He went down on one knee, as if stumbling, and Belle lunged forward for the kill, and an eye less trained than Laura's wouldn't have caught what happened next. Belle cried out in delight as her marker scored along Gabriel's neck, landing a killing blow. Laughing and whooping with delight, she offered him a hand to help him back to his feet, magnanimous in victory. Gabriel hugged her, pleased with her performance. "Well done Belle. You're coming along fine. I have a present for you," he grinned, going over to one of the benches and pulling open a drawer. He took out a walnut box, which he handed to her.

Belle's eyes opened wide with delight as she opened the box, to find two matched throwing knives which Gabriel had made himself for his daughter. She lifted one out of the box, hefting it. "I think I've got the weight just right for you. Why don't you give them a try?" he suggested, indicating the silhouette pasted up on one wall.

Hardly had he finished speaking, than Belle whirled and threw the first knife. It sank home right between the eyes of the paper target. "I think so, too," she laughed. "Thanks, Dad. Love you," she hugged him fiercely, tears starting to well up in her eyes before she broke away. Laura put an arm round her.

"He let you win, you know," Laura later explained to her daughter, as she followed her into the showers.

"I know, and he knows I know," she chuckled. "I felt his finger tracing along my tummy when he could have used the marker. I should have been disemboweled before I connected with his throat. But he wanted me to win, and he knows I'm getting better. One day I'll be as good. Well, maybe almost. He does have a few years on me after all," she smiled. It was good to hear the sounds of Belle's laughter once again. Perhaps now, the three of them would have the chance to grow into a real family. Laura smiled, and the two women embraced, hugging each other affectionately, until Laura lightly broke away.

"Hurry up and shower. Manuel has prepared a 'family' dinner. Let's not be late."

A Long Way To Die

Spring was slow coming to this part of northern Pakistan, and the cold March winds coming down off the mountains still stung with the biting cold of winter, bitter and harsh to anyone unprepared for the vagaries of weather in this part of the world.

The two Mossad agents struggled head-on onto the wind, wrapped up in their thick sheepskins, Their eyes stung as they trudged wearily onwards. The village could be seen in the distance, and a young boy tended a herd of goats in one of the nearby fields, but he paid the men little heed. A village like many others in this region, but one in which they finally hoped to find their prey. If it had a name, it wasn't on any map they knew of, situated on the northern bank of the Indus River valley. To the south, the peaks of Nanga Parbat could be seen, still covered in snow. It was a bleak and inhospitable place.

Mullah Ali Bin Wazir was one of the last surviving Taliban who had sought sanctuary in northern Pakistan, where many of the people openly supported his former regime, still declaring their allegiance for Bin Laden. This was a volatile part of the world, as Bin Laden's followers frequently crossed into Kashmir, engaging Indian forces and generally fomenting unrest in a region inhabited by two religions, where both nuclear powers claimed sovereignty. It was now a very dangerous part of the world.

Bin Wazir had fled here from Afghanistan, seeking to consolidate a new power-base, whilst avoiding the long arms of the American President in his self-declared 'War on Terror'. Like most Americans he talked big, but delivered very little, and the Mullah thought himself safe here, for he knew that President Musharraf would not dare allow any American operation within Pakistan's own borders, for fear of an uprising against his regime by the more extreme religious elements, all followers or supporters of Al Qaeda.

Israel did not respect international borders when it came to anti-terrorist operations, and a quiet word from the American CIA was all they needed to mount an operation of their own within Pakistan. President Musharraf was indeed aware of it, but would never publicly admit it. He was playing a delicate political game, only too aware of the extremists within his own country who were trying to undermine his rule. Should the mission become public knowledge, he would publicly condemn the Israelis, who knew they walked a thin line across international opinion. They had been walking such a thin line ever since the foundation of the modern nation of Israel, and they weren't afraid to cross it if the need arose.

Ali Bin Wazir was one of Osama Bin Laden's Military Commanders, responsible for planning a number of atrocities. Lots of different nationalities had died when those two mighty towers fell. A lot of them had been Jews.

For all the unrest and claims of persecution from the Muslim world, 95% of the world's terrorists were Muslim. That was a fact that couldn't be argued. Only the reasoning behind such acts could be argued, not those responsible for them. Religion was ever an excuse for acts which it's own faith forbade, yet one man's martyr was another's terrorist.

Al Qaeda was worldwide these days, as the world emasculated itself by allowing the terrorist organization to proliferate, hiding behind supposedly 'legal' front-organizations. Much of the funding came from the rich Saudi families that Bin Laden was connected to, who looked upon Israel's very existence as an affront.

Too many countries opened their borders too freely, and both legal and illegal immigrants, or refugees, were allowed free access. Not many even pretended allegiance to their new homelands, but continued to live their lives the way they had always done, knowing they were free from persecution under many countries' laws. Muslims now spread over the earth much further and more freely than they had ever done under the Ottoman Empire.

Western countries gave too much weight to ethnic and minority groups, and politicians were too afraid of losing votes to be seen to do anything against any of these groups, yet in places like America and even England, whites were now considered ethnic minorities in some towns and cities.

Islam was slowly being allowed to spread across the face of the globe almost unhindered, and it's followers were intent on spreading it's doctrine by any means necessary, for it was a very unforgiving religion and would suffer no others.

For sheer fanaticism, Islam couldn't be beaten, because children were made to learn the Koran before being given any other education. Indeed, some never got any further education, as the Koran was supposed to contain all the knowledge it's followers needed. Islam looked on the rest of the world's religions with scorn, particularly the Christian faith, often ridiculing the Bible as a prophet's disciples' versions of the Word of God, whilst their own Koran itself was looked upon as the Actual Word of God, though they conveniently forget to mention that it is 'as told by the Prophet Mohammed' so no more reliable, really.

All Muslims were devout, at least in public, and most sincerely believed in its doctrines, sure that their reward for carrying out Allah's Will would be a place in Paradise.

Allah's Will, unfortunately, was not usually dictated by Allah himself, but by a variety of Mullahs, who were more practical than devout. Allah's Will was more hearsay, if truth be told, but none dare disagree openly with a Mullah's interpretation, for fear of reprisals by the rest of the Faithful. Blind faith was never blinder.

Anyone critical of Islam could be condemned by a Fatwah, for the Koran told that it was a Muslim's duty to slay any and all followers of any other religion, if they couldn't be converted to Islam, and thus save their souls. Conversely, anyone converting from or denouncing Islam, automatically sentenced himself to death in the eyes of the Mullahs.

The two Mossad agents knew what their fate would be if they were caught on such a clandestine operation deep in a Muslim country. Yet, knowing that, they had volunteered for the mission, and had been dropped into Northern Pakistan at night by one of the American Black Hawk helicopters flying covertly. Three other teams were operating across the area, but their whereabouts were unknown, and the single-burst one time radio they carried was to be used only for extraction.

They had followed the trail diligently for the last four days, listening and observing, fluent in the northern dialects. Bin Wazir and one of his three wives had been staying in this village, stationary finally, to attend a meeting of some kind. They would observe this meeting, and then make a decision on whether to take out their target or not.

*　　*　　*

Inside the house, Bin Wazir and his followers enjoyed the warmth of a fire, whilst listening to the wind outside. The house had windows of glass, keeping out the elements, unlike most of the dwellings in the town, which put up shutters in the colder months. He had a good view out across the valley and surrounding hills. So did his bodyguards.

Bin Wazir took the first small cup from his wife and sipped, nodding to the other single man in the room, who sat on the broad sofa across from him. Masoud Al Asmi took up his own cup, and drank also, though he now had a taste for western coffee in preference to this strong bitter brew. The woman offered him fruits, dates and nuts, which Masoud respectfully sampled. She left them on the low table when Bin Wazir dismissed her from the room to talk in private with his guest.

"The West thinks itself strong, secure even, now that it has broken our power base in Afghanistan," Bin Wazir began. "If they know of our reach across the world, they will certainly not publicize it," he chuckled to himself. Al Asmi nodded. "But the world weakens itself from within. It is corrupt, and has not our strength. Islam is the word of the one true God, and this 'War on Terror' will not silence us. Islam is the one true religion, and as the rest of the world wages war on us, we in turn will wage war on them!" Bin Wazir's eyes blazed, reflecting the inner fury he felt. "Islam is about to wage war on the very religions of the world," he told Al Asmi. "Centuries ago, the Christian Pope authorized a Holy Crusade against the Ottoman Empire, to control trade across the Mediterranean, and the Moors and Turks were expelled from their conquests in Northern Europe. Our religion suffered serious setbacks at the hands of these heathens," he went on, fervently. "It is time we embarked on a crusade of our own, and showed the nations of the world that our time is coming." His voice, well used to oratory, was having the right effect on Al Asmi, reaching deep inside him. "I want you to spearhead that crusade, Masoud Al Asmi. I want you to take the fight to the Infidel!"

*   *   *

The two Mossad agents befriended the boy with the goats, talking to him fluently, with not a trace of any accent. It wasn't long before he had revealed to them the location of the house used by the Mullah. In their backpacks and within their clothing, as well as the radio, they carried some explosive charges, two machine-pistols, and one broken-down sniper's rifle. The lie of the land would determine how they planned their assault.

*   *   *

"Imagine if you will, the religions of the world brought down by the power of Islam." Bin Wazir went on. "Not just the religions of the West but those of the East too, all of them falling in turn, as we strike against them, one by one." He had vision, and no mistake, thought Al Asmi, a part of him reacting to the Mullah's words, and yet his western upbringing rebelled.

His parents, Arab father, Pakistani mother, had raised him in the English town of Keighley, in North Yorkshire, where there had been much racial tension, as his own race soon grew to outnumber the native white community. Answering the call of the Taliban, he had made his way to Afghanistan to fight for Bin Laden against the Americans. After the rout, Bin Wazir, on hearing of his bravery and his background, had arranged this meeting, deeming him highly suitable for the mission he was about to bestow upon him.

"I want you to wage war, Al Asmi," Bin Wazir exclaimed. "Your first target will be the Holy Catholic Church, as revenge for the Crusades which drove us out of Europe those many years ago. You will take a small squad of hand-picked men and women, and infiltrate the Italian sub-continent. Once there, you will bring that country to its knees by a series of well coordinated strikes against the very heart of its religion," he revealed. "Your code-name will be Torquemada, and I want you to test the faith of the Infidel like never before. Let him feel the fires of the Inquisition."

*   *   *

The town-house was on the very outskirts of the sprawling village, halfway down the slope of a low range of hills. It had a commanding look across the valley beneath it. Three cars were parked up outside the house. Vegetation was scarce, and there was no way the two Mossad agents could approach the house in daylight without being seen. They could only observe from a distance until nightfall, and even that in itself was dangerous, lest their attentions be noted by the villagers.

There was an abandoned car, long since burnt out, by the side of the road, but it would not give either of them sufficient cover in the light of day, for there wasn't much of the bodywork left.

They went back into the town, and managed to find a small bar cum coffee shop on the road which led back out to the Mullah's house. It was the best they could do till dark. At least in here their presence would be disguised, and they could watch the traffic to see if any of those cars came back along the road. It also helped shelter them from the bitter wind, and so was a welcome relief.

*   *   *

Back inside the house, Bin Wazir and Al Asmi were deep in conversation whilst the bodyguards did their rounds, alternating their positions every hour, lest they became too complacent watching the same piece of terrain for too long.

"I'll need a list of operatives," Al Asmi insisted. "People who can pass themselves as Italians, or foreign exchange students. They all must be able to speak Italian. Fluent would be best, but not essential. Italy is a cosmopolitan country which sees a lot of tourists. It should be easy enough to move around. Two cells of four. I'll need cars buying. No rentals. They're too easy to trace. Forged documents, good ones. Cell-phones to communicate, pay as you go. They can't be traced or located unless they know who's got them. We keep it as simple as we can," he advised Bin Wazir, who was pleased to see the reports about the man's tactical strategies lived up to expectations. "Co-ordinate attacks in different parts of the country, which we publicize to force them to accept their own helplessness." He indicated towns and road-systems on the map, making notations here and there as Bin Wazir looked on, nodding in agreement.

Bin Wazir smiled. "I will look forward to hearing of your exploits on CNN," he chuckled.

"What about weapons and munitions? How will they be arranged?"

"Many of the Arab nations are sympathetic to our cause, and one in particular hates Italy with a vengeance. They will assist your efforts," he grinned. "I have an asset in place, and I have already spoken to contacts in the Balkans to arrange delivery of the more important items," Bin Wazir assured him.

"I am ready to give my life for Allah," Al Asmi assured the Mullah, who smiled knowingly.

"The home of Catholicism will be destroyed, and if it is necessary, your martyrdom will assure you of a place in Paradise," he promised the devout younger man.

∗   ∗   ∗

Dusk was coming, and the three cars all passed the coffee shop within seconds of each other, as the two Israelis shook their heads in frustration. So near and so close, but Fate was cruel. There was only a slim chance that anyone was left in the house, but they had to check it out.

Back out into the cold wind and dying light, they retraced their steps along the pitted road, seeing no lights in the house in the distance. Cautious, they approached carefully, taking their time and using what cover there was. Finally, satisfied that if they hadn't drawn any fire by now, they never would, they ran the last hundred yards to the house, alert as ever for anyone inside.

Controlling their breathing, they waited for nearly sixty seconds outside the door, but could near nothing inside. One of them put his shoulder to the door, and it fell in over, splintering the frame, and breaking the poorly made lock.

One covered the other as they conducted a quick search of the place, but their suspicions had proved correct. There was no one left in the house, no clothing. Only foodstuffs had been left behind. They searched for information now, and any documents that the Mullah had left behind to reveal his plans of movements.

In the fireplace, in front of the embers of a dying fire, lay a burnt remnant of a map, which must have fallen out of the fire. The outline of the southern coast of Italy was unmistakable. Still visible in the bottom corner of the map were four still-legible lines of Arabic script, obviously names, written in ink.

One of the men carefully picked up the map, and slipped it into a small plastic bag which he then sealed and put inside his clothing. A further search revealed nothing else of value in the house. The place was otherwise sterile.

Leaving the house, the two men climbed the slopes of the hill, seeking clear high ground, and one of them pulled the single burst radio. He thumbed the ON switch, and spoke softly into the mouthpiece. "Taxi . . . repeat . . . Taxi . . ." and he gave the co-ordinates legible on the GPS device built into the side of the radio, for the Americans to pinpoint their transmission point. Then he switched the device off, and hunkered over against the cold wind to wait for the helicopter extraction.